Sine Timore proudly presents

HOPE SPRINGS ETERNAL

From The Case Files Of Hannah Singer,
Celestial Advocate

The image used for the cover of this volume is believed to be in the public domain in the USA. It is a painting of the Kilauea Caldera by French painter Jules Tavernier, who died in 1889, and as such, the copyright has expired. If this is incorrect, contact me and the image will be replaced immediately.

"Hope Springs Eternal" copyright © 2013 by Peter G, all rights reserved. "Hannah Singer, Celestial Advocate" and all related characters and content are copyright © Peter G (2010). Unauthorized reproduction, in whole or in part, if prohibited (i.e. Fair Use is allowed).

All persons, places, and events depicted herein are entirely fictional. Any resemblence to actual persons, places, or events, living or dead, is entirely coincidental.

For those who know the real me, and love me anyway.

From the case files of

Hannah Singer

Celestial Advocate

Hell On Wheels
7

A Penny For Your Thoughts
29

Self-Made Man
53

Repeat Performance
75

Running From The Family
101

Many Happy Returns
115

Sins Of The Father
121

The Darkest Secret
135

Ace Of Clubs
163

HELL ON WHEELS

Strictly speaking, there's no such thing as having a "bad day" up here.

The sun is always shining and never sets, there's never any inclement weather unless it is somehow required, the birds are always singing, the grass is always green, and best of all, no more periods. It can boggle the mind what kind of paradise Heaven is because the Afterlife is pretty amazing unto itself.

"Bad day" is usually metaphorical. Like me. I have constant bad days. Not that I complain. See, I'm a Celestial Advocate. My job is to stand up for souls when they are judged, seeing mercy done and saving the deserving from going to Hell. But I'm not any ordinary Celestial Advocate. I'm a grey, which means I get to handle the toughest cases where what should be done isn't so cut and dry. I'm also senior, both Celestial and grey, which means there's only one in the entire Celestial Court system who outranks me. Hannah Singer is the best of the best. So I get the toughest of the toughest. You can't say I don't ask for this.

That said, some days are worse than others. And I got my first hint that this would be one of them when I heard that voice.

I was sitting on the wall of the Great Fountain at the center of the Archives on the Celestial Court grounds, going over some recent cases other greys had handled. I like keeping up with what the Church Advocates, the opposition, are arguing. No one has successfully ambushed me in court yet, and I take steps to keep it that way. Usually, when I'm that wrapped up in a trial record, I could be sitting between the amps in a battle of heavy metal bands and I'd never notice. So you can imagine how irritating the voice was that punched through my thoughts.

Standing in front of me a few yards away was a older white man. As is my habit, I started examining him, learning what I could. He had energy but his body hadn't started resisting his commands yet. Best guess? Probably late sixties. He smiled like a guy standing next to a river with a sack of live kittens, and the wrinkles on his face indicated he smiled like that a lot. Carrying enough weight to keep him from buying off the rack at regular stores. Bald head, stubble pattern indicated it was shaved to disguise pattern baldness. Grey business slacks, white shirt, red tie. Alterations to the body don't make it up here, so his fingertips didn't look like a heavy smoker's, although the way he held his fingers gave his habit away. At least two packs a day, and since he was upper management, probably the occasional cigar. What made me so sure he was upper management? He was sporting a Rolex on his left wrist. People who like to flash their Rolexes are shocked to find out no one up here is all that impressed with them.

The appearance told me a lot, but his body language and voice told me more. This guy was a close talker. It appeared involuntary – he wasn't trying to intimidate anyone, he just naturally figured he was everyone's center of attention. His accent was southern United States, complete with colorful colloquialisms that you aren't sure if they are real or if he's making them up on the spot. Nice and loud, too, punctuating his points with barks of laughter. Not only did he figure he was the center of attention, he relished being the center of attention. His attitude made him drown out everything else around him.

He had sort of cornered a trio of people. They were too polite to just tell him to zip it, but their eyes were looking around desperately for some sort of escape hatch. One of them saw me, and before I could think, "Oh, THIS is gonna be fun," I was pointed out. The guy started moving towards me like he couldn't wait to convert me to the Church Of Him as the trio sped away.

Given his demeanor and that I looked to be in my early thirties, I mentally wagered that the first thing he'd say was something referring to me as "little lady." He got up to me, extended his hand to me, and said, "Good morning, little lady!" That gave me one dollar. Did I want to try for two?

I decided to keep things neutral. Well, as neutral as I get. "I'm busy."

He let out a loud guffaw. "Boy, you Yankees sure do talk funny!"

It took me a moment to figure out what he was getting at. Some Americans mistake my British accent for New England.

I could feel my patience starting to wear thin. "My name is Hannah Singer. And you are?"

"Gary Sledge," he said, putting his hands on his hips and angling back slightly. Jesus Christ, why me? "And what do you do here, little lady?"

"I'm a Celestial Advocate," I told him.

He looked at me like a little kid who could do trigonometry. "Well, don't that beat all? I guess you women have it in you after all!"

I've been doing this for almost seven hundred years, so I've learned to keep a grip. And he was bulldozing his way through my coping mechanisms. I decided to end this until I could learn more about this guy and shut him down. I grabbed my scrolls, got up from the wall, and started walking away, not even looking at him as I said, "Well, it was nice talking with you, but I must be going."

He fell into step with me. "You must be one of the ones who has things to do."

I had to remind myself I could talk better without my teeth clenched. "Duh."

"Bet you regret that now."

Don't look, don't make eye contact.... "Why would I regret that?"

"Because you could have just been a housewife and let us men do the work."

"Burn," I sneered.

"Aw, come on, honey, lighten up!" And as he said that, he gave me a solid slap on the butt.

Suddenly, everything was in slow motion as I immediately pivoted around while cocking my fist back. I was partway through the turn when I

8

started bringing my fist forward, and I used the momentum to add force. I hit Gary in the jaw hard enough to launch him several feet.

I stood there, staring at the prone form, in complete shock as the scrolls dropped from my hand. This is the Afterlife. There is no physical body to render unconscious. And yet, Gary just laid there on the ground like a sack of flour. Life conditions certain behaviors, so I must have done enough for his mind to trigger unconsciousness. All I could say was, "Oh...my...God...."

Suddenly, my fists felt different. I started to panic. Was I about to be punished? I looked at my hands, and saw they were now encased in a set of boxing gloves.

Before I could even register who was behind this, St. Michael appeared next to me, dressed like a boxing referee. He held up one of my hands in the air and declared, "The winner by a knockout!"

Any other time (...well, sort of...), I would appreciate him bringing humor into a situation. But all I could do was look at him with abject terror. Eyes wide, I told my boss, "I'm sorry. I'll never do that again."

Michael looked at me strange as he let my hand drop. He looked at Gary and said, "Well, I guess there's no point in waking him up then." He stuck two fingers in his mouth and let out a loud whistle. Immediately, a pair of ministering angels showed up. They simply looked at Gary, trying not to look at me.

"Take him to the Equilibrium," the archangel ordered them. They nodded and flew off with him.

Once we were alone, I turned to Michael. "So I'm not in any trouble for that?"

"Are you kidding?" Michael laughed. "I'm going to ask God to preserve that so all the angels can experience it!"

"Really?"

Michael leaned towards me conspiratorially. "Let me put it to you this way – Camael may actually like you for a few minutes."

Only now did I start to relax. Michael noticed. He asked, "I'm finally getting you to calm down?"

"Not you," I told him with a smirk. "The fact that just about every angel wanted to see him clocked is what's doing it."

Michael straightened and turned his head away from me while sending his nose into the air. "Tough crowd," he sniffed.

I couldn't help it. I threw my arms around my surrogate big brother's waist and hugged him. I put myself under a lot of pressure, so having someone to just be human around is wonderful. I felt his arms go around me. "You know you have to do worse than that to lose your post or get Cast," he said with warmth and humor in his voice.

I forced myself away from him. "It's still not cricket," I told him.

He poked his finger into each boxing glove, making them pop like balloons and freeing my hands. "Nervous baker," he smiled.

"'Nervous baker?'" I asked as I picked up the scrolls.

"I've never used that expression around you before?" he asked in surprise as we started walking together. "I guess not, you would have remembered it. You're a nervous baker. 'Did I use the right amount of ingredients?' 'Should I make the oven a bit warmer?' 'Was there something else I could have added to the mix?' 'What if they don't like it?' You want it absolutely perfect, and you obsess over every detail."

"It's what makes me so effective in court."

"And neither of us wants you any other way."

I could only nod. He was right as usual. "So, who was the noodle?"

"Gary Sledge," he said with a shake of his head. "Head of one of the big American automobile manufacturers. Had the audacity to credit God with his success. Like God approves of treating people like trash and backroom deals with regulatory bodies."

I rolled my eyes. "Oh, my God! Why are we getting so many of these dipsticks nowadays?"

"Because people think religion is as simple as paying dues," he said. "In order to be inclusive, churches started teaching a simplified way of being religious. People don't have to do as much to be considered Christian, just give some money, go to church, and do some basic charity. Living in accordance with God's Word is just too inconvenient."

"Their lives move too fast for God?"

"No. It just doesn't pay well enough."

We got to the court buildings and split up, Michael heading for his chambers and me heading for the Office Of Records to return my scrolls to Russell and, something told me, to get a leg up on Gary Sledge.

Gary Sledge liked to call himself an American success story. His qualifications were where he ended up, not what he did to get there.

Gary was born in the southern United States, in South Carolina, to be exact. He was the middle of three boys growing up. Dad did okay as a foreman at the factory, mom stayed at home. Older brother was career Army, younger brother fixed cars on his own and ran around the local racing circuit.

Gary hated it.

Oh, he loved his family. But he didn't like lower middle class life. He saw people who could afford nice cars and nice houses and entry into the exclusive social circles and thought, "Hey, why not me?" He examined them shrewdly, and they all had one thing in common – they were businessmen.

Gary focused his efforts on his studies to get a full ride scholarship to an Ivy League school. He had to. His dad would never be able to afford it. He didn't really interact with the other students, no real friends, and he didn't date anyone, graduating high school with his virginity intact. He felt he was better than those hayseeds.

Once in college, Gary really went to work. He carved a place in a tight little club where no regular people would ever understand their problems so they leaned on each other. Gary's professors were impressed with his drive and business sense. His classmates were impressed by his charisma. The school was one of those that put out lawmakers, CEO's, the people who pluck the strings that hold the world. Gary understood the importance of networking with these people, of doing things for them and getting them to do things for you. It was easy for him, making deals, introducing people, and sometimes just providing some sympathetic aid.

Gary never had to look for work. Before he even graduated, a recent grad contacted him. An American automotive company had some openings. People do not work their way into those positions, they get them because of connections, and this guy was part of the Old Boy Network there. His boss was always looking for people who graduated from his alma mater, and the recent grad looked out for those who "got it." Gary had done a lot for the guy, including somehow scoring the answers to the final exam. The resulting score made him valedictorian. Gary graduated on a Saturday, and was in Detroit in his new office on Monday.

The post-World War II America had caused a social shift. Companies and unions made money hand over fist due to the war effort. People equate success with survival, and with the Great Depression still fresh in many people's minds, business became the new hunting ground. It gave rise to the nuclear family and corporations becoming societal deities. Just to make clear that the things that happened with Gary in charge would have happened anyway, it just became focused under him.

Gary rose through the ranks at the car company quickly. Part of it was his handling of the employees. Gary just had no respect for regular people, full stop. They were manual labor. If they had any intelligence or ambition or talent, they'd be working in an office instead of a job anyone could do with some basic training (yes, he treated store clerks and food servers and such the same way for the same reason). He offered a bribe...sorry, I mean, bonus program, giving gift cards for attendance and actually telling people they could use the money on "liquor or beer." I've been dealing with bosses for seven hundred years, and this was the first time I had ever heard someone think it was a good idea to treat his employees like a bunch of winos.

The union was good, but Machiavelli Jr. was better. He knew the rules better and basically blamed the union for it. "I may not like it, you may not like it, but it's right there in black and white," he would say as he implemented changes that resulted in weird hours, changes in benefits, whatever. "You don't like it? There's the door." "Why are you so upset by all the overtime? You're making money. You actually lose money spending time with your family." Some people quit in frustration, enabling the hiring of cheaper replacements. Others hung on, but even the little bit he shaved off them translated into bigger bucks when lumped together.

What's that? Why didn't the union fight it? Gary had key people in his pocket, either people in the rank and file who would keep quiet with a little...restitution, or the people the union stewards reported to. Filings to the government were done and talked about, with no mention of the incomplete forms and such to prevent them from being followed through on. All the plebeians knew was that the government didn't seem to actually care. (Of course, even if one got through, Gary had enough connections to keep it from finding the company at fault.)

That was a good start, but it wasn't enough to put Gary on top of the mountain. That came as people in administrative positions became aware of the financial straits the company was in. Everyone at the company had political connections, but Gary had ones in certain positions that came in handy. He engineered a federal bailout of the company that his buddies made happen, making the company president look good. The money saved on labor was touted as an example of them getting serious about turning the company around, so it looked good to the press and the regulators and they left them alone (the bailout was paid for with a second bailout after the press lost interest).

Gary was on a real roll, and eventually, a new CEO was needed. Companies promote based on people embodying the ideals they exude or how much money people bring in. Gary fit both criteria. He made it to the top, and people around the country celebrated the straight talking guy who had saved the proud American automaker, patriotism and success stories being more interesting than looking further.

This, however, was actually the beginning of the end for Gary. The combination of making money and disregard for humanity culminated in one of the worst decisions ever made. Because the American economy was having problems, new car sales were sagging. Not helping was the decision of car makers to make features "standard", pushing up the price of the car and preventing the existence of a cheaper alternative. Gary decided America needed a cheap car to help boost his company's sales, and the result was a four-wheeled failure called the Garrano.

The design process was classic Gary. The design was finished, and Gary wanted additional cuts to be made. Instead of removing standard features, a cheaper engine design was used, one that hadn't been used in a while because of its unreliability. Instead of proper electronics, the "circuit boards" were printed on cardboard. Cheap and made to stay that way, it was also seen as a boon to the franchise dealership's repair businesses. While slimy, it wasn't evil. The part that made it evil was the Garrano design also put the gas tank in a position to easily rupture and create a fire in the event of an accident. People who argued against the placement were met with Gary's judgment – with the expected sales, they would be able to more than afford to pay the projected number of wrongful death suits. Yes, projected -- he knew people would die.

Well, you can only use the public for so long. As word got around, people were less likely to buy a deathtrap just because it was cheap. The casualness of the lawsuits damaged the public image of the company. Spin doctors deployed to manage the damage were constantly undercut by Gary's "I'm just living out loud," philosophy. Reporters would hang near Gary's table, waiting for him to start talking. He would, they'd take notes, and the articles wrote themselves. The stockholders weren't thrilled, either. It was cutting into their dividends, and people were asking how they could support such an unethical company.

When people started saying, "Yeah, I own tobacco stock, but at least it isn't THAT company," and saying it without irony, there was a shareholder revolt. Gary tried to hold on. He was openly contemptuous at the meeting. He was annoyed that these people didn't understand what was really important. After all, they were still making money, and it's not like important people were dying. A vote was taken. Unanimous decision, Gary was to be thrown out. Gary's rage and indignation blew up. He stormed out, cursing these stupid people who weren't interested in being successful. He was already fighting the effects of stress because he was a tough guy, he could take it, not realizing how much damage he was doing to himself. Between ulcers, hypertension, lung damage...the fury Gary stoked and maintained made his body pull a, "You can't fire me, I quit!" on him. He dropped three days after he was sacked.

Gary's case was pretty straightforward. He had no empathy for people, cared about nothing but his own success, and considered the final score of money to be the measure of a man. Michael was waiting for Gary to petition so he could contest it and get it over with. I filled out the recommended fate, reincarnation as a pauper for several lifetimes until he learned his lesson. However, there was really nothing to the case. I decided to give it to Clarence Jones to lead for the Celestials. No muss, no fuss.

Alas, nay, it was not to be, for a fine jest was to be played upon this fair maiden. I was in my favorite spot in the Water Gardens, going over some life scrolls and deciding whether or not they needed my representation when I heard heavy footsteps coming along. I know Michael's gait.

He came around the corner. He knew exactly where to find me. He came up and said, "Hannah! Let's play a guessing game!"

I squeezed my eyes shut as I began rolling up and tying scrolls. "Oh, goody," I said with a monotone that would make Ben Stein proud, "I love guessing games."

"Great! Here's your clue!" And Michael did a pirouette.

"The American government keeps the brains of all deceased Presidents in a tank, and Millard Filmore's brain got Gerald Ford's pregnant?"

Michael didn't miss a beat, I'll have to try harder next time. "Close enough! You are leading the opposition to Gary Sledge's petition!"

I could feel my face contort. "...whut?"

"I thought you'd never ask," Michael stated. "You are leading the opposition to Gary Sledge's petition."

"Why me? There's nothing in his scroll that requires a grey."

"It's not his scroll that made me reassign it."

There was only one thing that would make Michael reassign a seemingly simple case to the best Celestial ever. "Fairchild is leading?"

Michael nodded his head. Jeff Fairchild was senior Church Advocate, and the two of us mixed together about as well as ammonia and bleach. In an

13

Afterlife full of angels singing, we were the biggest show in town.

I started reviewing details of the case. There was something here if Fairchild was suddenly opposing, and I quickly locked on to it. "What is Fairchild doing now?"

"Consultation with Sledge."

"And where are they now?"

Suddenly, we heard that familiar annoying guffaw. I didn't even look at Michael as I grabbed the scrolls and walked in that direction. As I passed Michael, he said, "By the way, the brain thing was great. You almost threw me off there. Consider it stolen."

"Burn," I told him as I passed. I said it a bit crossly, but Michael knows me well enough that he knows it's not personal. I'm always like this when I have to deal with Fairchild.

I found them just on the Campus grounds where the Churches reside. They were coming from the direction of the court buildings on the Archives grounds. My guess? Fairchild was making a beeline for his chambers in hopes of shaking off the barnacle yakking up a storm next to him.

I was just a little behind them, so I wasn't noticed. I sped up, fell into step with Fairchild on the opposite side of Gary, and said, "'Morning, Fairchild. How's it going?"

Fairchild came to a dead halt and his face looked like his bottom lip was trying to climb up into his nose. Gary continued to prattle on (no idea what he was talking about, I was listening around him), but stopped walking just like I did.

Fairchild slowly swiveled his head to me. His eyes had a look that said, "Death, where is thy sting?" And given he was already dead, he knew there was no mercy. "Reassigned to you?" he asked like he didn't need to hear my answer.

"Wait, you're opposing?" Gary asked. He then stepped around Fairchild and stood in front of me. "Miss, I would like to apologize for my behavior earlier. It was inconsiderate of me."

I only shifted my eyes to him. "Don't bother, I'm still contesting."

"Why? I didn't do anything wrong."

"How about, 'lack of humanity?'"

"My company gave record amounts to charity every year I was in charge."

"Giving to charity isn't enough."

"Should have expected this from a peasant."

Now I turned my head to him. I grinned evilly. "Doing your homework on me, huh? Did you also uncover that I used to be an Atheist?"

The friendly demeanor had vanished. He was now the conqueror, the guy who would get what he felt he should have, one way or another. "I got where I was because I knew how to get to people. No one gets in my way. I have earned a Heavenly reward, and Fairchild is going to get it for me."

I turned fully to face him. "His case is a loser."

Gary moved in so his gut was actually bumping against mine. "And how do you know that?"

"Let me explain what his arguments are and why he's doing it," I said, stepping forward and bumping his belly back. "He's going to say that God wants His children to be successful, so what you are doing was what was expected. He tries that with televangelists and other preachers who live richly. And it doesn't work for them. And it won't work for you."

"I'm not a preacher," Gary shot back, leaning into my face. "There's another angle."

"No, there isn't," I said, leaning in and bumping his forehead with mine. "Fairchild isn't defending you because he thinks you deserve it. He's defending you because he knows, if he doesn't, Celestials like me will use it to our advantage. We'll say the standards are inconsistently applied and start potting his precious brethren in record time. He's defending you because he has no choice."

"We are all important to God!" Gary yelled into my face.

I rapidly jammed a finger into his mouth and poked the back of his throat. He started gagging and fell back as I said, "What about the people you abused? The workers you disrupted the lives of? The jobs you kept away? The money you took from them? The time they'll never get back? The success you hoarded from them? They're important to God, too."

Gary got himself under control enough to say, "They deserved it. They're lazy. They want more out of life? They should put some effort into it. Like I did."

I turned to look at Fairchild to ask if he could believe what he was hearing, and saw he was gone. My last glimpse of him was him going up the steps into the Campus building where his quarters were.

I turned to look at Gary, who was now advancing again, trying to reclaim the physical space. I waited until he got up to me, same position as before, breathing heavily in my face. As he communicated his rage, I communicated my determination. "I'm going to nail you to the wall," I said. "I've taken on bigger and more powerful than you. Popes. Kings. Mobsters. Billionaires. Generals. Union leaders. Gods among men. Anyone who took advantage of those who couldn't fight back. And I made them pay. Each and every one of them. And you're going to be no different. Enjoy the Afterlife. It's the best you're going to feel for a long long time." And I turned on my heel and walked away, listening to his heavy breathing fade the further I got.

I marched down the halls of the court buildings, ready to drop the hammer on Sledge. God's mercy is for the deserving, people who genuinely tried to do right. Maybe they just didn't follow through. Maybe they made a mistake. But those who got God's mercy were not willfully evil. Sledge was. He was not getting into Heaven on my watch.

Fairchild's situation added an interesting wrinkle. When the Churches know they have a disaster on their hands, someone that they cannot in good conscience allow into Heaven, they will present a token case that any moderately skilled Celestial can rip to shreds. That way, they can say they did their jobs and stood up for a good Christian (whatever they meant by that) without trying to get them in. But Fairchild never threw cases that way, his involvement meant he was going to fight tooth and nail. He had to....

...my pace didn't slow as a thought struck me. Something wasn't right here. Fairchild argued the way I said all the time and he's never won. Not once. There was something different about this case. What was it? It had to have something to do with Gary, something he had that the church officials Fairchild represented didn't. I caught the faint whiff of a scheme, something that would establish a precedent, and likely grease the skids for the corrupt church officials seeking to get away with the heartlessness they exhibited in life. I shifted my brain into overdrive – I had to be ready to think on my feet.

Entering the courtroom, it was actually pretty sparse. Not a lot in the Gallery to watch the trial, just some juniors taking notes and a couple of angels. No one seemed to suspect what I did, that this simple case was going to go big.

Well, except Michael. He was sitting in his customary seat in the Gallery right behind where I stood at trial. We just smiled at each other. He had the same bad feeling I did.

Fairchild was already at the Church table on the left. Sitting to his left in the Petitioner's seat was Gary, looking as friendly as he could. The last two seats were occupied by Fairchild's favorite flunkies, Edward Fiedler and Burke Finley. Standing by the divider like a hired gun was Jacob Palini. His appearance was never fun.

I got down the aisle that split the Gallery, just past the divider, and took a sharp right, putting me at the Celestial table of the courtroom and in my usual spot. My two juniors were already here. Harold "Smack" Kowalski, his wide-brim fedora adding a touch of cool to his robes (so he claimed), was a former sportswriter when he died at seventy-five. He had a lightning quick wit, and given that he was working class his whole life and proud of it, I wanted him to step on Gary's arrogance. Also there was Clark Horvis. Clark was a Midwesterner who was a faithful churchgoer and studied the Bible well when he was alive. I was hoping Clark's working class background would provide some needed perspective.

I had several scrolls with me. I thought they would be relevant to the proceedings, but I noticed I was spacing them out on the table. I didn't think they'd be much use to me anymore. And I know Fairchild noticed.

I sat and swiveled my head to look at my juniors. They looked at me like I was about to put on a hockey mask and start swinging a machete. "What?" I asked, sounding as innocent as I felt. Honest.

"Nothing, boss," Smack said. Smack isn't usually nervous around me, but his demeanor, combined with the pen being held perfectly still by compressing teeth, said he was.

I turned to face the front, steepling my hands and resting my nose on top of them. "Sorry. I got a bad feeling about all this."

Clark leaned around. "Don't worry. You need us, we got your back."

I looked at Clark. His voice had a determination I hadn't heard before. "Gary bringing back some bad memories?"

"Worked for someone like him," Clark said, his voice lowering to a rumble. "Couldn't get work in home construction for a year because of him. Made sure anyone who called for a reference thought twice."

"One of those, huh?" Smack said, turning to Clark. "I had editors like that. 'Oh, we can't do THAT, it's ILLEGAL.' Like they don't have other ways of sticking it to you."

"Yeah, and then people act like you're paranoid. You know, my wife had to go back to work and I was stocking groceries until I charmed my way onto my last job. Had to move in with my brother until we got squared away. Two years it took."

"Stupid desk jockeys," Smack harrumphed.

"Yeah. Let's see them actually work for a change," Clark harrumphed back.

I leaned over to them and wagged my finger in a, "Come here," motion. They leaned to me and I whispered, "We've got a bigger problem. Drop the class warfare." Tribalism can make you stupid if you aren't careful.

They didn't exactly look contrite. "Sorry, Hannah," Smack said. "Life."

I didn't say anything. I could have shut them down by pointing out I was a peasant, but I hate the thought of winning at being the most piteous. I just forced them to refocus. I went over their roles in the trial to make sure they knew what their limits were and where they might be needed.

Smack noticed how specific my instructions were. "You're expecting an ambush." It was a statement, not a question.

"Got that right," I said. "I might use you to flush Fairchild out so I can get him."

"Got it," they both nodded, and we straightened up. I lost myself in my thoughts as I tried to figure out where Fairchild was going and why.

I remained in my loop until I heard the chimes sound to signal the start of the court session. Everyone in court rose, and Smack dropped his fedora off his head onto the table in front of him. Angels, Advocates, and juniors deployed their wings. We human souls don't have wings like angels, so we get ceremonial wings. They aren't attached to our backs, but float behind us and move like they are. Mine are the simplest design, each looking like an upside down tear drop with a smaller upside down teardrop on the outside and a flat line along the top filling in the gap. I call it modest and a statement of my position in relation to the angels, although Michael insists they are "aggressively minimalist." Don't ask me, he can't explain what he means by that, either.

The door on the right side of the court next to the Tribunal Box opened, and twelve angels, wings already out, entered. It was one of the few times I didn't get caught up in the beauty and wonder of their presence. My brain was using any time available to process the situation.

The door at the back of the court opened to admit the presiding angel.

Aces! It was Pahaliah! Pahaliah and I go way back, as he was the presiding angel at my own trial seven hundred years ago. In order to avoid a mistrial, he lets me get my points out and argue fiercely. I get away with a lot more direct confrontation in front of him than I do almost any other angel. I suspected Michael pulled a few strings to get him assigned to the case. If I was going to foil Fairchild's plot, I needed room to move.

Pahaliah got up to the bench and struck the gavel immediately. The Gallery sat down with him as he readied a record scroll and got situated. He looked at Fairchild and called out, "Who is the Petitioner?"

"The Petitioner is Gary Tiberius Sledge."

Pahaliah knitted his brows. "'Tiberius?' Seriously?"

Fairchild attempted to be smooth. "I can think of nothing more fitting to call him."

Oh, that was the wrong thing to say. Two angels on the Tribunal coughed and covered their mouths with their hands. Pahaliah pinched the bridge of his nose and shifted his eyes to me. This was gonna be a looooooong trial.

He dropped his hand and looked back at Fairchild. "And who are his Advocates?"

"Jacob Palini, Edward Fiedler, Burke Finley, and Jeff Fairchild, acting as lead."

Pahaliah turned his attention to me. "And who Advocates for the Celestials?"

"Clark Horvis, Harold Kowalski, and Hannah Singer, acting as lead."

"Will the Petitioner please take the stand?"

Gary strode up to the dock, a raised platform ringed by banisters except for the side entrance, and climbed inside. Angels can sense emotions from humans if the feelings are strong enough. His general demeanor was friendly, but he looked at me as if to say, "You stupid nothing." I know Pahaliah picked up on it – Gary didn't see Pahaliah suddenly look at him with surprise on his face.

Pahaliah then looked at me quizzically. He was expecting me to be thrilled Gary was making the trial easy for me. I wasn't hiding my emotions. Gary was the least of my concerns. Fairchild's secret plot was the real problem, and I still needed to figure out what it was.

Fairchild gave me some big clues with his opening arguments. Once the Tribunal, Gallery, and our juniors sat, he cleared his throat and said, "Gary Sledge is being unfairly maligned for his disinterest in other people. Gary had garnered a lot of hatred. And all of it is pure jealousy. 'He was the head of a company with vast resources. Why didn't he use those resources for good?' Well, he did, just not what the detractors feel is good.

"God wants us to be successful. And there is no shame in being successful. He wanted the tribes of Israel to be successful. Lot. Job. The Bible is full of stories of people who were successful. They had riches. Power. Job was even restored after demonstrating his faith and love of God. And no one ever says they shouldn't have been, that they should have given up everything.

Not even Jesus criticized them or others. He just said they should dedicate themselves to charity.

"Gary has done that. He kept a company that thousands of people depended on for survival thriving in a tough world. He gave millions to outreach programs helping those in need. His pull in the field of trade disrupted embargoes or put safeguards in place. He was a guardian of man's well being.

"What Gary has done isn't evil. His disregard of other people is no worse than the disregard other souls in positions of power have exhibited, other souls who have gained entry into Heaven. Distancing yourself from people is not a sin. As such, he has done no more wrong than others who have seen their petitions granted. He worked hard and shared his wealth. Charities with millions of dollars they wouldn't have had without Gary in charge. Allow him entry into Heaven. Do not punish him for living as God wishes. Thank you."

I momentarily lost track of things, focusing on Fairchild's last sentences. I turned them over a few times, and suddenly, I had it. I understood what his endgame was. On the outside, I was cool as a cucumber. But on the inside, it was sunbeams and rainbows. I still had to push this in the right direction, but I now knew there was a way to shut Fairchild down. And I had to. Losing this would create a disaster in the Celestial Courts.

I rapidly rewrote my opening arguments to keep my knowledge to myself. I wanted Fairchild to get overconfident. "The Church is trying to distract from why exactly Gary is on trial.

"Here are the cups they are using. First, God wants us to be successful. Second, Gary was Christian enough, going to church, saying prayers, giving to charity. Third, he gave people a way to survive, to advance, to continue, in a harsh world.

"Now, here's the pea those cups are hiding: none of that has anything to do with why Gary is on trial. The things he did, he did at the expense of other people's humanity. He cost them time with their families. Success that they had earned. Benefits to make their life easier. And he didn't do it because there was no balance, that those people had too much at the expense of the company or others. He did it to make himself impressive in the eyes of others. He gained from everything he did, and he gained things that ultimately did not matter. He gained praise and attention from people who were either more impressed with success than what the person did to gain that success or by disregard for the people stepped on during the trip to the top. THEY aren't important. THEY aren't doing anything no one else can do. 'The poor are disliked even by their neighbors, but the rich have many friends.' Proverbs 14:20.

"The Church is attempting to move the cups, preventing you from keeping track of what you are supposed to see, enabling them to win their little con game. As you consider the arguments, as you listen to the debate, keep in mind the basis of mercy. It has never been the *what* of people's actions, but the *why*. And the why of Gary's actions is to validate himself. He has done worse than just disregard people, he has exploited them. He has destroyed them. He has trapped them in a cycle of just barely getting by, of making life a punishment instead of a gift.

"This is what the Celestials oppose. What you must oppose. It is not the things he did, it is what made him do what he did. And that was his own ego. Gary should be reincarnated to learn regular people matter, that they have more value than just for other people to compare themselves to. Oppose his petition. Thank you."

The horses were in the gate, and they were off. Fairchild turned to me and said, "You are punishing him for being successful."

"Amazing. I didn't know you could get delirium up here."

"You not only feel he should have been forced to give up things he earned and achieved, but using a standard he was unaware of because people on Earth do not know what we know. How can you in good conscience defend your judgment of him?" This was not Fairchild's usual MO. He was well rehearsed, coming out swinging, and putting words in my mouth. I needed to come up with something out of left field. If it wasn't something in his script, he'd focus on that and lose the plot.

Thinking about some of the things other Churches have argued, I decided to build on that. I started laying breadcrumbs. "The standards are established and available for people of Earth to know."

"Yes, and he's followed those standards."

The trail was up to the trap. "Such as?"

"Do I really need to rehash my opening arguments with you?"

He was almost in. "Giving to charity and such, sure. But where in the Bible does it say building up their position with disregard for others is the most important thing?"

"'The parable of the ten minas!" Fairchild declared triumphantly. "'To all those who have, more will be given!' Written by Luke and Matthew!"

Gotcha! "That was about faith, how dedication reveals more to you, not about wealth. As always, people are taking Biblical passages out of context."

"And where in the Bible does it explicitly state financial success is shameful and wrong?"

"Another quote frequently taken out of context. It doesn't say, 'Money is the root of all evil,' but 'The love of money is the root of all evil.' It isn't his success that is wrong, it is the reason he made himself successful. The why of his actions, not the what."

Fairchild looked to the bench. "Move to strike Singer's last argument."

Pahaliah asked, "On what grounds?"

"Privacy Of Mind," Fairchild smiled.

You have GOT to be kidding me. Pahaliah looked like he was fighting to keep his reactions in check, too. I shifted into "Oscar performance." "Motion should be denied!" I pleaded. "His motivations are central to this case! We need to...."

Pahaliah interrupted me. He was stern, but I caught the twinkle in his eye as he said, "God respects our privacy and doesn't hold our innermost thoughts against us. Therefore, we shouldn't, either. Struck."

I looked back at Fairchild. He was looking at me like he owned the world. "He went to church. He gave to charity. He provided jobs and preserved peoples' wellbeing. He was a good Christian man and should be allowed into Heaven."

I didn't become senior Celestial and senior grey by being stupid. "Move to strike Fairchild's argument."

Pahaliah was resting his head in his hand, holding the gavel up, and not even looking at me as he asked, "On what grounds?"

"Inconsistently applied," I responded as a formality.

I would swear I saw blood vessels throbbing in Fairchild's temples as he yelled, "Motion should be denied! He was a good Christian man! He believed...."

Pahaliah and I said in perfect unison, "Privacy Of Mind." Great minds think alike.

Pahahliah hadn't changed position, and remained that way as he lowered the gavel gently and simply stated, "Struck." He then angled his eyes to me and said, "Please continue."

Fairchild just stood there, staring in numb shock. He suddenly realized that, by winning his last motion, he just put himself in the trick bag (this is why good Advocates argue so much instead of constantly moving to strike – a double edge sword means you're always on the sharp side). Fairchild was now forced to only explain and interpret Gary's actions and things he said to others, and build that into a profile that supported his conclusions. Oh, I was forced to do that, too. But I had a lot more to work with. And he knew it.

I turned to Fairchild and smiled. "So, a good Christian man, huh? You want to tell me where in the Bible it says, 'Thou shalt make a car expected to kill people and thou shalt be blessed?'"

Palini to the rescue. He shot to his feet and declared, "It's not his fault people died."

I hate Palini. His mind does not work like anyone else's. He will come up with all kinds of strange and illogical leaps in order to win his point. "He made a machine with a critical flaw," I said, fighting the urge to pinch the bridge of my nose. "He could have made a slight change and prevented a lot of deaths."

"Everything can kill anybody," Palini said imperiously.

"Is that so?"

"People overeat and clog their arteries. Is the cook responsible? Electricity shocks people or kills them by burning down their houses. Is the electric company at fault? Do we hold gun manufacturers responsible when people use their tools to hurt or kill people? No, we hold the criminal responsible. Things get made, it is up to the people to use them responsibly and protect themselves."

"'Am I my brother's keeper?'"

"Exactly!" Parini beamed. "People misuse things all the time, like sleeping with a hair dryer on under the blankets, drinking and falling asleep with a lit cigarette...what are people supposed to do? Do nothing for fear someone is going to do something stupid and send them to Hell instead?"

I had to shut down Parini fast. The longer he talked, the more time Fairchild had to organize his thoughts. I played my highest card. "People weren't misusing the cars."

"Oh, they meant to get in accidents?"

"Cars have safety features to make them safer in the event of accidents. They are there to give people a reasonable chance to survive. Not only was the gas tank a known hazard, Gary didn't figure it was a risk. He expected people to die, and even included the projections in his budgets. He made the cars riskier despite things meant to make them safer. People didn't misuse the cars by getting in accidents, Gary misused them by making them dangerous."

Palini's eyes darted around. "People could have made them safer."

"By that logic, they can make any car safer. They get the vehicles expecting to be safe. They weren't. The decision was Gary's. The fault is his."

Fairchild got a sudden light in his eyes. Hang it all, he had an idea. As the defeated Palini sat back down, Fairchild turned back to me. "It is not actually his fault. His obligations to the company required him to do it."

"Are you actually advancing that the company itself was evil and not him?'

"Yes," Fairchild said with certainty.

Smack rose to his feet. He held his arms straight by his side and declared in a fake German accent, "I vas only following orders, mien fuhrer!"

Palini found a second wind, too. Back on his feet, he declared, "Companies, by their very existence, are affronts to God! They exist just to make money! Nothing more! People can't help but be corrupted by them!"

"Plenty of people exhibit greed without being part of big business. Must be something else," I said.

I caught movement from Horvis. I made a subtle motion with my hand, a secret signal that he could jump in. He shot to his feet and said, "I worked construction. My company wasn't evil, the person running it was."

"The company existed to make money, didn't it?" Palini sneered.

"It made plenty of money before. The new boss felt it wasn't making enough money and started fu...I mean, rooking us over."

"So, he took over, and he couldn't help but become corrupted," Palini said happily.

"Yeah, just like his previous boss," Smack countered.

"Sounds like conscious choice to disregard humanity and not surrendering free will to me," I said.

As Palini took his seat again, Fairchild said, "The things he did were part of his duties. Just like we have our duties."

"It was his duty to influence government and restrict trade?" I asked as my juniors sat.

"He didn't restrict trade," Fairchild countered.

"He used patriotism and claims of economic authority to have taxes and tariffs placed on foreign vehicles. That's called 'protectionism.'"

Fairchild smiled. "Look at history. Economies have always used protectionism. In fact, they thrive better with it."

"Then why did Gary keep promoting himself as a free market economist?"

Fairchild was quiet. I filled in the blanks. "Because it was never about protecting the economy, but protecting his job and his paycheck."

"He was concerned about his workers."

"Busting unions, scaling back wages and benefits, his actions paint a very different picture."

"The charitable donations!" Fairchild practically screamed, like he'd discovered a new element.

"Tax deductions," I snorted.

"Maybe, but they still did good. The charities that benefited from him never would have had the money if he hadn't tightened the belt on his employees. The money went to people who would do far more good with it. After all, they were helping the poor. The workers would have spent it on beer and material things."

"So, the end justifies the means?"

Fairchild froze. That is one of the easiest arguments to shred – so much so, Advocates are taught it before they ever set foot in court. It is pitifully easy to reduce to absurdity. All you have to do is suggest an air strike on poor neighborhoods. Suddenly, there won't be people suffering. Anyone who walks into that never does it more than once. I continued, "Paying other people so you don't have to care is heartless and counter to God's Will."

I saw Fairchild working his jaw. He was calculating his odds. The longer he argued with me, the better my chances of figuring out what he was up to. So far, I hadn't addressed his secret motive. If he moved for closing arguments now, he had a good chance of swaying with his last word. I wanted him to move for closing arguments. I would hit him when I made mine, leaving him struggling to rewrite his closing arguments on the fly to address the points I made. Come on, Fairchild, you always pick the worst option. Don't let me down now....

Fairchild stated, "Move for closing arguments."

I kept still for a moment more, to make it look like I was unprepared. Finally, I said, "I concur."

We both turned to face the Tribunal box.

It's star time.

I declared, "The Church position hinges on a simple fact of life: God wants us to be successful. This is true. He doesn't want His children to suffer, but to enjoy life. Not everyone can, so those that do have a very special gift given to them.

"But there's a difference. Serving God is not as simple as just giving things away and saying, 'There, that should be enough.' That is not serving God, it is simply making it look like you are serving God.

"This is where people get confused. It's not success that is evil, but the lack of charity, as we have seen by people without money who have had to atone. Charity is a mindset, of considering other people and what they are going through, not just giving stuff away when you don't need it or letting someone else have it. It's doing things because other people are precious, not because, 'What else am I going to do with it?'

"The Church position states the obvious that people cannot live for everybody else in the world. It's just not possible. Not only is it not practical, but distance adds isolation. People will be more concerned for a car accident down the street than an earthquake half a world away, even though far fewer people are killed in the collision than the cataclysm.

"So the question is, what can be done? How much is enough? The problem isn't how much is given, as the poor woman Jesus saw give what she could demonstrates. It is when is something simply done without even a thought to whether or not it does good? Think about the logical conclusion of this. There are religious leaders around the world who are resistant to the changes and challenges their congregations go through."

I heard a sharp gasp from Fairchild. I was bang on the money. He was hoping to use a corporate executive as a precedent for what people can do, and translate that into defenses for other church authorities who cared more for their social positions than leading and guiding their flock.

Some of the angels on the Tribunal arched their eyebrows in contemplation. No one looked at me as if I was talking crazy. Good. I had them eating out of my hand. I continued as if I hadn't heard Fairchild's reaction. "On Earth, there is an expression – 'There, but for the grace of God, go I.' It is said by people who see a horrible tragedy occur to others and realize that, with just a little change in circumstances, it would be them suffering as well. Natural disasters, financial ruin, family strife. These things can happen to anyone. And people like to fool themselves into thinking they can control it or deal with it, that the people in harm's way just aren't willing to do what it takes to get out of it. That the world doesn't operate independently of them and will wait for them. People who don't evacuate for fear of their houses being looted. People who live in dangerous areas because there is nowhere else to go – no jobs, no housing, no nothing. People who put up with abuse in the hopes that maybe, someday, by some miracle, the abuser will realize their error and things will get better and be happy again.

"Not all of those people can be helped. Few of them can. But even if there is nothing that can be done to help, people need to keep others in mind, and if they have the opportunity and the means to help somehow, even at the very least through a quick prayer, they have the responsibility to do so, regardless of if they get anything from it. Thanks for the help are nice, but making it the primary consideration turns charity into bartering. That is abominable.

"That is what Gary did.

"Gary's position of power, authority, and success insulated him so he would never have to feel sympathy again. He cut himself off from humanity.

THAT is his crime, the one that determines his fate. The Churches are attempting to use guilt to shield Gary from reaping what he has sown. Like the TV preachers who guilt their flock into giving them money, even if their flock needs it to provide for their families and survive, Gary took from people, people who deserved consideration, and treated them as he never should have, whether they worked for him or bought the products he instructed be made. Gary turned their world into Purgatory, where they wait out their time until their true reward. It is time for him to live in the world he helped forge. Send him back as what he hated. Thank you."

I positioned my shot at Fairchild's big reveal where I did to give me time to make my points while limiting his time to think of new closing arguments. Fairchild now had to address the points I raised or the Tribunal would dwell on them, overshadowing his other arguments and sinking his case. He started off the way he usually does when he's rattled – sloppily. "'A bribe is a charm to the one who gives it; wherever he turns, he succeeds.' Proverbs 17:8. There! That is proof that Gary did nothing wrong! He had the chance to become successful! He used his resources correctly! What Singer is proposing will punish him for something he had no control over – that others didn't have access to the tools he did!

"So he didn't give the right way! No one knows what the right way is, so they do the best they can! In a way, Gary helped the public gain God's favor! The money that they would have wasted went to charities that did good work! So they did without a few things! Suffering is good for the soul! It teaches humility! How many of these people, knowing God would approve of them giving the money Gary used, would have given it away?!? They would have kept it! Gary saved them from their greed!

"In this case, things have ultimately worked out. Each of those people still have roofs over their heads, food on the table, and clothes on their back. Even those fired by Gary found work elsewhere. They didn't suffer, they were inconvenienced. Big difference! And those who were suffering got a break. Gary is no more heartless than a person who doesn't give half his money to a charity on the other side of the country. They can't know everything! And they aren't supposed to give up their own livelihoods, either!"

I caught a couple of angels on the Tribunal knitting their brows at this. Fairchild likes to say people don't give enough, that they could eat a little less or drive a little less or something, they just don't sacrifice enough. For him to suddenly say otherwise was so ironic, everyone in the court needed a tetanus shot.

"Every time someone stands before the court and the subject of sacrifice comes up, we always have to wrangle over their intent. Singer likes to say it is the why of their actions, not the what. And the result is inconsistency, scaring people as they wonder if they did enough. And how often do they do enough, or their isolation is understood? Instead of making this about the why, it should be the what. Gary did the best he could in his situation. A situation with no idyllic answers like Singer is saying there should be. He was a captain of industry, the head of a collective. He had responsibilities and duties that the people under him would never understand. And they would never understand why he made the decisions he had to. What happened was not his fault.

"Some people have been allowed people entry into Heaven for making mistakes. They've committed crimes out of desperation or lack of options or whatever. Gary is just as much a victim of his environment, of his situation, as they are. His activities are no more illegal or unethical, they are just covered by different statutes. All are deserving of mercy, be they lesser people or great people. Show Gary the same mercy we show others. Grant his petition. Thank you."

Pahaliah stared at the Tribunal. So did I. They had that Buster Keaton thing going on, their faces betraying no emotion or inner thought. Pahaliah said, "You have heard the Advocates for Gary Sledge state their recommended fates. You may now make your decision. You wish to confer?"

The Tribunal whispered among themselves for a moment, then the lead Tribunal stood. "We are ready to rule."

"And what is your decision?"

"Petitioner is to be reincarnated in accordance with Singer's recommendation."

I heard Fairchild let out a groan of frustration. Gary just stared at the Tribunal in shock as Pahaliah declared, "So be it!" and slammed the gavel, ending the session. Pahaliah and the Tribunal exited out their respective doors.

Gary continued to stand in numb shock. He wasn't even trying to move. The two Guardians walked over from in front of the bench to help him on his way to the Petitioner's exit on the left side of the court. They were just about up to Gary when he realized what was happening and snapped out of it. He grabbed the railing in front of him, his eyes darting between the Guardians. "No! Don't! Don't make me one of them! Please! Have mercy! I'll start another business! It'll change the world!"

I got the trio's attention as I said, "What was your reaction to your employees wanting to do things their way instead of being forced to do it your way?" I snapped my fingers. "Oh, yeah! That's right!"

Gary wasn't letting go, but a human is no match for the strength and will of angels. They simply held Gary at the wrist, and his grip went slack. They gently pulled his hands off the railing. Not really looking at anything, Gary wandered out of the dock and headed for the Petitioner's exit with the Guardians behind him.

I turned to look at Fairchild. All his juniors were already leaving. That's weird, Finley and Fiedler usually stick around and walk with their boss. My juniors stuck around as Fairchild said, "You aren't being fair, Singer."

"Neither is Sledge," I shrugged. "He's getting the same treatment he dished out."

"Objectivism doesn't become you," Fairchild said.

"You're just jealous I can rely on it to win and you can't."

"Singer, please," he said, sounding pained. "People are constantly having to validate themselves just for being successful."

"No," I said, stepping on his last syllable. "It has nothing to do with being successful, it has to do with preventing others from being successful. Get yours and take his. It's not simple disinterest or unawareness like for others. Gary refused to care. He refused to listen. When confronted with a situation where humanity and understanding were important, he disregarded it for no good reason other than they didn't matter. That's monstrous, no matter how you truss it up."

"Some people would rather take than earn," Fairchild said.

"So the best thing is to treat everyone as takers? Yeah. That'll show them. All it does is make the takers move to easier targets and the earners feel insulted."

"You don't get it," Fairchild said. "You don't deserve to be senior. You don't deserve to be in charge of anything. If you ever had to choose between what is supposed to be done and what needs to be done, what would you do?"

"Same thing I always do – I would do my best."

Fairchild just wandered away at that point. My juniors and I gathered the scrolls and we left the court.

I was sitting outside, against a shade tree in the Blooming Meadow. It's nice here, very fragrant from the flowers. The Water Gardens make my mind focus. This makes my mind wander. For example, the jasmine flowers. They made me think how nice a spot of jasmine tea would be right about now....

It wasn't the jasmine flowers. I looked down and saw a nice cup and saucer of jasmine tea being held a bit under my chin, the aroma drifting right into my nostrils. The hand offering it was attached to Michael.

I gently pushed the tea away. "No thank you. You don't have any tea."

Michael suddenly produced another cup and saucer with his other hand. I rolled my eyes, graciously took the tea, and sipped it as Michael leaned on the tree next to me. The trunk wasn't thick enough for us to sit side by side, but we were as close as we could get.

"What's on your mind, Hannah?" Michael asked.

"Do any of us truly do enough?" I asked.

"Elaborate," Michael gently commanded.

I thought for a moment, then said, "Here. Take animal rights. People who crusade for animals make all kinds of personal sacrifices. No products that came from animals. Nothing tested on animals. No food made from animals. It's an admirable principle. And yet, it's just not possible. They step on insects without realizing it. Their bodies slaughter germs by the millions. And some things they do, they don't realize the environmental impact and how it can hurt the animals they try to protect with their actions."

"So what's the question?"

"When absolutes are impossible, where is the middle ground? When are you going overboard, and when are you just being lazy?"

"Ah, yes. Hannah, you are asking a question people have been asking since God gave his Commandments. You want to know something funny?"

"Sure."

"No one ever knows the answer. They think they do, and they move forward based on that. But there's always that element of doubt. And it exists for every choice. You fight for self-defense? You wonder if you should have fought sooner to dissuade the attacker or tried harder for a peaceful resolution. You bought something. Should you have invested the money instead, or bought something else?"

"Should you take a cup of tea when you have nothing to offer in return?" I asked, rolling my head so I could see Michael.

"That's the problem with guilt," Michael said with a chuckle. "It's great for keeping your actions in check. But it also turns simply sharing and giving into bartering. That no one can just do something nice for someone else. That reciprocating is the only way to validate generosity. Especially when giving back pretty much contradicts the whole 'generosity' thing."

"So what do I do? When am I doing enough?"

"The questions you are asking put all the responsibility on you. And you can't do that. You shouldn't. If you don't give enough, it's your problem. If someone is demanding too much, it's their problem. You decide what to give and what to allow all the time. You just don't realize it because, most of the time, it's pretty low stakes. An inequity isn't a big deal. It's only when it starts adding up, become constant, or becomes huge that you notice. And because you are now thinking about what you are doing instead of simply doing it, it shakes you."

"Like when professional athletes choke."

"Exactly. You do the only thing you can do – you do your best. Stand on your own as much as you can. Keep the unnecessary exploitation to a minimum. Don't be wasteful. And if you are truly in the wrong, make it right. You can't see beauty if you spend all your time looking at a measuring stick."

I held my tea cup over to him. "'Be excellent to each other.'"

He clinked his cup with mine. "'And party on.'"

A PENNY FOR YOUR THOUGHTS

I was marching across the grounds of the Archives, heading for St. Michael's chambers. I was mad. Furious. Absolutely livid. Yes, Hannah Singer was a lowly human who had only recently died and Michael was an archangel, but I didn't care. I was going to give him a piece of my mind.

I was inside the court building and had just gotten around the corner to Michael's chambers when I saw his door open. Michael was just starting to come out, holding a scroll with a tie around it in his hand. He was smiling and whistling a happy tune, everything just fine within his little bubble.

Out came my pin. "St. Michael!"

Michael looked up and over at me. "Lady Singer!" He was still smiling, but obviously a smidge confused as to my behavior. "It's great to see you! What brings you around?"

By now, I had closed the distance between us and was standing right in front of him. "May I please have a moment to speak with you in private?"

"Sure. Anytime." Michael stepped back into his chambers and stood aside for me to enter. Once I cleared the doorway, he shut the door and locked it. I went to one of the highback chairs in front of his desk and plopped down. I jumped up with a yelp. I glared at him as I picked up the tack there and set it as gently as I could on his desk. He just shrugged as he took his chair and set the scroll on the left side of his desk.

"So, what's on your mind, Singer?" he asked.

"I'm junioring cases."

"Yeah. So?"

"When do I start leading cases?"

"You don't have the experience to lead grey cases yet."

"I'm not asking about grey cases. Not yet, anyway," I responded tersely. "Before I can lead those, I have to lead regular cases. But I'm still junioring. And very infrequently at that. I haven't even juniored on a grey case yet. I'm just sitting on trials, not even consulting. I might as well be sitting in the Gallery. I want to know why."

Michael looked at me sympathetically. "Singer, I understand your frustration."

"Do you?" I challenged.

For a moment, I wondered if I shouldn't have been so obstinate. But when Michael gave me that kindred spirit smile, I knew he not only understood, he expected me to behave that way. "Yes, I do. Your first trial, you saved yourself and stopped a scheme to dismantle the Celestial Courts. So this is kind of a slowdown for you."

"'Slowdown,' nothing. I feel like I'm marching through a bog."

"Singer, I see the potential in you. Everyone does, even the Churches.

Believe it or not, I want you to be a Celestial. But I'm moving you slowly because I want to make sure I'm not overwhelming you."

"You aren't even preparing me to be overwhelmed," I told him. "I've spent more time watching trials from the Gallery than doing anything officially Celestial related. Frankly, I'm better than this, and you know it. You don't have to treat me like a fragile little egg."

"Everything happens when the time is right."

"I know. That's what God used to tell me."

"'Used to?' He's not telling you that anymore?"

"Just now, I was praying to Him and He said to come talk to you."

Michael looked to the scroll he had set to his left. He then looked up and laughed, "Okay! I get the hint!"

When Michael looked back at me, the kindred spirit smile was still there, but there was an extra element to it. Anticipation. "So, you want to see if you can handle the advanced course?"

Without hesitation, I said, "Yes."

Michael stood up, taking the scroll with him, and came around to me. "Then I propose a mock trial."

"I'm open right now."

"I don't mean in my chambers, Singer. I mean in the practice courtroom." He held the scroll up for me to see. "This trial has already been heard. Sort of a grey area, no danger of being Cast or anything. I will sit in judgment, Holman will defend, you will oppose. You will have time to file your request for trial, recommended fate, everything. It will be just like a real trial." He craned his head down at me. "You up to it?"

I sprang to my feet, rising until I was on my tiptoes and my nose as close to Michael's as I could get. "Name a time, name a place, I'm there."

Michael put the scroll on top of my head, balancing it just right. As he turned to go back to his chair, I took the scroll off and started stalking to the exit, with Michael calling after me, "See you in court, Singer."

The scroll described the life of one William Feeders. The case should be simple, except for one little detail – Feeders had bought an indulgence.

I was very familiar with the idea of buying indulgences. Pardoners would come around to my villages once in a while to offer salvation for just a nominal offering. It offended me then when I was an Atheist, and it offended me now that I was an agent of God's mercy. However, all I knew was what came with me from Earth. I clearly needed to do some digging. I grabbed a book on church history to see what exactly I was dealing with.

Huh. Isn't that interesting? Indulgences originally had a much different purpose. Initially, the Catholic church was big on harsh punishments for redemption. Indulgences were supposed to help soften that. They didn't originally buy you out of a sin, you couldn't get an indulgence until your sin was forgiven. If it wasn't, all the gold in the world wouldn't help you. Once the sin was forgiven and you were given a penance, THAT was when indulgence became an option. And not without precedent on Earth. For example, knights could avoid service if they paid their lords enough.

At the time of my death around the middle of the 14th Century, the Catholic Church was seen as corrupt, an affront to God instead of an extension of His grace. Indulgences were one of the biggest complaints. Despite the official position being unchanged, many people saw indulgences as what modern people would call a "get out of jail free" card. It didn't help that many churches saw indulgences as an easy way to get money to finance various endeavors or crusades. Not only was the purpose of indulgence being corrupted, but so were the agents. Falsified documents attesting that someone was a church official abounded, and many of the relics they sold were fake.

The result of all this, as far as the Celestial Courts were concerned, was a total clustermuck. People would petition and find out their sins hadn't really been forgiven. That was bad enough. It was even worse for the people in Penance Hall, where Petitioners went to repent. It was almost as if Guardians were seeing the inside of Penance Hall more than the actual courtrooms. The indulgences couldn't be disregarded, since that would have eliminated all penances, both the sincere as well as the tainted. Hearings became massive arguments as everyone debated whether or not those particular indulgences counted.

William Feeders was lord over a fairly sizable tract of land. Just like his neighbor. Thanks to the Black Death killing so many, people who could still work the fields were becoming highly sought and pursued. Feeders didn't like competing with his neighbor, so he somehow managed to live trap a pair of does going into heat and tethered them in his neighbor's fields. Guess who showed up for a party. By the time the bucks were done, they had trampled a considerable portion of the crops. Feeders was able to charge more for his own untouched crops, didn't have to pay his peasants as much, it was perfect. Still, he was aware that maybe he shouldn't have done that, so he bought an indulgence with some extra food. Not the money, he was keeping that. Not that the pardoner asked any questions anyway.

It was here that I made my first visit to the Office Of Records and met Russell, who was there before I turned up and will likely be there long after I've claimed my Heavenly reward. I requested a couple of dozen scrolls, all dealing with indulgences, both accepted and denied. I read through them while I was there and jotted down notes. This was a test, and I was determined to ace it.

After checking different options and pursuing lines of logic as far as I could, I felt I was ready. I filed my trial request with Michael, complete with my recommended fate, reincarnation for Feeders as a peasant, once for each peasant that got rooked by his little scheme, preferably working for his rival, if he was still available. A short time later, I had come out from watching another trial when I saw Michael. Usually, there was a comfort or friendliness to his expression. This time, he looked dead serious. He simply said, "This way."

I immediately got serious. This was it. Time to show what I was made of.

Michael led me to one of the practice courtrooms. He stopped at the door and just waited. I went past him and held the door open for him. After all, he was going to be the presiding angel.

Practice courtrooms can be a bit claustrophobic compared to regular courtrooms. There is no Gallery, so as soon as you enter, you're in court. The tables are right there against the back wall in their customary layouts, no dock or Tribunal box. Noah Holman, the senior Celestial and senior grey, was already here, standing at the Church table. He didn't even smile at me, he just looked at me, sizing me up. It was his game face. I didn't change my expression. This wasn't a social gathering, and if I even looked like I was trying to use the friendships we had to win my case, I could kiss my career as an Advocate goodbye. Michael had said this would be just like a real trial. I put myself in the right mindset.

I went to the Celestial table as Michael climbed up to the bench. I simply sat down, folded my hands, and looked at him. Michael looked back. We waited, I don't know for how long. Finally, the chimes sounded, signaling court was in session. I stood and all three of us deployed our wings. Michael watched me carefully. "Who is the Petitioner?"

"The Petitioner is William Feeders," Holman called out.

"And who are his Advocates?"

"Noah Holman, acting alone."

"And who Advocates for the Celestials?"

"Hannah Singer, acting alone," I responded.

"Advocate for the Petitioner goes first. Mister Holman, your opening statements, please."

I expected Holman to throw his turn. I was right. "Feeders has nothing on his record to contest. He has repented and atoned for his sins. His petition should be approved. Thank you."

Michael looked at me. I started off. "The Bible states that the love of money is the root of all evil. Feeders schemed to ruin another purely for his personal gain. His sin is beyond the scope of his penance. His petition should be denied. Thank you."

Michael sat back as Holman and I turned to each other, nerves forged from iron. Holman started off. "Beyond the scope of his penance, you say."

"That is correct."

"His indulgence covers his sin. It is forgiven."

"An indulgence is granted after the sin is forgiven, it does not actually forgive the sin. As such, the indulgence is inappropriately applied."

Holman wasn't shaken. "The pardoner forgave him. It was before the indulgence was bought. Ergo, he is forgiven."

"But the indulgence is insufficient," I responded. "He didn't just get a leg up on his neighbor, he actively destroyed his livelihood. Not only did he not recover, but what about his workers? They had to move or accept a lower pay with Feeders. A lot of evil came from that one act of hubris. Sharing some of the crops harvested at the end of that year is hardly making things right."

"That's not for us to decide," Holman said. "That was for the pardoner to decide. He decided no further questions were necessary."

"Feeders was not restricted from trying to make things right on his own, without a pardoner telling him what to do."

"Why should he? The pardoner told him that was enough, and that was all he needed to know."

I saw my opening and moved. I turned to face Michael. "Move to strike the indulgence from consideration."

Michael's eyebrows arched in surprise. Moving to strike is not a rookie move. "On what grounds?"

"The pardoner was not an actual agent of the church. He was a shyster looking to take advantage of people looking for indulgences. As such, he had no authority to grant the indulgence."

"Motion should be denied," Holman responded calmly. "The pardoner was believed to be an agent of the church. It is well established that church authorities can still perform works and call blessings even if they are in a state of sin themselves at the time."

"Those are still officials of the church," I countered. "The pardoner was not."

"It was Feeders' sincere belief," Holman responded. "The covenant God made with us states that what we hold true on Earth, he will hold true in Heaven. People do not always know who is a legitimate church official and who isn't, so they act on faith. That faith is enough to validate an indulgence acquired in good and true faith."

Yes! Holman opened himself up to a bigger attack. I just looked at Michael and played dumb as he declared, "Denied," and struck the gavel.

I returned my attention to Holman. "You just proved Feeders hasn't atoned enough."

Holman looked at me in confusion. "How so?"

"If what is held true on Earth is held true in Heaven, many many people will feel that Feeders hasn't atoned enough for his misdeeds."

"Majority rule?"

"Far more would feel Feeders is rotten than those who feel he did the right thing."

"Doesn't matter what the consensus is. If it did, we wouldn't need church officials to make official proclamations and guidance. It would just be what most of the followers felt was right."

"But you just advanced that you don't need church officials," I responded. "People believing someone is an official is good enough. Therefore, there are no standards by which to judge the indulgence as sufficient."

"If we accept that argument, then that means no indulgence has worth, even those that are appropriate."

I felt my insides turn to ice. It was over.

I blew it.

I numbly restated my position. Holman simply restated the Church's

33

official position. Michael made the simple ruling granting petition immediately, and that was that. He declared, "So be it," and cracked the gavel. I willed my wings away, bowing respectfully to Michael and Holman. I don't know if they even acknowledged it, I couldn't really see anything. I exited the courtroom and walked outside the Archives.

The entire time, my mind replayed that joke of a trial. God, that was so stupid of me! Why did I do that!?! I started thinking of other possible arguments I could have made, other ways I could have outfoxed Holman, anything else to keep the feelings of failure and worthlessness at bay. I didn't want to think about that. I didn't want to admit that I was in over my head. I wanted to be a Celestial. I had to find some way to get better. There had to be a way. Right?

I eventually wandered to the Ancient Forest. I traveled pretty far into it before I found a nice shade tree. I sat beneath it, my back to the trunk, and periodically hammered the back of my head against it. All I could say was, "Stupid! Stupid! Stupid!"

"No, it wasn't stupid, Singer."

I reacted with surprise to Michael's voice. He was just standing next to me, looking down at me. But he didn't look like he was judging me. He was smiling sympathetically. "I was worried."

"About what?" I asked.

"I asked St. Peter to let me know if you decided to claim your Heavenly reward."

"I'm not," I told him with certainty, leaning towards him. "I'm going to be a Celestial. I'm going to be the best. I'm just...." I leaned back against the tree. "I'm just having trouble figuring this out is all."

Michael went and stood in front of me. He held his hand out, palm up, and acted like he was lifting something. A rock big enough to sit on rose through the grass behind him. He got comfortable and I ducked my head. I didn't feel I could face him. After everything I did in my own trial, only to flame out so spectacularly....

"You could have saved that, you know," Michael said.

I didn't look at him. "How?"

"You're being too hard on yourself, Singer." The friendly smile in Michael's voice made me look at him. I saw the kindred spirit smile, and for the first time since the practice trial, I felt actual relief. "You actually started off really strong. I can tell you caught Holman by surprise. Even I was shocked. You definitely researched. You took this seriously. We were afraid you were just going to rely on the natural talent that got you through your trial." He leaned closer to me. "You showed us you're more than that."

Michael shifted back. "The problem was you got overwhelmed. You didn't know enough to keep your momentum going."

After a pause, I spoke. "I should have read more trials."

Michael chuckled. "No, that wasn't the problem. The problem is you've only been here for a couple of months. Time passes differently up here, but you're still new. First, you were an Atheist, so you don't really know the Bible in depth. And now, you are looking at a system that you have no preparation for and trying to fit in instantly. Even those with natural talent still need to refine themselves to be the best they can be. You're trying to skip that step."

"I should be able to skip that step."

"No. Just because you are a great spirit doesn't mean you are required to do everything different. You aren't any less just because you need to learn more. Everyone knows you should be a Celestial. God, me, the Churches, Holman, everyone who has seen you in action. You are learning as fast as you can, but you aren't getting the context. You aren't seeing what you have to prepare for, what you have to adapt to, what you have to do to sew things up. You're great now. Think how much better you'll get with time."

I let my head sag and took a few deep breaths. As much as I hated to admit it, he was right. I had potential, but I didn't know how to use it properly. To get real guaranteed results. "So how do I get better?"

"It's not what you can do, but what I can do. And for starters, I'm going to tell Holman to start including you in consultations and brainstorming sessions."

My head snapped up. Michael was leaning back a little and beaming. I could only say, "...what?"

"You're right," Michael said. "You aren't a fragile little egg. You are better than what you've been doing. And it's high time I ended your frustration."

I just stared at Michael, my arms moving a little and trying to fight the smile trying to burst onto my face.

"What is it, Singer?"

I didn't have it in me to duck his question. "I...want to...to hug you."

Michael didn't say a word. He just opened his arms to me.

I launched myself forward and felt Michael enclose me in his embrace. I felt so relieved. "I thought I wasn't good enough."

"You are good enough," I heard him say above me. "You thinking that is my fault. So, to make up for it, how about I treat you to a little lunch on Earth? I know a great French bistro."

I pulled back enough to see him, but I didn't let go. He didn't, either. "Oh, no. You don't have to do that."

"God ordered me to."

"God ordered you?"

"I was planning to do this anyway since you accepted the challenge to the practice trial." He smirked and looked up. "God's just reminding me who's boss is all."

"Well, I'm not going to argue with God."

Michael smiled, stood, willed the rock back into the ground, and everything around us shifted and swirled.

The French bistro was great. The food was great. Or, at least, I hoped it was.

"Why would you think that, Singer?" Michael asked.

"I was a peasant. What do I know of good food?"

"It is good food. Jesus Himself loves this place."

Jesus is a foodie. "Good enough for me."

As we ate and drank, I felt my spirits returning. I was debating whether or not to say what was on my mind. Admittedly, I had no problem challenging Michael, but this was a more personal thing.

"Ask me," Michael stated.

I looked at him. "No."

He smiled at me. "Why not?"

"It's...it's not court related."

"It doesn't have to be court related, you know."

"...it's not proper."

Michael leaned in. "Hannah," he said, using my first name for the first time I could remember since my original trial, "things don't have to be so formal, so strained between humans and angels. You can reach out to me as a friend. I want to be your friend. Would I have even brought you here if I didn't?"

I just looked at him for a moment. "What about duty? I'm supposed to be a Celestial, not making friends."

"Life is about friends. The Afterlife, even more so. We aren't meant to only do our duties. We wouldn't be what we are if that were true."

I thought for a moment, then said, "I'm a failure."

"Says who?"

"Says me. I know other Celestials do what you say, you train them, and they turn out fine. I'm not...reacting, I guess, the way they do. Maybe there's something wrong with me."

"There's nothing wrong with you, Hannah," he said. "I just made a mistake."

I smirked at him. "Angels make mistakes?"

"Sure, they do. Look at Lucifer."

I shivered a little when he said that name. "I'd rather not, thank you very much."

He let out a little laugh and said, "You aren't a failure, you're different, and I wasn't adjusting for that. The failure is mine. I was actually holding you back."

"You were doing what works. I wasn't picking up. How is that your failure?"

"I was doing what works for shields. Of course you weren't picking up on it."

"'Shields?' What do you mean by that?"

Michael shifted back in his chair and got comfortable. "You see, Hannah, there are two kinds of people. There are shields and there are swords. The difference is in how they react to trouble. Shields are defenders. They protect. They nuture. Holman is a shield. One of the best. Swords, however, are a different breed. They are attackers. They don't protect against trouble, they seek it out and destroy it."

"Swords don't love," I said.

"No, they do, just not in the same way. Shields and swords both want to see the things they love protected and prosper. They both want to see them develop, become great. Shields do it by building up and reinforcing what they love. Swords do it by destroying the things that would harm what they love."

"So which is best?"

"Doesn't matter," Michael said. "Both approaches not only have their merits, but both approaches are needed. That's why nobody is both, why the world is filled with both. You are different because no one can be everything. You are to help each other become safe and great. It's an obligation to watch out for others."

"I seem to run into more shields than swords."

"You're right. There are more shields than swords."

"Because it's easier to defend."

"No, it's not easier," Michael said with a shake of his head. "People only think it's easier because it's reactive, not proactive. That you don't have to do anything until a problem develops. Good shields are proactive, watching for ways to improve."

I thought for a moment. "So they don't have to react."

"You got it, Hannah. But because there are so many shields, the swords out there? They have to be bigger. Stronger. They have to be more so they can balance things out with their fewer numbers. And because there are fewer of them, their loss is felt more keenly."

I took a sip of wine. "So I'm a sword, huh?"

Michael rolled his eyes. "Oh, my God, yes. Think about how you operate in court versus how Holman operates. He simply defends against the Churches' assertions. He reduces them. You chase after the Churches' assertions. Holman simply defends his stance. You make the Churches defend theirs. Holman swats down their arguments. You turn their arguments against them."

"And that's why you were holding me back?"

"Sort of. Defensive skills are vital to any Advocate. When you get cornered like Holman did to you, going defensive gives you time to reorganize your thoughts and salvage your case. But you don't learn like everyone else does, you need a different approach. And since you are so good at figuring things out as you go, I'm thinking letting you swim in the deep – not throwing you in, letting you swim, you'll still have Holman to back you up – is the best approach."

"Thank you. I really want to be a Celestial."

"I know, Hannah. So do we. So it's time we did things to make that happen. But keep in mind, if this isn't working, we'll have to figure something else out."

I just started smiling. Michael just said, "We don't give up on humans in trouble. Did you really think we'd give up on you?"

"I was afraid of it."

"You don't have to be afraid anymore."

And we finished our meals in companionable silence.

As always, Michael was true to his word. Holman was receptive, but wasn't quite sure what to do with me. At first, that is. He quickly started making me junior on grey cases. He sought my advice more. Shortly after that practice trial, I lead my first official case and won. It didn't take long for me to start junioring on grey cases, not to learn, but as an actual participant. Holman and I worked out little signals so I could let him know if I was ready to jump in and if he thought I shouldn't. Then I was leading simple grey cases and junioring on the tough ones. No one expected me to advance as quickly as I did.

The entire time, I kept watching other trials, reading other trial records, and learning every trick I could. I had faced Victor Spire, lead Church and someone with a real axe to grind, or his schemes several times by now. He was a fire and brimstone type, the kind that believe the church is supreme, the true extension of God. He didn't like me for being an Atheist, and he sure didn't like that I'd shut down his chance to make the church the true determiner of the fate of man instead of the Celestial Courts. The serpent in the Garden Of Eden had nothing on him.

It was another interesting day. I had just lead a couple of regular cases and won them both. By this point, I had a little under two hundred years under my belt. The Churches were seeing me as a real threat to their goals, and seeing Spire's face turn red as hot iron was happening almost every time we faced off. I had returned my scrolls to the Office Of Records. I was allowing myself more downtime now. What did I want to do to relax a little?

I didn't get a chance to think of anything, because a putto, Simon, came flying up to me. "St. Michael requests you in his chambers immediately," he said.

"Tell him I'm on my way," I said. The childlike angel flew off, and I ran as fast as I could.

When I got to Michael's chambers, I saw the door was shut. I raised my hand to knock on it. As soon as my knuckles hit the door, I felt the door grip and start to pull me. I was a little shocked, Michael didn't set his door for pass through very often. It enabled only certain persons to enter or leave, and because the door didn't open, any conversation inside would be kept secret. I had just thought this was something big when I finished going through the door.

On the other side, I saw Michael, Holman, four Celestials, and two angels. They all looked at me. Michael and Holman seemed to relax a little. "Thank you for coming so quickly, Hannah," Michael said. He flicked his hand at his door, and it vanished into the wall. Now, only angels could enter at will.

I marched up to the desk, standing between the two highback chairs in front of it. Michael didn't sit. "Real barn burner, Michael?"

"Doesn't even begin to describe it," Michael said. He reached onto his desk and grabbed a life scroll. He presented it to me without preamble. I took it, untied it, and started reading about the life of one John Farmer, a humble man from my native England. I got halfway through when my eyes popped and I stopped.

All I could say was, "Oh, no."

"Oh, yes," Michael said, finally sitting down.

Holman interjected. "You lead, I'll junior."

I reeled back a bit as I looked at him. "You sure about this?"

"Has to be this way," Holman said as Michael nodded at me. "We need someone who will take the fight to the Churches on this one. A lot of souls are at risk with this one."

We started brainstorming right there. Farmer's petition was being contested by the Churches for selling fake indulgences.

John Farmer was a devout Christian and pretty typical of such people of the era. Martin Luther and the Protestant Reformation had been on the radar for a while, and now it was close enough to be seen, although it hadn't happened yet. People were becoming frustrated with the Catholic Church and its corruption and were ready to strike out on their own.

Farmer was actually fairly affluent, and it was this affluence that gave him a unique view of indulgences. Thanks to things like the Western Schism with two competing popes based on politics instead of ideology, he started questioning the whole "immutable authority" thing. He also saw plenty of officials collecting extra money if they needed it and giving a pass to professional pardoners, including one who wasn't even indoctrinated into the church, he just went around selling indulgences. When he complained about how people's sins weren't actually forgiven and they were going to Hell, he was told about the covenant, how God said what we held true on Earth, He would hold true in Heaven. As long as people believed the pardoner was a real church official, God would let them pass.

Well, that was the wrong thing to say to a creative thinker like Farmer. Farmer did some looking around, seeing what passed for phony documents. Actually, there wasn't much to them, some of them he was surprised anyone fell for. Getting a few things together that could pass for relics and blessed objects, he started going out into the countryside as a pardoner. Big difference, though – while he was no less fake, the indulgences he ordered were very easy to do. Well, for the most part. Like us Celestials, most of the sins he came across were small, simple ones, ones with no real harm done. Chiefly crimes against themselves. Anything that was really bad, he would say he didn't have the authority and point them to a proper church. People would say rosaries or give spare time or any of a variety of things, giving of themselves instead of giving the money and objects they needed to survive.

Farmer made a mistake, however – he was horning in on professional pardoners' turf. They didn't like that villages they came to suddenly had all sins forgiven so there was nothing to confess, and at a discount price to boot. In the tradition of honor among thieves, the others kept their eyes out for this renegade who was ruining their livelihoods. They eventually found him. In the dead of night, the pardoners committed one of the greatest sins, murdering John Farmer. In their arrogance, they felt they had nothing to atone for. And those that did? Well, for a handful of coins, they pardoned each other.

Farmer turned up in the Valley Of Death and realized he was going to meet his maker. He did it, he knew he did it, and he knew he didn't feel guilty about it then, so feeling guilty about it now wasn't going to do him any good. He went, petitioned, went to Penance Hall, and went to the Interim to await his fate.

When the petition got to Michael's desk, he knew it was trouble. He filed "No contest" and immediately contacted Holman. The two of them sat and went back and forth. In the eyes of the Churches, Farmer's sins were just too great. They were going to roast him on a spit. There was only one solution...

...this shield needed a sword.

I walked across the Archives, carrying a note scroll and heading for the Interim. I wanted to talk to Farmer for a while, get inside his head. I already knew Victor Spire, the most senior Church, was going to lead. After all, fire and brimstone were his specialty. He'd never turn down a case he could just coast through.

I had just gotten on the Interim grounds when I saw Spire coming out. He had the most evil smile I'd ever seen on this side of the Afterlife. He saw me, and his expression became angry, but no less evil.

I walked easily up the steps as he came down. He stopped right in front of me, blocking my path. "Going somewhere, Singer?"

I unrolled the scroll, put it on his shoulder, and pushed him aside without touching him. "You know why I'm here."

I had stepped past Spire, but he moved to try and get ahead of me again. I simply blocked his path. He was still lower than me, figuratively as well as literally. "Farmer, right?"

"Yup."

"Good."

"How's that?"

"Because you're going to lose badly. To me."

"You're sure of that, are you?"

"Oh, yeah," he said as he slithered away.

My brain shifted into overdrive. Spire doesn't behave that way unless he has some scheme in mind. Did talking with Farmer give him some ideas? Let's find out.

Farmer was leaning against the wall of the Interim's residences. He was a decent man. His clean shaven face emphasized his hooked nose and tiny eyes. He reminded me of a bird, ready to pick and dig to locate what it was after. He had brownish straight hair swept back. He looked resolute, ready for face whatever it was.

"John Farmer?" I asked.

He looked at me as if to say, "Oh, goody, another one."

I extended my hand and approached. "Hannah Singer, Celestial

Advocate. I'm leading your defense."

It was only after I said "defense" that he extended his hand. We shook. His grip was resigned. Nothing to it. Just going through the motions. We separated, and I gestured to the ground. "Why don't we have a seat?"

"I'm fine," he said.

I bluffed. "I've just finished several trials and I've been on my feet for a while. Please don't make me beg."

With a sigh of resignation, Farmer sank down on the ground. I joined him, checking the note scroll to make sure it was taking things down. Spire had to have mined something out of him, I just had to figure out what. Finesse clearly wasn't going to get me anywhere, so might as well start with the direct approach. "Why'd you do it?"

"Does it make a difference?" he asked.

"It must, or you wouldn't have done it, would you?" I smiled.

Farmer just looked at me. I continued, "I mean, other people were going around and selling indulgences and doing things with the money. You didn't need money. Why would you do that?"

Farmer looked at me like he was willing my head to catch on fire. "I didn't do it for the money!"

"What other reason could there be?"

"You said the other reason!"

"Did I?"

"I know about church officials! I deal with them! Bribes! Upkeep on their homes! Blessing their own and sticking it to the humble! And just...just...."

"'As soon as a coin in the coffer rings, the soul from Purgatory springs.'"

He turned to face me, leaning in. He wasn't challenging me, he recognized my mindset. "Exactly! Jesus says He is the way to forgiveness, that through Him, we are made pure! Salvation can't be bought! He gives it to us! It can't be...."

"Ransomed?" I offered.

"Yes!" Farmer sprang to his feet, his outrage bringing him to life. "'The pope says this!' 'The pope says that!' The pope has no authority! Jesus has authority!"

"He's supposedly acting for Jesus," I pointed out.

"Well, he isn't!" Farmer spun to me and glared. "He is acting in his own interests! Jesus' laws are immutable! The pope can't change any of them! Jesus forgave us, there's nothing for the Pope to forgive but laws and edicts he himself makes! And they aren't selling indulgences for that!"

I didn't need the note scroll anymore. I was listening and burning everything Farmer said into my brain. "Then why sell indulgences yourself?"

"Because my penances are just! They come from the goodness of people, not from their possessions that they need! There are people who will do without things to feed their families for the sake of their salvation! That's wrong! My penances have people giving the glory to Jesus! Not to the pardoner! Not to the pope! To who it really belongs, to who really forgives and saves us! And it's not the guy in the funny hat!"

"A miter."

He stopped short. "What?"

"The funny hat is called a miter."

He just stood there, apparently trying to figure out how to get his little red choo choo back on the tracks. I helped him. "So, you're saying the pope should go suck mud."

"That's exactly what I'm saying!" Yup, he was back in action. "Think about it! Charity! We are to give our worldly goods to help those in need! That means clothes! Food! Not money! We aren't supposed to buy salvation! We earn salvation by helping others! By being there for them! Not by leaving our own misery behind, but by helping others leave theirs!"

He continued along those lines until he finally ran out of steam. I stood, smiled at him, and said, "Don't worry. You aren't going to Hell."

He looked at me. "How can you be so sure?"

"For you to go to Hell, I have to lose this case." I leaned towards him. "And there's no way I'm going to lose this case."

He seemed a bit reassured when I left him. Once I was off the Interim grounds, I raised my hand and held up two fingers. A pair of putti zipped up. I told the first to please have Holman meet me at Michael's chambers, and the second to tell Michael I needed to talk to him and Holman in his chambers. They left, and I ran for the Celestial Courts.

When I got to Michael's chambers, the door was wide open. I saw Michael and Holman inside, watching for me in anticipation. I got in, shut the door, and jerked my thumb at it. Michael flicked his hand at it, and it vanished into the wall.

"We need to do more brainstorming. Right now," I said without preamble.

"Why? What's wrong?" Holman said.

"Spire's got another scheme going."

"Big shock," Michael said with an arch of his eyebrows.

"It's worse than you think," I told Michael, taking one of the chairs in front of his desk. "I just talked with Farmer. All the things that motivated him to sell indulgences? They are the very things Martin Luther is contemplating right now."

Holman's jaw dropped in surprise. So did Michael's. Michael spoke first. "He's going to use the trial to undermine Martin Luther."

"And if he does that, he can establish a precedent that can be used against anyone who follows him," Holman finished the thought.

I asked the question I dreaded but had to ask. "Do you want me to step aside so Holman can lead?"

They looked at me like I was mad. "Out of the question!" Michael boomed, making me jump.

"Absolutely not," Holman said, quieter but no less forcefully.

From there others were brought in as we examined and prepared. Spire was playing fast and loose. Spire was going to fail. And hot dog, I was going to be the one to make it happen.

The shield and the sword, Holman and I, strode through the hallways of the Celestial Courts, determination etched on our faces. We had been over everything. Arguments. Strategies. Signals we could use to communicate with each other. We were fired up and ready to go.

Getting around the corner to our courtroom, we saw Mark Freedman come around the corner. He was one of the Churches from my original trial. We got to the door to the courtroom at the same time. Holman opened the door for us. Freedman just marched past, I gave Holman a curtsy as I went. I waited for him inside until he fell in step next to me again, and we resumed our walk to our arena.

Standing at the Celestial table, talking and gesticulating, were our juniors. There was George Burkeshire, the resident Celestial expert on Catholic doctrine. Since this case was going to be used to reinforce the authority of the Catholic church, Holman and I both wanted him there. Also there was George McCreedy, one of my choices. McCreedy knew Christian history and how it had changed over time. With the Catholic church not the only church in history, he could come in handy. Holman's other choice, David Macht, was also there. Macht was a German with plenty of experience under his belt. Five Celestials, ready to go.

The Church table had its own vibe. Spire's juniors were also talking. With Freedman joining them, it was now four at their table. Spire, Freedman, Richard Chapel, and Hunwald Gire. Spire's usual line-up.

Holman leaned up to me and whispered, "See anything interesting?"

Holman knows I look at the opposition to get a read on what they might be up to. Spire was giving a lot of orders, but his hand gestures were focused on the table, not his juniors. I whispered to Holman, "He has a master plan and expects the others to follow it. There's no clear division on who is to argue what other than Spire is the boss. Interesting."

Holman whispered, "Thinking you can take advantage of that?"

"He's chosen people who think like him. It's a very real possibility."

We finished our walk down the aisle and took our places at the Celestial table, me in the lead spot, Holman on my right. We continued to talk amongst ourselves, making sure we were ready.

Our patter was interrupted by a clearing of the throat. The two court Guardians were standing there with Farmer. I motioned for Farmer to take the second seat in. He did, and the Guardians took their place in front of the judge's bench.

I had noticed the seat in the Gallery directly behind me was open. I kept my eye out, and sure enough, Michael eventually turned up and took it. I felt a little more relieved. Michael had become like a big brother to me, and knowing he had my back was always good.

Eventually, the chimes sounded, and everyone took their positions on the proper sides of the tables. Out came the wings. The Tribunal door opened and twelve angels, wings already out, entered. I smiled as I watched them enter the box, I just couldn't fight it.

The door at the back of the court opened and the presiding angel entered. It was Gabriel. Spire's jaw dropped. Gabriel is God's herald and radiates honesty and integrity. Gabriel is also one of only two angels allowed to sit on a trial that specifically concerns Catholic doctrine. Michael was sending Spire a message: good luck saying that this ruling doesn't stick. And Spire heard it loud and clear.

I forced confusion from my mind. Raphael almost always sat at Catholic trials. Gabriel did it very rarely. As such, no one really had any idea how to prepare and argue specifically for him. I decided to focus on the facts and keep God's will towards the front. It was the safest course of action. I would see if I picked up on anything else as I went.

Gabriel sat down at the bench and tapped the gavel. The Gallery and the Tribunal sat down. "Who is the Petitioner?" he called.

"The Petitioner is John Farmer," I responded.

"And who are his Advocates?"

"David Macht, George Burkeshire, George McCreedy, Noah Holman, and Hannah Singer, acting as lead."

"And who advocates for the Church?"

"Mark Freedman, Richard Chapel, Hunwald Gire, and Victor Spire, acting as lead," came the response from my left.

"Will the Petitioner please take the stand?"

Farmer walked out like he was facing a firing squad, resolute and ready to face what was coming. Hold tight, Farmer. I'll get you out of this.

With Farmer in the dock, the juniors sat. Holman took the now empty Petitioner's seat, and McCreedy was left standing, my orders. Gabriel said, "Advocate for the Petitioner goes first. Lady Singer, your opening statements, please."

If Spire had any doubt we knew what he was up to, my opening statements eliminated it. "Man does not live alone. It would be so easy if that were so. We are born, we live for a while, and then we die, all without setting foot outside our boxes. It would be so simple to make sure everyone lived a good life that way.

"But we don't. Man lives in a society. We are supposed to interact with each other. We are supposed to look out for each other. We are supposed to use our strengths to protect each others' weaknesses. It is part of the Divine Plan. We serve God by serving each other.

"John Farmer looked out for and protected his fellow man. We all know about professional pardoners. We keep dealing with the results of their actions in our trials." I snuck a look at the Tribunal. Some of them were nodding their heads in agreement. "Some of the things people were atoning for weren't even sins. They knew it, but some person who claimed to be an official from the church told them it was. They erred on the side of caution and bought indulgences that weren't needed. Or weren't adequate. Or were just flat out conned.

"Farmer knew the Bible and canonical law well enough to see what was happening. He couldn't teach people the truth. He isn't from the church. He doesn't hold their salvation in his hands. So he tried a different idea. He sold his own indulgences, no less valid in the eyes of the buyers, and far more in line with what the Bible says is appropriate. He made himself an extension of the church for the good of his fellow man. People were no longer sacrificing what they needed to survive. They did good works. They affirmed the glory of God. Farmer's service is above and beyond the call of duty and his petition should be granted. Thank you."

I turned my head to look at Spire. He looked ready to spit nails. Good. That moved it into the realm of the personal, where Spire was sure to lose. He launched into his opening arguments. "Let's suppose, one day, we get a person who claims to be the Messiah. He starts his own religious following. People worship him. People do as he says, even when it contradicts established church teachings. These people do fine and lead good lives.

"It doesn't matter how much good they did. The person still impersonated a holy being. He misled.

"He *lied*.

"This is John Farmer's crime. Not only did he falsify his identity, not only did he call down blessings he wasn't authorized to do, but he denied the authority of the Catholic church. The one true church, founded when the Holy Spirit came upon the Apostles. He has committed an egregious fraud, placing himself as greater than actual servants of God. He made himself God, determining who was worthy and who wasn't. He helped people. Doesn't matter. These people had it in them to be worthy and repentant with true church leaders. He overstepped his bounds. His usurped authority. And he had no compelling reason to do so. He should be Cast Down. Thank you."

Spire liked to overplay his hand during opening arguments. The guy loves being dramatic. Spire had neatly summarized the three points I needed to chip away at – false identity, no right to call down blessings, and defying the Catholic church. And I had to take them all down, none of them could be left standing or Martin Luther and the others would be sunk. Defying the Catholic church was going to be a philosophical argument. Spire's thoughts were too lucid right now, the fight would be too protracted. Better to shake him up first. And Spire gave me the opening on a silver platter. "Farmer was fully authorized to act as an agent of God."

Spire turned to me fully. He wanted to make me sorry. "By who?"
"By God."
Spire was incredulous. "God never said he could be an agent."
"God has implied it."
"How?"

"We all have the light of God within us. We benefit from His grace. We can do things in His name, such as calling down blessings."

"Wrong," Spire sneered.

"Holy water," I said simply.

Spire looked taken aback. "What?"

"Holy water. Take some water, pinch of salt recommended but not required, and say a prayer. If a person's faith is strong enough, it becomes holy water."

Spire saw where this was going, and he didn't like it. "Only priests are allowed to make holy water."

I didn't dare close my eyes. I enjoyed the sight as a lightning bolt streaked through the ceiling and hit Spire right between the eyes, throwing him back against his juniors. They heaved Spire back onto his feet. As the char marks vanished, Spire straightened his robes and tried to act like nothing happened. But something did. "You know that was a lie, Spire."

Spire glared at me. "Holy water should come from church officials. It's authority. It's chain of command."

"So the point of the church is to take abilities God gave man and restrict them?"

"It's not restricting, it's regulating. Otherwise, everyone will be making holy water."

"Oh, no. A world full of people who can make holy water. Might as well open the seals and start the Apocalypse."

Spire closed his eyes. It wasn't anger, he was thinking. He knew he had to come up with perfect arguments or my holy water gambit would literally wash away his moral high ground.

He opened his eyes. I saw uncertainty in them. "The church is authority. It exists to help teach people. What you are advancing means that the church has no authority. People don't need it because they can do the things it offers themselves. The church is to have a place in people's lives. It is why the church should make holy water instead of common people. Why the church should establish marriages instead of common law. Why the church should lead people to spiritual enlightenment."

"You are simply reinforcing my point, that the church exists to take away abilities and privileges granted by God."

Spire brightened. He had an idea. "If people have all these abilities, why have Jesus? He said He is the light and the way. In other words, man does not save himself, Jesus saves him. Not everything is within us, some things needs help. Focus. Someone in charge. It is why Jesus gave us the church and referred to it."

"If the church is absolute authority, why isn't participation compulsory?"

Spire's face dropped. I was about to reverse his momentum. "It is compulsory. You can't get into Heaven without it."

Gabriel started coughing, the kind of cough that almost but doesn't quite cover up a laugh. Everyone in the court knew I had been an Atheist but I had a Heavenly reward waiting for me.

I didn't make myself the focus, I had a better idea. "Christianity is founded on Judaism, correct?"

Spire dug in. "Correct."

"And Judaism taught that good people get into Heaven, be they Jews, Gentiles, or Atheists, correct?"

"Old Testament," Spire countered. "Jesus established a new covenant, where He is the light and the way."

"Which He established by acting as an independent agent of God," I countered. "Remember, He challenged the Pharisees for being more concerned about maintaining their place in the social order than the spiritual development of their followers. He not only called down blessings by Himself without being a church official, but defied an established order because He felt it was in the wrong." Two with one shot. Not bad, if I do say so myself.

Spire was finally getting wobbly. "He was Jesus. He was the Son of God. He wasn't human."

Holman shot to his feet. "He was human. He lived among us as a man, not a god. He sought to understand us, not for us to understand Him."

"He didn't need to understand us. He was all. He knew all."

I moved. "Then why did He have His doubts about God's plan and His own death? That's not the behavior of a god, that's the behavior of a man. A man who is scared."

"Jesus feared nothing!" Spire yelled.

Yes! Spire finally lost his focus. I pressed. "He asked His disciples to stay awake with Him the night before His capture, didn't He?"

Spire tried to salvage things. "Which has nothing to do with any of this. It's not Jesus that is on trial here. John Farmer is on trial."

Bull, I thought. But I said, "Your whole Catholic church is founded on the idea that there are times when the church is wrong. That there are times when man not only needs to take action for himself, but for others as well. That the reason these blessings and abilities God gave us all are never surrendered to the church is because we may need them someday to do the right thing."

"Plenty of people regard the church as right," Spire countered.

"Majority rule?" I smirked.

"There's a reason things are popular."

"The church spread in popularity thanks to the efforts of Paul. It wasn't some great enlightenment that everyone understood or accepted. Otherwise, Jesus would have been welcomed and not killed, would he?"

"You are talking about salvation," Spire grumbled. "There are ceremonies. Rites. We are trained to do them properly. Regular people are not."

Holman scratched the center of his forehead with his ring and pinkie fingers. He was signaling to me he could take this if I was stumped. I made a fist with my left hand and put the top against my mouth like I was suppressing a burp. I was signaling to him that I was setting something up, just play along.

First order of business, keep Spire fired up so he wouldn't realize the golden openings he was making. "You are building a moat between God and His people. And church officials are the only ones who will take things across."

"Absolutely not," Spire said. "Would you trust someone untrained in weapons to wield a sword? Would you trust someone untrained in how to be a king to run a country? Christianity is about more than people's individual faith, it involves matters spiritual that people don't understand or don't have the background for. That is why we are what we are."

"And all those other indulgences you argued for and got accepted? The ones by people who weren't part of the church?"

Spire looked like his insides had turned to ice. He turned to Gabriel. "Those had extenuating circumstances."

Gabriel looked completely disinterested. "Each of which has had to be argued and judged on its own merits. You always have to validate why indulgences should or should not stand. This time is no exception."

Spire looked at me. I could feel the feral look my face had twisted into. "Go on," I growled. "Argue."

Spire meekly said, "He impersonated a church official. He had no right to call down blessings. His penances were too mild."

Spire had just closed his coffin. I just had to nail it shut. "Which has not been grounds to contest certain indulgences. If we accept what you say, then ALL indulgences, even the sincere and official ones, are invalid."

I caught the movement of Holman sitting back down. The movements were calm and relaxed. He knew this was over. So did Spire. "Move for closing arguments," he mumbled.

"I concur," I said to Gabriel.

Gabriel gestured to Spire, and he started. "Singer makes a convincing argument. No doubt about it. She presents what Farmer did as being about mercy, about understanding. That he did nothing wrong in the eyes of God. But he did. His error was his belief that he was just as good as the church. That he understood humanity just as well as the church.

"The church was created to be God's representative on Earth. To help tend the flock. To guide people to the truth. We have seen plenty of examples of what happens when people think they know better. Faith is corrupted. The glory of God is corrupted. The Gnostics. The various groups during the time of Jesus. All based on competing with each other instead of presenting a united front, giving people one answer instead of several confusing ones.

"Farmer ultimately did nothing wrong. But it only worked out that way. Had he tried for anything further, he could have given out indulgences out of proportion for the sin. He could have worked the crowds for monetary gain. The only reason we don't know for sure what would have happened was he was murdered. He didn't live long enough to go astray.

"He would have. Many have. Many will.

"Singer is attempting to redress what Farmer did as no harm done.

Doing so creates a dangerous precedent. It opens the door for others who think they know better to overthrow the established order. An order created from care and dedication, from consideration over centuries, not a spur of the moment, knee jerk reaction. This is the danger, that things are being done as a reaction, not as a reasonable conclusion. This is Farmer's crime. This is why he should be Cast Down. Thank you."

Gabriel looked at me, and I was off. "Spire's arguments posit there is a difference between a knee jerk reaction and a reasonable conclusion. He overlooks that one can and often does inform the other. When you grab a rose and get stuck by a thorn, your immediate reaction is to not do that. The reasonable reaction is grab in a way that won't stick you next time. The knee jerk response in this case is completely validated.

"The knee jerk response to Spire's statements is to dismiss them for being too vague, too general, to strip away Farmer from the proceedings. However, that informs the reasoned response that comes when you actually attempt to take what he says seriously. Spire undermines himself because he has defended phony pardons and corrupt pardoners with the very reasoning he now decries. The only difference is, who gets the credit, the church or the person?

"Farmer's indulgences were completely in line with the teachings of the church, Jesus Christ, and God Himself. They were far more appropriate than the church's own indulgences. They protected the faithful from predators who sought to exploit them. This is actually what the church itself teaches – that there are times when doing the right thing in defiance of authority is most important. The church did this themselves with the Crusades. Should they have fought? Doesn't matter, the point is, they did, and everyone was pardoned for it. For doing what they felt was right.

"Farmer didn't do what he did as an act of petulance. He wasn't out to show the church's hypocrisy or stupidity or evil. He did it to help others. No one can know everything, so those with knowledge are obligated, by God's design and by compassion for their fellow man, to share and help those without it. Does this remind you of another man? It should. Jesus Christ. Born into an era with a religious order that He felt was more concerned with its own place in society, He defied them and taught something new. A new path to enlightenment. He didn't do it because He was Jesus, He did it because He felt things had to be different.

"Farmer, obviously, isn't Jesus. He didn't perform miracles. But from the standpoint of trying to educate people, he did the exact same thing as his Savior. He didn't seek to destroy the order he disagreed with, only to help others see a better way. He arrived at his conclusions with the very knowledge the church teaches and defends. The issue Spire is making is that this knowledge was used counter to what was good for the church, and who cares if it was good for the faithful. The church is not absolute. God is. And when the church does things that violate His will, those who recognize it have an obligation to do something about it. Farmer already served God. His actions were to serve his fellow man. He has acted in the best tradition of the saints. He deserves nothing less than Heaven. Thank you."

Gabriel looked to the Tribunal. "You have heard the Advocates for John Farmer state their recommended fates. You may now make your decision. You wish to confer?"

The lead Tribunal shot to his feet. No one tried to stop him. "We are ready to rule."

"And what is your decision?"

"Petition for entry into Heaven is granted immediately."

"So be it!" Gabriel declared as he slammed the gavel. Everyone rose as Gabriel and the Tribunal left the courtroom.

Once they were gone, Farmer raced out of the dock and shook all the Celestial hands he could, and made sure to thank Michael. He went through the Petitioner's Exit as fast as he could.

Macht looked at the now empty Tribunal box. "That was fast. They didn't even deliberate. Maybe we didn't have to prepare so much."

"Not at all," I smiled at him. "You saw how general those arguments were. If we hadn't fought them, who knows who they would have been applied to?"

Holman and Michael smiled at me as if we say, "Oh, we know."

Everyone was congratulating each other when we heard someone clearing their throat. I turned and saw Spire looking at me. Only it wasn't the way he always does – barely restrained fury. He was looking heartbroken.

"Do you have any idea what you've done?" he asked.

"Yes," I said. "I kept a soul from being Cast Down."

"You know about Martin Luther," Spire said, starting to shake. "You know what his philosophy will teach."

"He will teach what makes sense to him."

"He will destroy the holy church! Saying that only God can forgive sins and not the church!"

"But that's true. Even if someone is absolved of murder, they must still account for what they've done up here."

Spire looked pained. I almost started to feel sympathy for him. "The point of the church is to act as an intermediary. We have a more direct link to God. We can make things happen for the good of our flock."

"Then why don't you? Money taken in from indulgences goes to pet projects instead of the good of the parishioners. How can you stand there with a straight face and say everything you do is beneficial?"

"Think about the alternative Luther will present!" Spire was practically pleading. "Only God can forgive, so the Christian life he will present will be harsher. Less forgiving. He rejects anything not in the Bible. He will reject science, a gift from God so people can live better. He will reject any new religious philosophy. He will present closed mindedness as the path to salvation!"

"Which is already happening," I said calmly.

"And that makes it okay?!? The solution to uncertainty is more uncertainty?!?"

I leaned into his face. "People are to search for their answers. Some come from the church. Some come from other religions. Some come from their own hearts. People will go to Luther because they want to learn. And they will learn what they need to."

"And then what? They'll move on?"

"Some will," I said. "People don't need formal learning to be close to God. They just have to want to be. To reach out to Him, and He'll be there."

"People don't realize that," Spire said. He sounded deflated, knowing he would never change my mind. "They go to church and think attendance is good enough."

"Well, whose fault is that, then? The church teaches that it is supreme, not God. It harnesses God. It controls His mercy. The Afterlife is what really matters, and people are taught that not listening will cost them that. Luther's church and your church both seek to control people. The only difference is which church they serve."

Spire simply shook his head. "You are so focused on letting people do what they want. Don't you understand there are times when liberty is wrong? When people have to be restrained? It's for their own good."

"But it's not God determining that liberty. And it's not the people themselves. It's you. You and your little exclusive club. I don't buy that. And neither does God. The Celestial Courts, the sacrament of forgiveness, liberty itself, none of those things would exist otherwise."

Spire just shook his head and walked away. I knew what he was saying. But it had to be this way. There had to be choices. There had to be ways to learn. There is no one path to God. And bad though the future was, restricting it was worse.

The rest, as they say, is history. Martin Luther sent bishop Albert of Mainz his 95 Theses. Contrary to popular belief, he never nailed them to a church door as a public proclamation. In fact, it wasn't until early the next year, when the theses were translated from Latin into German and with an assist by the printing press, that things started taking off.

It was centuries later that I was sitting on the steps of the Eternal Sunrise, a beer stein full of jasmine tea with me. I held it with both hands and sipped as I thought.

"Here you are, Hannah," said the familiar voice of Michael on my right.

I didn't look at him as he came down and sat just above me. "You're upset," he commented.

I tried to deny it. "No, I'm not."

"You are sitting in your favorite reading spot without a book," he said simply.

He had me. My big brother knows me too well. I took a sip of jasmine tea and asked, "Do you ever think we made a mistake?"

"Like when?"

I reached to my left, where I had a scroll with a clasp holding it closed. I handed it to Michael, then took a big drink of tea, holding it in my mouth and swishing it around for a few seconds before swallowing.

Michael had unrolled the scroll and looked it over. "The John Farmer trial, huh?"

"Spire was right," I said glumly. "Luther's philosophy gave rise to ugliness. People think God is merciless now." I took another sip of tea. "We could have saved Farmer but left the points Spire wanted to use against Luther."

"What good would that have done?" Michael asked me. "We would be the only ones who knew Luther's splinter group was ruled invalid. Those on Earth wouldn't have a clue."

"There has to be some way to reach them," I said. "To let them know. I mean, look what happened. The Vatican used to promote the sciences. The arts. They were losing followers, and had to become strict like the others. That's not what God wants for us. He wants us to learn. To understand. To advance."

"Some people figure that out."

"And those that don't? They're intimidated into staying with their churches. Into being strict. Because of fear. They are afraid God will damn them just because they didn't do what the church said."

"That's why the church is an extension of God, but not Him. It's why the Celestial Courts are separate. It's the whole purpose of God's mercy – to save people from a life they thought they had to live."

I couldn't say anything. I just tilted to the side, leaning on my big brother. I felt his hand reach behind me and rest on my left shoulder. I watched the Eternal Sunrise as my mind went blank for a while.

SELF-MADE MAN

My bookcase is full of all kinds of great books. It's a relatively small bookcase, the only one in my small quarters. I prefer to just go to the library, where I know I can find whatever I want, return it when I'm done, and not have to worry about it. So anything that goes in my bookcase is a trophy of sorts. It holds a special significance to me.

If you look at it nowadays, you'll see all kinds of giants in there. Shakespeare, of course. Mark Twain. Douglas Adams. Noel Coward. Frank Herbert. (No Isaac Asimov, but only because I don't have room for all his books. In fact, I don't think anyone has room for all his books. And yes, he's still writing, even on the other side.) Charles Schultz. Neil Gaiman. Peter S. Beagle. Edgar Allen Poe. James Thurber. Terry Pratchett. All kinds of things.

Sitting on the middle shelf, all the way on the left, is one particular book. It is an original first printing of *Frankenstein; or, The Modern Prometheus* by Mary Shelley (you can tell the first printing because it was originally published anonymously). Some people see it and figure it's because it was the first science fiction story, and written by a woman to boot. Take that, patriarchy!

But that's not why the book is there.

The story of Frankenstein is not science fiction.

It's science fact.

It actually happened.

And I was the lead Celestial in the trial....

It was the very early 19th Century. I reviewed the scrolls on my table in front of me, the scent of parchment and jasmine tea filling my senses. I was putting extra effort into the cases, even though they were pretty basic. Henry Gallows had become senior Church, and things were going exceptionally smoothly. I'd never known such a lack of hassle from a senior Church. Well, other than Alfred Smith, but he wasn't on the job long enough to really be a problem. There was a lot more mercy and understanding from the Gallows regime, which made me suspicious. I know it's cynical, but I just couldn't believe things were this good.

It was in the middle of my eighth review of a particular life scroll, and me wondering why I had even read it more than twice, that I heard a knock on the door to my quarters. I went to open it, and was greeted by the sight of Joshua Hunter. Hunter was an expert Celestial, and I'm not just saying that because he was my protégé. Hunter was the Celestial who handled shadow court cases. These are sort of outside regular Christian considerations, such as beings that aren't human but are seeking a place with God. The existence of the court is a general secret among us up here, very few know about it. I learned about it when a mermaid needed help and Hunter wasn't quite ripe. I led the case and scored the win despite some very cruel manipulations on the part of the Churches that almost literally destroyed her. Since then, Hunter had grown into a formidable Advocate in his own right. The last time there was a trial in the shadow court, he led (I juniored just to make sure someone had his back) and he blew everybody away. Made me feel very proud.

I still saw Hunter every once in a while, and not just because I was senior Celestial and senior grey. He was a great guy with a competitive streak. Watching him, St. Michael, and I go at each other was always fun (although it really was the two of us competing for second place. No one beats Michael). However, he never sought me out in my quarters before. And coming to me meant only one thing.

I gestured for him to come in, and as soon as he cleared the door, I closed it and vanished it into the wall. Only angels could enter now. I looked at him. "Shadow court case?"

"Right you are," he said apologetically. "I just got done with a special consultation with Michael."

"I'm guessing you're here because you think you need my help."

"No. I *know* I need your help."

"Hang about," I said, a thought striking me at that moment. "What shadow court case? I'm senior Celestial and senior grey. I haven't seen anything like it, and Michael hasn't mentioned anything."

Hunter's hands shot up in "stop" gestures. "He's not keeping you out of the loop...."

I waved my hand and smiled. "Oh, I know he's not." If St. Michael didn't tell me about something, he had a good reason and I didn't question it.

Hunter relaxed a little as he continued. "You haven't heard anything about it because the shadow is still on Earth. He hasn't died yet."

"So Michael's keeping a close eye on him."

"Yes."

I thought for a moment. "I would suggest we include Michael in this discussion so I can get a complete overview."

Hunter nodded. "Sounds good to me. Besides, you'll probably be leading anyway."

I made my door reappear. "Nah, you're sharp enough. You'll do fine."

Hunter looked at me, dead serious. "I'm requesting you to be lead."

Suddenly, all of this took on a dangerous dimension. Even for shadow cases, this was going to be bad. "Time's awasting. Let's go."

We walked with purpose and a little more speed than usual to Michael's chambers. I knew he'd be there. Once Hunter and I got into the hall outside my quarters, I signaled a putto to find Michael and ask him for an emergency consultation. We had just gotten outside the building when the putto returned to say he'd be waiting for us.

Michael's door was open. Force of habit made me notice it was open too wide for there to be a bucket of water perched on it. I knew I didn't have to worry at a time like this, but I couldn't help it.

Michael was at his desk. He looked uncharacteristically worried. Hunter and I got inside, and Michael vanished the door into the wall. My eyes went to a life scroll on his desk. It was amazingly small, like a baby's scroll. I pointed to it. "Is that our subject of discussion?"

"Yes, it is," Michael said.

Suddenly, I caught movement in the scroll. The end was in a different position. Life scrolls are self-modifying, so something happened to the subject and the information was just added.

I felt my head shift back a little bit. It couldn't be a baby. Baby scrolls don't modify so dramatically. I mean, they're babies. They eat, sleep, and mess themselves. They don't do much of note. But it wasn't big enough to be a full grown adult. Hunter and I moved to the chairs in front of Michael's desk as I ordered, "All cards on the table, Michael."

"The shadow is named Adam. He wasn't born. He was assembled."

I felt my eyes fly open. "Someone did it. Someone actually created life."

"Yeah," Michael said.

I leaned back in the chair, holding my chin and looking aside. Michael and I had discussed what would happen if someone ever succeeded in creating life. Michael said that God would not just leave a body roaming around without any control. God would have granted whatever it was a soul. But shadow trials were usually about something not of God's creation requesting a soul. Adam already had one. "Why is this even a shadow case?" I asked.

"Because this is not only completely without precedent, but we have a relatively new senior Church. He could conceivably move to have the soul nullified."

Michael was referring to Henry Gallows. Through a series of strange circumstances, Gallows had become senior Church. Gallows was a good guy who tried to be understanding of people instead of going for the harsh punishments his predecessors sought. "You really think Gallows would oppose this?"

"It's not likely, but it is possible," Michael said.

I knew what he meant. Things we claim we will or won't do are largely academic in nature. A lot of those situations, like killing a home invader or having an unplanned pregnancy, we won't wind up in. So we are mostly guessing how we will react in those situations. True, our behavior is pretty consistent, so we have a good idea how we'll react and will follow through when the situation appears. But it's not absolute, and every once in a while, we do behave out of character despite everything in our nature telling us what we should do. It just seemed unlikely with Gallows. He was a straight shooter, he was considerate, and he genuinely sought to do right by God and people. I'd bet against it.

Suddenly, a thought struck me. I looked at Michael and Hunter, and saw they were looking at me with uncertainty. Ah, I get it. They weren't sure how I'd react to that scroll. To tell the truth, I wasn't sure, either.

I locked Michael's gaze with mine. "Let me see the scroll."

Michael took a deep breath, then picked it up and extended it to me. "I warn you, Hannah – it's not pretty."

"We're talking life here," I said as I took it and prepared to open it. "Life seldom is pretty."

As I started to open the scroll, I saw the top of a picture border. I was going to get a perfect view of Adam. I didn't want to spook Michael and Hunter by flipping at the image, so I let my eyes unfocus, turning the scroll contents into a blur as I stretched it. I got it to the point where the picture and the start of Adam's personal information was visible. I focused on the words, focused my eyes, and slowly moved my eyes up, building the image gradually to keep the shock value to a minimum.

The image would horrify most people. But it didn't affect me that way. All I felt was deep sympathy and heartbreak. I mean, yeah, he resembled a patchwork doll, with scars and lesions and bodily fluids seeping out. But that only made me want to help him somehow. I didn't know how, but I wanted to spare him any pain that I could, and comfort any I couldn't.

Based on the stitching I saw, the head was made from three separate individuals. And that was just the head itself. The eyes didn't match. The mouth was slightly twisted, like the jaw didn't fit properly on one side. My God, could he even talk? Did his eyes have close to the same visual range? Was his skin preserved, and if it was, could he feel anything, from a breeze to the warmth of the sun? His body was completely asymmetrical, with different muscle builds and even two right hands instead of a regular set. Some muscles bunched in ways they weren't supposed to, making me wonder if there were some additions made before the parts were attached. Most likely – someone doing this isn't concerned with the dignity and aesthetics his creation would be stuck with.

I started reading Adam's details. It was worse than I thought. Not every part inside him was human. He was literally using any organ that could be found to do the job, even if they came from animals (he had four sets of lungs to supply him with oxygen, coming from three different dogs). If this were the modern day, I would have been surprised that the creator somehow forgot to include duct tape in all of this. At least the brain was human, coming from a woodsman who was in the wrong place at the wrong time. He didn't have the woodsman's identity, though. The soul had it's own.

There was a strange fascination to this, seeing everything put together and struggling to work. It's like the joke about the dancing elephant – you aren't surprised it dances well, you are surprised it dances at all. But we have knowledge of the human body that the living have no clue about. These conflicting parts couldn't last. "How long has he got, Michael?"

"A week at the most," Michael said. He was fighting back tears. He also hated seeing Adam suffer. I stole a look at Hunter, and saw his head bowed in despair as well. Michael rubbed his eyes and continued talking. "His survival instincts are working, so he's finding water. He's scrounging just enough food.

Plants, small animals, even took down a few wolves that tried to get him."

"Physical failure," I said.

"Yeah. His whole body is at war with itself because of all the component pieces. It's only because of his will he's made it this long. Only thing that would kill him faster would be if villagers found him."

I looked at the scroll to get his location. "Middle of nowhere."

"Where else would anyone conduct unholy works?" Michael shrugged.

"I'm not running from him," I told Michael. "If Adam doesn't need me, fine. I'll be the first to have tea with him when I get to Heaven. If Gallows does oppose, I'm in, and I'll get Adam in if I have to drag him through the Pearly Gates myself."

Michael rested his head in his hand. "This can be so frustrating," Michael mumbled. "We angels love humans. If we could save you from all suffering, we'd do it gladly. If we could suffer for you, we would. I hate it that sometimes...."

"Sometimes, we have to bleed," I supplied.

He angled his eyes up and nodded sadly. We spent the rest of the time discussing the worst case scenario and what we would do.

Humans are an ambitious lot. This ambition has lots of positives to it. It is what fuels scientific advancement. Things that make life better come as a result of people trying to learn what makes the world tick and how to change that rhythm.

Nowhere is this more evident than with matters of life and death. Man is not meant to live forever. But most men aren't looking to live forever, just a little bit longer. Those that do want to live forever, though, get really interesting.

Man has long sought the Secret Of Life. Complete mastery over death. It was lucky Adam and Eve ate from the Tree Of Knowledge – the other tree they could have eaten from would have made them immortal (thankfully, they were too busy freaking out over what they'd done to think to do that). Other men have tried, bolstered by stories of people like Elijah and Jesus raising people from the dead. The official Catholic church, which for the longest time was a huge proponent of the sciences, realized this might be a Bad Idea, and said don't do it.

And ambitious people then did what ambitious people do now – ignore that.

Many tried to create life, but none of them really knew what they were doing. Even Giovanni Aldini's galvanism demonstrations on the body of George Forster were just simple parlor tricks until the muscles deteriorated from being seriously dead. But the first person to get way too close to the truth was a man born in the actual honest-to-God Castle Frankenstein. Johann Konrad Dippel was a Pietist studying theology, philosophy, and alchemy (yes, it was taught once upon a time). Dippel felt religious institutions were counter to the Will of God and advocated their abolishment. He also denied the Bible as the literal Word of God. For Dippel, this led to a rejection of any outside influence on his personal code of ethics, referring to Jesus as "an indifferent being." Dippel returned to home to Castle Frankenstein and began dark experiments at the turn of the 18th century.

Dippel did a lot of scary stuff, one experiment resulting in the destruction of one of the castle towers (anyone who tells you Dippel was playing with nitroglycerin, don't believe them, that stuff wasn't invented until 1847). Rumors abounded of him experimenting on animals, robbing graves, and maybe even making a deal with the devil. Dippel eventually would claim he had discovered the Elixir Of Life. Problem was, Dippel died of a stroke in 1734, so no one really put much stock in his claims. They should have.

Dippel's findings were published posthumously under the name "Christianus Democritus" in a 1736 book called *Maladies And Remedies Of The Life Of The Flesh*. Some people who had been paying attention to his lectures and his writings tried to carry on the tradition. And one of them succeeded.

No one kept official records for fear of being beset by angry Christians with pitchforks and torches, so the legends that sprang up got merged with Dippel's findings. Yeah, it usually takes a while for legends to get going, but let's face it, this one was pretty big. I can't tell you everything, but I can tell you this much: Adam, the resulting being, didn't live very long. It started with his brain. The creator thought the resulting Adam was insane. Nope, he was just experiencing what is now known as ICU psychosis, which happens when the brain has been inactive for a prolonged period of time and is trying to operate properly again (coma patients go through it all the time). The parts of his body rejected each other, even the human parts, because no one had even conceived of "donor matching" at that time. With them fighting what they perceived as biological enemies, Adam went through a staggering amount of pain and trauma. He died in the woods, where local animals consumed his Whitman's Sampler of a body. Adam had been through a figurative Hell.

And I had to keep him out of the real one.

I knew the exact moment Adam finally and mercifully died. I had taken out his life scroll to reread it yet another time again just to keep up on what was happening. Most of me figured this would be open and shut, that Gallows would just approve petition and that would be that. But Michael clearly had a funny feeling about that happening. And the truth was, I did, too.

I was sitting in the Ancient Forest, back to one of the majestic trees rising out of the ground like a wooden waterspout. I just finished rereading it and had rolled it up. I set it aside and tilted my head back, listening to the bird singing and getting lost in my thoughts. I suddenly felt a strange flash of energy at my side. I looked at the life scroll. It suddenly had a tie around it.

I undid the tie and read the scroll. It was over for Adam now. I said a quiet prayer to God – please, let this be simple. Let him go home.

Michael suddenly turned up next to me, the speed of angels making it seem like he appeared out of thin air. It stopped making me jump centuries ago. I simply pointed to the tie on the back of the scroll and said, "I know, Michael. Just happened."

"I'm on my way to find him," Michael said.

That got my full attention. There is no fixed entry point for the Valley Of Death. Where the souls go depends on their mentalities when they were alive. Where would Adam be? How did Michael know where he would be?

Didn't matter. Michael wasn't just telling me so I would know, he wanted me there. I shot to my feet, grabbing the life scroll as I went.

He touched my shoulder, and the world around us shifted and swirled. When it settled, we were in one of the remotest parts of the Valley Of Death. It's simply called, "Chroma." The land is perfectly flat. The sky is perfectly clear. No birds in the air, no clouds, no vegetation. The ground is grey and the sky is almost the exact same shade of grey, close enough you can lose the horizon if you aren't paying attention. The wind doesn't blow, footprints are not left. If you travel that far and approach on foot, you can see the grey bleeding out into the area around it. It doesn't take long to get far enough inside, no other colors, features, or details are visible other than the continuous grey. Because it is so neutral, this is usually where people who suffered from mental imbalances on Earth turn up.

It's still a large area, and searching it becomes even harder when you have no bearings. You just don't know where you've been or even where you are until you see what lays beyond. Michael, however, was attuned to the Divine and with his speed, we had searched the area in a flash. Adam was quickly discovered.

I steeled myself to see what he would look like, and was also just a bit curious. When people die, their souls turn up completely intact. Missing body parts are restored, piercings are gone, any physical deformity is undone. What would Adam's soul look like?

Turns out, not too shabby. Adam's completed soul had no scars, and in fact, looked nothing like any of the component bodies he was made from. He even had a proper set of left and right hands. He was muscular and well-defined, easy to see because the clothes he was wearing when he died were reduced to just a few shreds of fabric here and there. His face was clean shaven, and short blond hair curled out of his head. Don't know what color his eyes were. They were closed, and he was seated on the ground and breathing deeply, absorbing the stability he never experienced in life.

Michael and I stood in front of him, waiting patiently. It soon became apparent this was going to take longer than we expected. Michael looked behind him to make sure his wings were put away (yeah, he knew, but he checked anyway. Go check if your stove is on), then politely cleared his throat.

Adam's eyes popped open. I had never seen such uncertainty before. I understood. He was beyond scared. With the clarity of mind, he knew there was no clear cut salvation for him. What would happen to him?

Time for a little bravado. I immediately stepped forward, extending my hand to him. "I'm Hannah Singer. I'm here to save you."

Well, THAT sure got his attention. "'Save me?' How? How can you save someone that isn't human?"

"I've done it before," I smirked.

"You mean, there are others like me?"

"Not exactly like you," I said, continuing to hold my hand out to him for...I don't know what. "But other souls that weren't born human? They go to Heaven. And I'm one of the people that makes that happen."

He examined my hand, unsure what he was to do with it. "It can't be that simple."

"Not for me, but for you it is," I said. "I do the dirty work, you just go to court, stand there, and go to your Heavenly reward."

"Why would you help me?" he asked, a defensive edge entering his voice. "I'm not human."

I pulled my hand away and pulled myself up to my average female height. Times like this, looks have nothing to do with it. It's all about the attitude, if you can sell it. And I knew how to sell it. "Of course, you are. Why would you even be here if you weren't?"

"Same reason I was alive – it was a mistake."

"You don't think you have a reward after serving God?"

His head rocked back a bit. "How did I serve God?"

"People have been getting too close to making life. They needed to know how dangerous that was."

He rolled his eyes. "Writing a book would be more effective."

Well, maybe. Adam didn't know humans very well. But this wasn't the time for that discussion. "God does not allow a human to exist without a soul. You were a human. You got one."

Adam looked angry. "God made me to suffer?"

"No. The sorcerer who created you did. He tampered with things he shouldn't have. He put that shell together. He did it just to say he created life, he cared nothing of the life he was creating. People were made to take care of each other for those times when God can't get involved."

"Why not?"

"If God stops us from going through the bad, there's no point to life. The soul doesn't exist in those situations. But He doesn't want people to suffer. It's why we are to take care of each other." I leaned in, resting my hands on my knees, and gave him my best smile. "And I'm going to take care of you."

"I would have rather been taken care of in life," he growled.

"Don't try to scare me. You think you're the first person I've met with a chip on his shoulder?"

"I'm not a person!" he screamed at me.

"Says you. Everyone else here, including the angel behind me, says you are."

His head jerked to Michael like he was noticing him there for the first time. "You're an angel?"

"You have no idea how I wish I could have helped you," Michael said. "How much I wish I could have changed your life. You and millions of people around the world. To spare you from suffering. To make others see the real you.

To treat you with the honor and dignity and respect all people deserve."

Adam was starting to tear up. "Why didn't you?"

"We can't. No matter how much we want to, some things, you can't fix even with the power of God Himself. All we can do is help as much as possible once you come to us." Michael was starting to tear up, too. It wasn't an act. It's never an act with Michael. "I'm so sorry."

Adam cracked like a stone under pressure. All his fear, all his anger, every conflicting emotion boiling inside him burst at once. Michael and I both rushed to him, dropping to our knees and wrapping him in the best hug we could. It took him a minute, but he eventually wrapped his arms around us and just let everything run out.

I don't know how long we stayed there. I wanted to stay longer just to make sure Adam had purged himself of the poison that had been distilling inside him. But Adam eventually felt he was ready to go. Michael touched both of our shoulders, and we were outside the clerks' offices. Michael told Adam what he had to do, and that we would wait for him. Michael didn't ask me if I wanted to wait. He didn't need to. As Adam went inside, I told him, "I promise you, I'll be there for you."

"Is she usually this sociable?" Adam asked.

"Don't let her fool you," Hunter said with a smile in his voice. "She is very much aware of her surroundings."

I didn't even look up from the scroll I was studying. "Adam? You're starting to tilt your cards down."

I heard the fast movements indicating that I was right. I then heard a quiet but distinct rumble from Hunter, meaning I caught Adam before his opponent had a chance to peek.

Hunter had fallen in with Adam and I, not only to help with the case, not only to see what further pointers he could pick up, but also just to see The Master at work. But I was so focused, I wasn't really interacting with them. Any questions or thoughts dripped out instead of gushing. To help kill time, Hunter was teaching Adam to play poker, a relatively recent card game spreading through the Mississippi Valley like chicken pox through a kindergarten class. Hunter taught our guest a two player variant with twenty cards, and despite only just being introduced to the game, Adam was already running rings around his opponent.

A real fast learner.

I tried, but a sigh escaped me.

Adam picked up on it. "Stumped?"

Hunter's voice was sympathetic. "No. That's her sigh when someone died before they could even reach their potential."

I tried to rebury myself in what I was reading, but Adam's next question ruined any chance of that happening. "Why would she care so much about me?"

I just looked at him. "Because I do. I couldn't do anything to help you while you were alive. All I can do is help you now."

"Why do you have to help me? Why can't I just go to Heaven?" he asked in exasperation, tossing his cards between him and Hunter. "I did what I was supposed to! I mean, what was I supposed to do?!?"

"Everyone goes through this, even the pure and righteous," I told him. "You can't take shortcuts into Heaven. Much as we would like to stuff every deserving soul into a cannon and fire them over the Pearly Gates, we can't. We have to face adversity. We prove ourselves by facing it."

He sagged. "Then I'm doomed. What adversity did I face?"

I leaned closer, softening my voice. "You're facing it now. Believe it or not, you are asking the same questions everybody on Earth asks."

"Everybody?"

"Everybody. Everybody wonders the same thing. 'Why am I suffering? Why can't it just be over?' Everybody wonders it." I paused for a moment, then I continued. "People think they suffer because God doesn't care. He does care. It's why He made you to overcome obstacles and problems. He made people to fix their situations, to end their suffering, to help each other out. The world is set up so that everyone, on their own or together, can overcome obstacles. The crime is not that people suffer. The crime is in people allowing others to suffer."

"But I didn't stop others from suffering."

"Yes, you did. No one else is trying to create life after seeing the results. And maybe you didn't stop any suffering by those around you, but it's not like you added to it. Your case is a series of special circumstances."

"Maybe I'm not worth the effort."

"You are," I told him. "I know how terrible Hell is. I also know how beautiful Heaven is. And I'm going to cover every angle and get you in."

Adam ducked his head and started gathering up his cards. Hunter took advantage of the lack of attention to give me a look. We communicated so expertly on cases, we didn't need words. And I knew what that look meant.

He was afraid Adam wouldn't be granted Heavenly admission.

And Hunter had every reason to worry.

When Adam first came alive, his mind was in shock, and it still wasn't under control when his body died. You get into Heaven by understanding life, love, and preciousness. He had no chance to experience those things, and the window where he could show he did understand and appreciate them, his time in the Afterlife before trial, was rapidly running out.

I kept going over every avenue I could think of in hopes of minimizing the focus on Adam's actions and going for the general points. No one who had ever gone through the shadow court had ever been denied, but even among shadow cases, this was unique, so all bets were off. I would read, study, think, and when I had any spare moments, I would pray that it was unnecessary, that senior Church Henry Gallows would simply approve petition and Adam would just be on his way before the ink dried. I should have also prayed for a pony and an ice cream for all the good it did.

Gallows had filed his official contest. I told Adam and Hunter it was to be expected. Which wasn't a lie. I did expect it. I was just...disappointed, I guess, that it happened. I decided to have a little consultation. It would probably take me a little while to locate Gallows, so I decided to do things the easy way. I asked a Putto to arrange a meeting in the Ancient Forest, his favorite spot, and set off on my way.

The Ancient Forest is huge, but there's one place that Gallows always gravitates to. There's a nice hill partway through. The upward slope and most of the sides are grass covered, but the far side drops off and reveals a rocky outcropping, like the stone formation is pushing itself out of the ground and bursting through. The rocks have interesting shapes and cracks. Just like clouds, you can sometimes see images there if you let your imagination run. And unlike clouds, this never moves or changes, and yet I don't think I've ever seen the same thing twice in there.

Gallows had actually gotten here before me, which was surprising. Maybe he was already here. He was seated on the ground, crosslegged, just looking at the rocks. His gaze was different this time, though. He wasn't seeing what might be there. He was looking deeper. For answers.

I sat next to him. What I was about to do might be considered a risk, but I wouldn't do it with anyone other than Gallows. Collusion on any case for any reason was grounds to automatically Cast Down. Admittedly, a trial would prove you innocent, but no one wants to be labeled a troublemaker, even someone like me. But Gallows would never do something like that. It was strange how much I trusted him.

"See anything interesting?" I asked.

He didn't say anything.

"Nice day, isn't it?"

Nothing.

"Well, enough idle chitchat. Why did you do it?"

A long beat, then he asked, "You mean, contesting Adam's petition?"

This wasn't the time for me to be smart. I just said, "Yes."

He bowed his head, like he was praying for something. Not strength. Maybe wisdom. "I didn't want to. I honestly didn't want to."

"Seems an easy enough situation to fix."

"...I can't," he finally said. "I don't want to contest. But I do want to contest. And the only thing I can allow myself to do is contest."

"Why?" I wasn't acting at this point. Gallows was a good man. He was fair. He was wise. He understood human nature and didn't hold mistakes against anyone. I couldn't figure out why he was opposed to Adam.

"He's not human," he finally said.

"Neither are others that have been through the shadow court. Come on, you have history against you, and you know I'm going to lead. You know you have no chance of winning. Why are you doing this?"

"I don't know!" he lashed out at me. Well, not at me, I wasn't the target. He was frustrated. "I know I shouldn't! Adam's soul is real! He experiences joy! Despair! He's...."

"He's made, not born."

"I'm scared," he said. "I mean, we are still supposed to defend God's will. It wasn't God's will that made Adam, it was a human. Who knows what will happen next?"

"And that's why? Because you don't know where it will stop?"

"What if this is too far and we just don't know it? We view history differently than we do the now. You know the expression, 'It seemed like a good idea at the time?' How do we know not contesting Adam is such a good idea? Humans on Earth are pushing limits every day. Things that people used to never consider, they're being constantly considered. Divorce, for example. How do we stop things from going into dangerous areas?"

"We don't," I told him. "We protect people from the choices they make, or that are made for them. We can't control those choices, or even stop them. Those of us that can go to Earth aren't allowed to interfere like that."

"Then we are failing," Gallows said. "People need guidance. They need to learn. They need to know. And we're stuck up here, just picking up the pieces." He turned to face me. "Do ever think about what life on Earth would be like if we could go back there and talk about the things we've seen? The things we know?"

"We wouldn't be listened to."

"But some would! We could save some people! We could help them be good to their fellow man! Help each other out! Not tamper with dangerous things like making life!"

"Everyone learns their own way. Otherwise, God would live among them instead of waiting for them to return to Him."

He turned back to the rocks. "How do you do it, Hannah?"

"Do what?"

"When I was alive, I never had to deal with half this stuff. I never even knew gays existed. That people mix across races. I've had to force myself to accept it. You just do. How do you do it?"

"I didn't accept just everything," I told him. "Some stuff, sure. But other stuff, I had to get over it, to accept that people do what works for them, and for me to judge them simply because I wouldn't do it is wrong. You're only seeing me now after I've had time to come around." Well, truth was, I came around pretty quickly anyway, it's just how I am. But this wasn't the time to mention that.

"I want to accept it. I should accept it."

"But you can't."

He took a deep breath. "Hannah? You embody God's love and God's will far better than any other human."

"Not Jesus," I smirked.

"I don't mean like that," he said with a sigh of exasperation. "I'm talking about within the Celestial Courts. I'm...I'm going to ask you for a favor...."

"I will NOT Collude," I told him with some anger.

"I'm not suggesting Collusion," he said. He didn't even move or change his tone of voice, my reaction just flowed past him. "You feel Adam deserves Heaven. And you are at peace with that stance." He looked at me. "I'm going to ask you to bring your best. Prove me wrong. Don't make him pay for my biases. Obliterate my case at trial. If he truly deserves Heaven, the angels on the Tribunal will allow it. Don't give me the chance to take that away."

I stood up. "I'm already working on it."

Gallows didn't look at me as I walked away, so he didn't see me look over my shoulder with a sinister smile. Getting Adam into Heaven? Oh, yeah. Already working on it....

I walked casually towards the Office Of Records building, trying to keep my casualness unconscious. The existence of the shadow court was not general knowledge in the Afterlife, and if anyone saw me walking with the usual Hannah Singer Determination, it might tip them off that something special was around.

Not that I was needed to suggest that. The entrance to the shadow court was located on a blank wall at the back of the building. It is the only section without any windows, doors, or anything to disrupt it. I figured there was something unusual about it the first time I saw it, but then again, that's how my mind works. Plenty of others never saw anything strange. They didn't even notice how the hedges and shrubbery across from it actually acted as a screen to keep anyone in the distance from seeing anything.

I got to the wall and took a quick look around. No one watching. I touched the blank section of the wall, and a cast iron double door appeared, black as a bottomless pit and each with a glowing white cross on it.

I touched the door on the right and got pulled through to the hallway. The doors would be vanishing again as soon as I got through, and I started stalking towards the courtroom at the other end. The monochromatic passage, with black walls and white floors, ceiling, and supports, only reinforced the importance of what I was about to face. I got to the black double doors on the other side, and passed through.

I carried the feelings of the hallway with me. The shadow court itself is actually very nice. Instead of the clean white stone of regular courtrooms, everything was made of wood, and the walls actually showed the outside of the Office Of Records. The Gallery was only about a quarter the size of the courtroom instead of half, and only a handful of angels sitting there. It was more intimate. More immediate.

I was actually the last one to arrive. Gallows was already seated at the Church table, head bowed in prayer. Adam was in the petitioner's seat, second in from the aisle at the Celestial table, with Hunter to his right. Michael was already standing in front of the judge's bench where the court guardian stood. He saw me and gave me a warm smile. The blind faith he puts in me really makes me uncomfortable sometimes. I willed myself not to crack and sat down.

Hunter leaned forward so he could see me past Adam as I folded my hands in front of me and faced the bench. "Hannah? Where's your scrolls?"

It was a habit I had started with all the other Advocates, Celestial and

Church. A look at the scrolls on the table in front of the Advocate and how they are grouped can give you an idea what kind of fight they are expecting. My table was empty. I looked at Gallows, and saw he was looking in surprise, too.

I smiled at Gallows. "Don't need 'em."

Gallows had several scrolls on his table, as well as a Bible with several bookmarks in it. It was a King James version, standard size, so I immediately had a rough idea what many of the passages were. Not that they were going to do him any good. Or me. My whole trial strategy hinged on a gamble. Gallows didn't realize how easy his fight was.

To get into Heaven, a person needs to show, for lack of a better term, enlightenment. That they understand how important humanity is and how to act with it. To see the sacredness and beauty of life. Adam spent his entire time alive in the grip of mental illness, and he was only alive a short time. Precedents or no, the Tribunal would never approve his petition with the information at hand. I was going to have to get Adam to demonstrate he understood these universal truths on an instinctive level. If I did that, I had the whole thing in the bag. If I didn't, Adam would be the first loss a Celestial ever had in the shadow court. Not on my watch.

Gallows actually looked concerned. He genuinely wanted to lose this case. And he probably would have more confidence if I approached this case with the "scorched earth" style I usually apply in the tougher ones. In fact, the only one who didn't seem to think anything odd was happening was Michael. It was like he didn't know how things would get to the end, but he knew full well what the ending would be.

There wasn't much time for anyone to really wonder. The chimes sounded, signaling the start of court. Everyone stood, and those of us with them deployed our wings. The door on the right opened, and the twelve angels making up the Tribunal entered. I shifted my eyes to Adam to gauge his reaction. It would be my first indication of how hard I had to fight or if I needed to be ready for my Plan B.

Adam watched the Tribunal. It was subtle, but he was enraptured by the grace and beauty he saw. Okay. Not great, but definitely good. I had a fighting chance after all.

The door at the back of the court opened, and Pahaliah, the presiding angel, entered. Pahaliah is the angel prayed to to bring people around to Christianity, so he was the natural choice to be the specially appointed judge of the shadow court. Pahaliah and I go way back, when he presided at my original trial. He was very tolerant of my behavior in court. And I think he could tell, from how I wasn't beaming at his presence, that I was going to need every inch I could get.

Pahaliah got up to the bench and set the black record scroll he was carrying down on the left. He looked at Adam and gave him a smile and a nod.

I shifted my eyes to Adam again. He looked a little confused, like a little kid the grown-ups suddenly focus on. He gave a quick nod of his head. Not a rude one, just an uncertain one. Goooooooooooood....

Pahaliah sat, banged the gavel, and the Tribunal and Gallery sat. "Who is the Petitioner?" he called.

"The Petitioner is Adam," I said.

"No last name?"

"That IS his last name, sir," I smiled. I heard a quiet snort out of Adam. Still looking good....

I wasn't really acting jovial, so I knew Pahaliah would pick up. Instead of continuing the banter, he moved right along. "And who are his Advocates?"

"Joshua Hunter and Hannah Singer, acting as lead."

"And who advocates for the Churches?"

"Henry Gallows, acting alone," came the response.

"Will the Petitioner please take the stand?"

As Adam walked up to the dock, Hunter moved in to take the now empty seat. As he moved in, he whispered, with concern evident in his voice, "Are you sure you can win this without scrolls?"

"I have everything I need."

He smiled. "Yeah. Yourself."

"Better than that. I have Gallows."

Hunter turned his head to me in confusion, but before he could ask anything else, Adam was installed in the dock. Court was fully in session, and Hunter sat.

Pahaliah said, "Advocate for the defense goes first. Lady Singer? You're opening statements, please."

"God is love. He loves all. He forgives all. Even in the days before Christianity, you didn't have to be a worshiper of God for Him to love you.

"God so loves that He has created this, the shadow court, so that those that exist outside of His creation can still earn a place in Heaven. You just have to be the best you can be.

"Adam was the best he could be. What else could he be, given the short amount of time and limited abilities he had? For him to enter Heaven, he has to show that he has learned from the experiences, and he understands what makes humanity what it is." I looked Adam square in the eyes and smiled. "And I will prove that to you in the course of this trial. You are angels. You no doubt feel his apprehension. Once I remove his apprehension, you will see the beautiful soul God granted that body, and see that the only possible choice to make," and here I looked at Gallows, "is to allow him into Heaven. Thank you."

There was a significant pause before Gallows started speaking. It was like it was being dragged out of him. "As Singer has rightly said, the purpose of this trial is to find the truth. So what is that truth? What is it you have to decide?

"Each of us thinks we know the truth. It is based on our thoughts, our reasoning, our feelings. And the feelings of the Church are that Adam is not a proper soul. He is a construct made to do a job, which was to occupy a body until it fell apart. The body was not made through God's design. It was not made by a divine act between a man and a woman. It was cobbled together.

Adam did not go to Earth to learn and grow, he was there to fill a gap and that is it. As such, he is not like other shadows that pass through this court. He isn't a spirit that wants to be human. In fact, he didn't even want to be created. Understandable, given that his life was a literal nightmare.

"Shadow trials are always horrific, because one possible outcome is denying that most precious gift of all, the grace of God. But it is the only real outcome that can happen here. Adam has served his purpose. He is nothing more than a means to an end, and he should dissipate. Thank you."

I looked at Adam in the dock and gave him a smile and a nod. He looked confused. Did I really think I had this? Yes, I did. The Tribunal was already on my side. Gallows was in perfect position. I just needed to fix the only thing that could sink the case -- Adam himself.

Time was not on my side. The more time people have to think, the more they can convince themselves of things and reinforce their fears and doubts. Adam had his own ideas about why he didn't deserve salvation. Time to pave the road.

Gallows and I turned to face each other. Gallows, as usual, didn't want a fight. He actually wanted to lose. But I couldn't just squash him, or Adam would never be approved. I had to stall. But Gallows was ready to listen. He would give me the opportunities I needed.

I started with a softball, low and over the plate. "Let's talk about Adam."

"Very well," Gallows responded.

"Not this Adam," I said with a polite point of my finger. "I'm talking THE Adam. The first Adam. From the Garden Of Eden."

Gallows quirked his face. "The one you said you would punch in the face if you ever met him?"

I leaned my head around to the Tribunal and gave them a toothy smile. "Ha ha. He's such a kidder."

Most of the Tribunal immediately adopted Gallows' expression. I don't exactly keep quiet about my feelings on Adam betraying Eve. In my defense, most angels feel the exact same way.

Well, back to work. "Let's revisit the creation of the Biblical Adam."

"What's there to revisit?" Gallows asked, genuinely confused.

"Humor me," I said.

"Okay," he said with a shrug. "Adam was made from adamah, which is derived from the Hebrew word for 'dirt'. And before you say anything, 'Adam' is derived from the Hebrew word for 'humanity', his name does not mean 'dirt.'"

"Points accepted. Please continue."

"Very well. God then gave Adam the breath of life, and he became man."

Target acquired! "Wrong."

Gallows reared his head back in confusion. "What do you mean, 'wrong?' It's right there in the Bible."

"Adam was initially a golem."

Gallows blinked a few times as he struggled to process this. "Adam was a man, not a golem."

"The Talmud specifically states that Adam was initially a golem, created from mud as all golems are. The Talmud is a central text of Judaism. Christianity is based on Judaism. Therefore, the text of the Talmud is just as relevant to Christian history as the Torah which formed the Old Testament. So its statement that Adam was initially a golem is admissible as fact in the Celestial Courts."

Gallows hooked his finger under his chin, thinking this through. "But I cannot concede your point," he said eventually. "We are not golems ourselves. We are living beings born of other living beings, not made from mud."

"True," I said. "Adam did eventually become human. Pretty quickly, in fact. Golems cannot talk, and yet Adam named all the animals. The fact remains that God created a lifeless husk and chose to give him a soul and make him a living being."

I snuck a look at Adam in the dock. He was actually thinking about this. He clearly wasn't sure he bought it. Good enough for now.

Gallows kept mulling it over. "So you are saying that the Adam here now is like the Adam from back then, in that he was just a creation and God chose to give him life."

"That is exactly what I'm saying," I said.

"...no. Not the same thing," he eventually said.

"Why not?"

"The Adam from the Garden Of Eden was imbued with intelligence."

"Our Adam would have had intelligence if it weren't for biology."

"The first Adam wasn't animalistic."

"Be careful, arguing his cognitive functions is a bad move."

"How so?"

"Because Adam sold out Eve. He teamed up with the conniving serpent to get Eve to eat the forbidden fruit first. His intelligence was actually used for exploitation. Exploitation of the woman he loved. Our Adam may have lived a harsh life, but he never betrayed anyone."

"In fact," Hunter said, rising to his feet, "his actions prove that, even in a psychotic state, he understood enough of humanity to protect it."

Gallows looked at Hunter. "How did he protect humanity?"

"Look at his life scroll," Hunter said as he looked at Adam. "Our Adam recognized the threat he was to other people. His path took him away from them, where he wouldn't hurt them."

"But how do you know he just didn't think to do that?"

"He was created by a human. He was there. He knew what a human was. He didn't seek out vengeance on the man who created him. He didn't seek to disrupt people's lives. Just like now, he was aware people would panic. So, until he could figure out what to do, he left them alone. Consideration. Understanding. Love. The most important part of humanity."

Adam still seemed a bit confused, but he was clearly leaning towards it.

And his feelings were getting stronger -- I could see the members of the Tribunal were picking up on it. Hunter had just made a perfect shot.

I couldn't help myself. Sheer abandon overtook me as I closed my eyes, tilted my head back, and declared, "Taught 'im everything he knows!"

A sharp rap of the gavel brought my attention to Pahaliah. He was smiling at me with understanding, but still with authority. "Lady Singer? Please stay focused."

I bowed deeply and sincerely to Pahaliah. "My apologies."

"I want to agree with you," Gallows said, a pleading quality in his voice. "But I can't. He isn't truly human. He was made from spare parts."

"What makes him human is his soul. One that God gave him."

"God gave it to him out of necessity. He was forced to."

"God's pretty smart. You think He couldn't have found another way to handle the problem?"

Gallows was quiet. No one wants to sound like they might be insulting God.

"Besides," I said, "Adam understands humanity. He has a soul, he is enlightened, he should be allowed in Heaven."

"He hasn't demonstrated he is enlightened."

I smiled at Adam. "He's demonstrating it right now."

Adam looked shocked. I kept right on going. "Look at the fear in his eyes. He understands what is at risk here. He understands what he has missed out on. He's not standing there, wondering what the big deal is, why we aren't just getting on with it. He knows the terrible fate he faces. Emotional depth. Self-awareness. He qualifies."

"He's still doing nothing," Gallows countered.

"He's doing the only thing he can think of to keep from messing things up."

Gallows looked at Adam, as if viewing him for the first time. Gallows asked Adam, "What if God offered you vengeance?"

Adam just blinked. Pahaliah told him, "You have been addressed. You may speak freely."

Adam looked nervously at Gallows. "What do you mean, vengeance?"

"We can't have man creating life whenever they feel like it. The one who created you is dangerous. He may try again. Suppose God offered to send you back to Earth to stop him from ever do this again."

"By killing him?!?"

"If it comes to that, yes. You would stop him from doing this act again. And you would be able to punish him for the haphazard job he did. One that caused you nothing but pain. That put your eternal life at risk. Would you accept it?"

Adam looked shocked. "Why would God ask that of me?"

"Why wouldn't He?"

"Why would a God that wants me to have a soul tell me to do something that would destroy it?!?"

In that moment, I felt it. The entire mood around the courtroom changed. The angels practically beamed at Adam. Pahaliah, the Tribunal, the Gallery, everyone. Gallows looked shocked. He did not expect the answer he got. Adam looked to me for help. I just smiled at him. Slowly, Adam realized what just happened. He had proven my point.

He was in.

Gallows turned to face the bench. "Move to change my recommended fate."

Pahaliah ached his eyebrows. "And what do you seek to change it to?"

"Immediate entry into Heaven."

"Are you withdrawing your contest of Adam's petition?"

Gallows looked over at Adam nervously. He gulped and nodded his head.

"Lady Singer? Any objection from you?"

"None whatsoever," I said brightly.

"As there is no contest, this trial is moot. Entry into Heaven is granted immediately, court is adjourned." Pahaliah slammed the gavel, and he and the Tribunal left out their doors.

Adam dashed down from the dock. He shook my hand fiercely. "I don't believe it! I don't believe it! Thank you!"

"Get going," I told him, pointing to the Petitioner's Exit on the left side of the court. "Heaven awaits."

Adam went and shook Gallows' hand as well. Adam was so excited, he didn't notice the twinge in Gallows' eyes. Adam went through the door.

I walked up to Gallows and just looked at him.

Gallows refused to look me in the eye. "I'm glad Pahaliah did that before I had a chance to change my mind."

"You did the right thing."

"It doesn't feel like the right thing."

"The right thing isn't changing your contest. The right thing is reaching beyond, to do right by others instead of yourself. You still don't think it's right for Adam to have a soul, do you?"

Gallows looked at me, his eyes begging for forgiveness.

"And yet, you forced that down to do right by him. Even if you objected to him or the circumstances of his life, you knew it wasn't right to make him pay like that."

"I should get past that," he said. "I should be able to overcome that."

"Some people can't. Some people, the best thing they can do is let others live their lives. Lack of interference with others is still a good thing."

"I want to get over it."

"And that's what will make that happen," I smiled.

Gallows didn't look convinced. He just dragged his feet as he shuffled up the aisle and out of court.

Usually, when I write these memoirs, I focus as much as possible on the moment, to present things as they are occurring, no peeking from the future allowed. But Adam worried me and was on my mind, and no doubt on yours, too. So, from the present day where I'm writing this, I'll tell you what came next.

Adam didn't go to Heaven. When he met God, God offered to let him live. Shadows usually take their time getting into Heaven, and Adam proved to be no exception. He quickly sorted out that he wanted to give life a go. As I write this, he's lived two full lifetimes and is patiently awaiting his third. His two lives, he's wound up being the head of an orphanage, taking care of kids and proving to them they have worth, that people do care about them and want them. The guy is good. Although nothing is guaranteed in life, everyone's pretty sure what will happen with his next go-round.

I was back in my quarters, just sitting on my couch next to my reading light. I had finally broken down and replaced the bench I'd had for centuries with something considerably more comfortable. I wasn't sure I deserved it, but I did want it, and Michael talked me into taking the plunge. I'll tell you the truth, I'm not sure if, the first time I laid back on it, I really was meditating or if I actually fell asleep. Spirits don't sleep. And yet....

A knock at my door stopped me from pondering. "Come in," I called.

Michael stepped through my door. I guess my posture was a lot more relaxed than usual, because he just gave me a knowing smile when he saw me. "See? Have I ever steered you wrong?"

I turned so that I was leaning in the corner of the couch, up against the left arm and the back. Michael sat down next to me. I'm glad I picked a big couch, he almost took up the space of two people.

"What's on your mind, Michael?" I asked.

"Something about Adam's case is bothering you."

"What makes you say that?"

"You're here instead of the Water Gardens or one of your usual haunts."

"You're sort of right," I said after a pause. "It's not Adam himself. It's Gallows."

"Yeah, Gallows was a bit of a pickle, wasn't he?"

"But why was he a pickle?" I asked. "I mean, remember how I was when I first discovered gays existed. I had never even seen it before, and I was shocked. But it was just in that moment. After I processed it, I decided it wasn't wrong or a sin. I decided to accept it. And I became less and less shocked. Less and less repulsed. And I was defending souls the Churches were trying to punish for it without even blinking. For centuries now, when I see two guys or two girls kissing, I think it's sweet and emotional."

"You did come around extremely quickly."

"Don't be so impressed," I said dejectedly. "I should have come around immediately."

"Don't be so hard on yourself," Michael responded. "You were shocked, not being discriminatory. You didn't cling to how you thought things should be, you accepted and advocated for the truth."

"So why can't Gallows? Why can't everyone? Even if it's something you can't or won't do, if there's nothing wrong with it, why can't you support it?"

Michael smiled at me. "You just answered your own question. Because they think there's something wrong with it. God created our sense of ethics to ensure some sins are just not done. Incest. Beastiality. Torture. These acts are horrible and locked away in a box inside our minds. But just as some things can get out of that box, some things can get put in there. And some people voluntarily add to that box. Usually things they just don't understand. They confuse their reaction with moral outrage.

"There are a lot of things in life that people are unaware of, that they never have to face. So when they see it, they are basically rewriting their beliefs and what they knew about life. Some people can do it almost instantly, like you. Some take a while. And some never can."

"So what can be done?"

"Nothing. At least, as far as us. That's the downside to choice. Some people just can't process what is right. And some people refuse to. The best they can do is live and let live."

"That's not good enough."

"It has to be," Michael said with a shrug. "You know how many people who face discrimination would thank their lucky stars that people would leave them alone? That they would treat them as human beings instead of dismissing them over such a petty difference? Everyone needs to learn to live with each other. Some people make it easy to live with them. Some make it difficult."

I lowered my head. "I don't want to be one of them."

"One of the difficult ones?"

"Yeah."

I felt Michael reach behind me and pull me to him. I just hugged him back as he spoke. "Well, Hannah, that analogy doesn't apply to you."

"How so? I'm either easy to live with or hard to live with."

"That only applies to people you HAVE to live with. People WANT to live with someone like you."

I wasn't sure what to think about that. It had the vague wiff that I was somehow superior to others. But for now, I just went with it. I'd sort it out later.

REPEAT PERFORMANCE

What did I do wrong?

The question went through my head, again, as it did several times every time I stood in front of Camael. In court, outside court, everywhere. Sometimes, he didn't even have to be there for me to wonder.

When I first became Hannah Singer, Celestial Advocate, Camael and I got along just fine. We weren't the best of friends like I had become with St. Michael, but we were fine with each other. We could talk. We could laugh. We could reflect on human nature. We could discuss art. I loved reading. Camael loved painting. Any angel that wants to paint doesn't have to do anything more than touch their brush to the canvas and focus on the image they want. Not Camael. He used watercolors and would savor every stroke, every color, every mix he tipped his brush with. Especially when painting birds. He loves birds. His skill was so amazing, they looked more like photographs than paintings.

He was usually dominating, despite his size. I'm actually a bit taller than him. He's solid and stocky. I admired his resolve, and he seemed to admire mine. Or, at least, respect it.

I can't pinpoint exactly when things changed. I mean, looking back, there were subtle differences here and there. But I thought it was just some general annoyance. I didn't realize it was me specifically until sometime in the late 19th Century. It was a regular trial, not a grey case, against a Church who was overplaying his hand. I made some comment like I usually do to reduce an argument to absurdity. I then heard Camael say, "Silence is golden," and crack the gavel. Before I could register what happened, a golden thread darted down my throat and I couldn't speak.

I looked at Camael in complete shock. He'd never done that to me before in five hundred years of advocating. Camael just stared back at me in silent challenge. Whatever was going on, Camael was on a knife edge, and this was not the time to push my luck. I pulled myself together, calming down, pushing the fear and anger and indignation from my mind, aware that angels can detect strong emotions in humans. He smiled sinisterly at me and looked at the Churches. If they were any happier, they'd probably have to change their underwear. Luckily, the case was already in the bag and my juniors were able to take it home, scoring a win and immediate granting of petition.

It didn't stop there. There were more cases, each one with an undercurrent of unease. Then came a low-risk grey case. Henry Gallows, senior Church at the time, was my opposition. Camael was doing things that I felt unfairly influenced the trial towards the Churches and I told him so. He responded by barring me.

Yes. He actually barred me.

Gallows' jaw just about hit the floor. The Guardians stared resolutely ahead, but their mouths were agape, too. Gallows moved for mercy, but Camael had none of it. The Guardians came up to escort me from the courtroom, clearly not sure what to make of this. I didn't resist, and kept close to them. I didn't know what I would have to do to atone and be reinstated, but I didn't want to make it worse. Outside the court, the two Guardians at the door just looked at me, wondering what I was doing there. I just started stomping away to the Ancient Forest so I could calm down.

Once trial resumed, my juniors took over. Gallows scored the win, and the now lead Celestial called for a mistrial. It was upheld – God overrode the fate and erased my disbarment. I was an Advocate again and didn't have to do anything. I also heard through the grapevine that Camael was pulled from court by God Himself and got an earful.

When word reached me, my frustration got worse, which I didn't think was possible. St. Michael tracked me down in the Ancient Forest, looking at me like he was looking at a bomb with nothing but red wires inside. I forced myself to calm down as well as I was able to. I wasn't going to take out my frustrations on him. He didn't say a word as he whisked me away to his chambers. We got inside, he vanished the door into the wall, and said, "Anything you say now will not be held against you. You can say anything you want however you want."

I then launched into a tirade laced with every swear word and personal insult I could think of, all directed at Camael. And I mean, "every". I must have gone for a half hour easy. Michael looked genuinely impressed by the time I ran out of steam.

"Feel better?" he asked hopefully.

"No," I said, marching past him and heading for one of the chairs in front of his desk. I didn't even bother to check for a tack this time. I plopped down. No damage to my butt. Good.

Michael sat down across from me at his desk, concern and confusion etched on his face. "I reviewed the trial record," he said.

I looked at him, pleadingly. "Do you see what I did to warrant being barred?"

"No," he said. He picked up a scroll, probably the trial record. "It's not even a question of you've gotten away with worse. You did absolutely nothing to warrant that." He was silent for a moment, then looked at me over the scroll. "Would you like to lodge a complaint?"

I rocketed forward, leaning towards Michael and being more forceful than I probably had a right to. "No. You have the trial record right there. You know as well as I do that Camael did nothing he doesn't have the authority to."

"Just because he can doesn't mean he should."

"Doesn't matter. The investigation will conclude Camael was perfectly within his rights and nothing will come of it. And it will put a target on my head. You know Camael. He'll remember my defiance. As tough as this trial was, the next one in front of him will be worse."

"Oh, he won't get even with you on my watch," Michael said.

"And give the Churches a chance at declaring mistrials left and right?"

Michael sagged and the scroll dropped from his grip. Camael already had the highest turnover rate of all the angels. Anything I did that could suggest his hands were being tied would open the floodgates. For the sake of the Celestial Courts, I had to swallow my pride and let this go.

Michael looked at me, still resolute. "Nothing can stop me from starting an inquiry." I felt my eyebrows shoot into orbit. "You'll be kept out of it," he hastily added. "I have more than enough here from the trial record to validate it."

I leaned back. I could feel the fearsome expression on my face. "I don't know if you should do that."

"Why not?!?" Michael thundered in exasperation. "You shouldn't be afraid of him!"

I let out a sigh of resignation. "Michael, if it even looks like I'm pushing, he can bar me. And he can make some obscenely difficult penance that I might not be able to do. Or it would take decades, if not centuries, to do. And I won't be able to advocate until it is done." I looked at him. "I can't. I can't let him take this away from me. I don't want this to end."

Michael's face softened. He understood. "You can appeal anything he does, you know," he said.

"It won't stop him. He's well within the rules, and he knows what to watch out for. He is waiting for me to defy him."

"What will you do?"

"Same thing he does. Stay within the rules. I can at least deny him the opportunity to bar me. If he pushes too hard at trials, I can call for a mistrial. But I'll find a way to handle him. I have to."

Michael and I went our separate ways afterwards. As I walked back to my quarters, I got plenty of sympathy. Some would just nod to me sadly, others would give me a pat on the back, but everyone seemed to realize I was getting railroaded.

I had just gotten around a corner when I saw a group of people standing around, glaring at someone I couldn't see. They were holding scrolls, so they had work to do. From how they were shifting their attention between whatever and each other, whoever it was had moved past them and was pretty far down. I carefully made it to the corner. The group saw me, and I put my finger to my lips in a shush gesture. I then looked around the corner.

I saw Camael walking along further ahead. His wings were out, his head tilted up slightly, middle of the path, recognizing no authority except his own. He seemed completely oblivious to all the dirty looks he was getting. I mean, no one was even trying to hide them, it was open contempt. I ducked back around the corner and hoofed it back to my quarters. Angels can sense emotions that are strong enough, and I wasn't sure Camael would be far enough away for mine to not reach him.

From then on, every case, every trial, was difficult. I frankly consider it a testimonial to my skill that my record didn't suffer despite having one hand tied behind my back. I locked every thought, every emotion, away where Camael would never get them. I betrayed no emotion, no fear, no sign of weakness. I was courteous and professional, and gave him nothing to feed off of. Or, at least, nothing I couldn't use to score a mistrial or maybe even an investigation. If anything did get out, it was my confusion. I couldn't help it. I went over court records for trials, discussions we had out of session, everything.

What did I do wrong?

On this occasion, I was leading the defense of a regular guy the Churches were just looking to put through the wringer. Despite some rather leading questions from Camael and him blocking some of my arguments, I scored the win and got immediate approval of petition. Camael just kept glaring at me. There was a moment where he nearly struck part of my argument, but a subtle reminder that it was guaranteed to get a mistrial stopped him.

After court ended, I went back to my quarters. I brewed some piping hot jasmine tea and sat on my couch. I didn't even bother to pull out a book. I can't enjoy reading immediately after a trial with Camael. And I reflected, trying to figure out, once again, why he hated me.

And once again, I came to the same conclusion. Let him hate me. The courts needed me. He wasn't going to chase me away. It was going to take something really really big to get rid of me.

And in the early part of the 20th Century, it almost happened.

It was the day that I was dreading. Dreading ever since the start of the 19th Century.

Henry Gallows was stepping down as senior Church.

God, I hated that thought. Gallows had somehow wound up as senior Church following a particularly scandalous court case that saw an exodus from the ranks. Gallows became senior, and the dynamic between the Celestials and the Churches changed. There were still skirmishes, but for the most part, there was an air of cooperation instead of antagonism between the two sides. Gallows wasn't interested in wielding an iron fist. When there were disagreements between the sides, there was respectful discussion. He truly was the best.

It didn't help that everybody coming up behind him was his complete opposite. They were anxious to hold people's fates in their hands. They wanted to reward those who they felt were worthy. Talked about having "standards." Never mind the whole set-up of the Celestial Courts meant everyone was worthy of Heaven, it was just a question of if they'd done enough to get it. They felt not everyone was worthy, and couldn't wait to decide who was or wasn't. Needless to say, they couldn't wait for Gallows to step down so they could install a senior Church who "got it."

Gallows' retirement party was huge. He had already petitioned, shortly after he arrived in the Afterlife, in fact. It had been approved, and he put it on hold so he could advocate. So there was no doubt what was coming up next for him. The turnout was unusual because it featured everyone. There were Churches, Celestials, and angels there. Usually, each group sticks with their own, Churches on one side, Celestials and angels on the other. The mix was truly beautiful, and the best testimonial to Gallows' character he could have ever gotten.

The Earth country of America was going through what they were calling The Roaring Twenties, and they had nothing on this. Streamers were everywhere, a big band, great food, and champagne flowing like Niagra Falls. Fruit punches with the greatest variety of flavors sat at ready. Doves would take flight from among flowers in full bloom, every color of the rainbow in attendance. I had never seen anything like it before in my six hundred years, and I doubted I would see anything like it again.

The crowd of well wishers had thinned out a bit, giving Michael and I a chance to talk to Gallows. Gallows had already stepped down, the only question was who was going to be the new senior Church. "Anyone want to place bets?" Michael asked brightly.

I rolled my eyes. "I'd rather not think about it," I said.

"Vacation's over, huh, Singer?" Gallows smiled.

"Sure seems like it," I said. "Sure we can't persuade you to stick around for...."

"Another few decades?" he laughed.

"More like another few eons!" I laughed back. We talked about our favorite cases and our most memorable ones, reliving the close calls and the good times. Soldiers from the trenches, sharing experiences no one else could understand.

While we were talking, I noticed it. The crowd on one part of the room was getting quieter. I looked at Michael. He noticed it, too. We both turned to look in the direction of the silence. Gallows noticed our gazes and followed.

Slowly parting the crowd was Camael, flanked on either side by a Church. On the left was Jeff Fairchild, an up and comer who was no end of trouble and he was only a junior. On the right was Pierre Devereaux, a French Church who was known for being a Christian hardliner in traditional French fashion. Camael was carrying a rolled up document. I had a very bad feeling. From the display, I suspected we were looking at a retrial.

The trio got up to us. Silence crushed down on the party. I fought the urge to stand in front of Camael and say, "A little going away gift for Gallows?" Michael moved to do the talking. "Hello, Camael. What brings you around?"

Devereaux gave a very pronounced bow. "Greetings from the new senior Church." He straightened, and his smile showed all his teeth. "They say the senior Church's first trial sets the tone for how everything else is going to go."

Camael held up the document. "Retrial. And I'm the presiding angel."

I started running through options in my mind. Gallows wasn't in much danger as far as I could tell. There was nothing in his record the Churches could really contest. If they were doing it just to harass him, it was a waste of time....

Camael then turned to me and tapped the scroll just above my chest, right where my heart was. "Hannah Singer. You are being retried."

The entire crowd gasped. I was fighting to keep my reactions in check.

Part of me wanted to pass out. Part of me wanted to run. Part of me wanted to scream in rage, and the last part wanted to punch those smiles off the trio's faces.

I stood rigid as I fought through the mess of reactions and tried to keep from acting out. Michael grabbed the document from Camael and started reading it. When he looked up from it, his face was dark fury. The Churches took a step back. Camael took two.

"Get out. Now," Michael clipped.

Camael gulped nervously. "We are here on official business...."

That was all anyone heard. Michael's wings exploded from his back and he rushed the two Churches out. He then grabbed Camael and literally threw him across the way and out.

I barely registered the activity around me. I felt lost, swimming in an ocean with no land in sight, storms closing in, and my body feeling exhausted. How could I survive? Could I survive at all? Camael was the presiding angel. Devereaux not only didn't like me, but taking out the senior Celestial, the senior grey Celestial, and the best Celestial the courts had ever seen would make him a legend.

I felt myself being shaken violently. I came around and saw myself staring Michael in his otherworldly blue eyes. "Hannah!" he yelled.

I started moving, enough to get him to release my shoulders. "I'm fine. I'm just...overwhelmed."

Michael yelled at the top of his lungs, "Party's over! Everyone out!"

No one complained. They just shuffled out, casting worried looks at me as they went. Once the place was empty and putti started flying in to clean things up, Michael touched my shoulder, and the world around us shifted and swirled. When it resettled, we were in his chambers. Michael vanished his door into the wall, then waved at the two highback chairs in front of his desk. They moved together, merged, then settled into a very large sofa. Michael led me over to it and made us sit at the same time. His arm never left my shoulder.

I was still too stunned to react. I couldn't move. I couldn't even think. I felt Michael pull me into a hug, but I didn't even try to return it. I just sat like a statue. It went like this for a while until I told Michael, "I need some time alone. To sort this out."

Michael reared back and looked at me in fear. I told him, "I promise, I won't do anything. I just need to think."

Michael studied me for a long moment, then released me. "Take all the time you need. I'm reassigning your cases."

"That won't be necessary," I said. Besides, the thought of routine was comforting to me.

"You're too distracted right now," Michael said, and it was clear from his tone that there was no point in arguing. He said goodbye, and simply left when I didn't say anything.

I don't know how long I sat there. My options were limited. Unless there was a ruling that said otherwise, my petition was still mine. I could simply pray to Jesus at any time, even in the middle of the trial, and claim my Heavenly reward. Eternal peace, no one would be able to do things like this to me ever again. Not Camael. Not the Churches. No one. But to do that, I'd have to quit being an Advocate. Once you cross over, you don't come back. And that meant standing up for scared people and against bullying authorities would be over. Forever. And as much as I wanted Heaven, I didn't want this to end.

Eventually, I decided to just get up and walk out. I mostly kept to less traveled paths, I didn't want anyone to see me and try to engage me in conversation. Then it hit me. The shadow court! I'm authorized to go there, and there were no cases coming up to be heard there. The perfect place to not be found.

I went to the Archives, to the wall at the back that was empty of any detail. I got close, and a set of black iron doors with a white cross on each appeared. I put my hand on it, and poured through to the entrance hall of the shadow court.

The hallway was complete empty, devoid of anything except anyone standing there. And it acted like a speaker cabinet, amplifying the voices I heard on the other side of the doors that led to the shadow court itself. And I recognized the voices. They belonged to Michael and Camael.

I locked up my emotions to keep them from being detected and crept closer to the door. I didn't have to get close, the two angels were bellowing at each other.

"You put them up to this, didn't you?!?" came Michael's voice.

"You know me better than that!" Camael responded.

"Bad enough you constantly throw her in the deep end! But having her removed from office?!?"

"I didn't give them the idea!"

"Which is why you're the presiding angel already even though only one side has filed a request for trial!"

I felt my emotions returning. I blocked the yelling from my ears and ran back to the exit. I didn't even slow down as I touched the door and emerged on the other side in a full sprint. I got around the building and finally slowed down. People were milling around, all of them trying not to notice me.

I shook my head and started walking to the court building. I went inside and went to Michael's chambers. I took a deep breath and reached out for the handle. Only certain people can enter Michael's chambers when he isn't there. I'm one of them. No matter what, Michael instantly knows if anyone is his chambers and who they are. I said a quick prayer to him that he didn't need to worry, I just wanted some time alone. I then went to the back of his chambers, where his bookcases were. I just kept looking over the different books, seeing the titles but not reading them.

I don't know how long it was. It might have been moments, it felt like hours. But Michael turned up. I didn't look at him. I couldn't bring myself to.

"Hannah? You okay?"

I took a long breath before I spoke. "Camael's the presiding angel, right?"

"He doesn't have to be," Michael said, his voice turning slick.

"No. He has to be."

"What are you talking about?" Michael sounded like he was ready to put me in a straight jacket. "I do have some pull. I can get you someone less likely to be harsh."

I closed my eyes and tilted my head down. "No. It has to be him. If I win the retrial with him, it's over. No more retrials. No mistrials. No nothing. If I want this over, I have to go through his Hell."

I soon felt Michael's hands on my shoulders. "You don't have to face this."

My right hand went up and covered his left. "Yes, I do."

"No, you don't," Michael said with finality. "There won't be a trial."

My head straightened and my eyes popped. I batted his hands off my shoulders and spun to look at him. "Don't even think about it, Michael."

"I am head of the Celestial Courts," Michael said. "Nothing says I have to grant a trial. Even if I sign off on the retrial, it will never make it on the docket."

I looked at him levelly. "Michael? Don't make me go over your head."

Michael suddenly looked scared. More than I thought I had ever seen him. "Don't do this. Devereaux is just flexing his muscles."

"Michael, this has to happen. You know it does. Otherwise, the Churches will think I'm dodging."

Michael viewed me judgmentally for a few seconds, then stood straight and tall. He was facing the firing squad and ready for his fate, no regrets. "Do what you have to do. I will not do this voluntarily."

I appreciated the gesture, then closed my eyes and said a prayer to God. As soon as I finished, I opened my eyes and looked at Michael. He tilted his head and looked upwards. Incoming message from God. He closed his eyes, let out a sigh, then walked over to his desk. He took out a document, and started writing. He watched me the entire time. "I can defend you."

"No. This is a retrial. They might use me to dismantle the courts again. I have to do this alone again."

Michael looked at me for a long moment. "Please, if you have to, just claim your Heavenly reward. I can still see you there."

I nodded and walked out of the room. I hated to force his hand like that, but there was nothing else I could do. The Churches wanted a showdown. And I had to participate, whether I wanted to or not.

I continued to avoid everybody, trying to figure out what to do. I was scared. Terrified. I was looking at going to Hell. Not only the most horrible place imaginable, but Lucifer himself wanted me. I would be his ultimate prize, someone he loved and stole away from Michael. That thought hit me hardest.

I was outside in the Blooming Meadow when I broke. The pressure was too much. I started running, across the Blooming Meadow and into the Valley Of Death itself. I didn't know where I was going, I just wanted to run and not stop.

But I did stop. I was starting to cry. My whole future, my whole existence, in the hands of an angel who would hand me to the Churches on a silver platter. All the people who needed my help. All my friends in the Afterlife. Michael, my big brother. Jeanne. Gallileo. Everyone. Stripped from me and no way to even contact them. Hear them. Let them know I was thinking of them.

The crying became sobs, disrupting my rhythm. I started stumbling, and finally fell forward on the ground. There was no stopping it now. I was on my knees crying in despair. In anger. In fury. In complete and utter helplessness. My sobs were punctuated by my fists striking the ground to words I couldn't say.

I finally collapsed on the ground, my anguish coursing through me like whitewater. After a little while, I felt different. I forced myself back under control as I felt weightless. I couldn't see through my tears, but I could see the green colors around me were changing to pastel blue and white. And I felt a presence. It was one I don't feel very often, and feel guilty about that. It was the Holy Spirit, taking me away. I started crying again.

"Don't cry, Hannah," the Holy Spirit said. "There is no need."

I couldn't say anything.

"Think your answer, Hannah. Why are you crying?"

Because I ignore you, I thought.

"You don't ignore me."

I talk to God and Jesus all the time. I don't talk to you unless I think of it.

"I am always there, am I not?"

...I don't deserve you.

"Nonsense," the Holy Spirit laughed. "You don't think about me as much because you don't need me as much."

I was having trouble processing that. I forced myself under control and opened my eyes, wiping my eyes and nose with my sleeves. I was eventually able to see though. The Holy Spirit has no real form. He's like a ribbon of light, pouring around in smooth motion. He floated in front of me, a shape of light waiting.

"I should," I finally said. "Ignoring you is wrong."

"I'm not ignored, Hannah. You misunderstand my role in God's Creation. You've been here almost six hundred years. How much do you know about me?"

I thought hard. "...not much."

"So, you do not know my purpose, correct?"

I bowed my head in shame. "...correct."

"That's okay!" He laughed as He poured into a long ribbon of light and began encircling me. "God is love. Jesus is redemption. I am faith. People already believe and trust. For the most part, I'm not needed. But everyone falters once in a while. Everyone. And when their faith is weakest, when their despair is greatest, I am there."

I thought about that. "So the reason I'm not familiar with you is that I haven't needed to be."

"Exactly," he said. "Everyone knows about me. I'm part of the Holy Trinity. But they don't know what I do unless they need me. It's just how it works out. It's nothing to be ashamed of."

"But I should be paying some attention to you, shouldn't I?"

"It's the thought that counts," He said. "You want to honor and respect me, you just don't know how. But you would if you knew how. And what you already do, keeping me in your thoughts and prayers, that's more than enough to show that you care. Expressions of love don't have to be flashy. Just sincere."

He then poured himself into an almost human shape, the "head" leaning close to my ear, as he whispered, "Besides, right now, you need me."

I went defensive. "My faith is strong."

"Hannah, you can't fool any of us. That was the cry of a fallen angel."

"I'm no angel."

"Which makes it even worse."

The cry of a fallen angel is the absolute worst sound in Creation. If you hear it once, it will haunt your mind. "I was hoping no one would notice."

"I know. That's why you came all the way out here. But remember, no matter where you are, I am always with you."

I looked at Him in confusion. "I didn't notice you."

The Holy Spirit poured in front of me, then faded from sight. "Of course not. I didn't want you to notice me. But I'm always right there."

I was silent for a moment, then He asked, "Want to see me again?"

I could only nod. The light returned, then started streaming, orbiting around me. "I know why you are terrified."

I felt like I was getting smaller. I squeezed my eyes shut, trying to keep the tears from falling. "What do you think will happen?"

The streaming stopped directly in front of my eyes. "What I think and what I know are the same thing – you will win."

"How can you say that?!? Camael is ready to hand them my head! How can you have faith in me?!?"

"Because I see humanity for what it is. God made you, all of you, the way He did for a specific reason – so you could survive."

I just sort of sat there, trying to process this. The Holy Spirit poured around me, His end never moving. He continued to move around me until I was cocooned by His comforting light. The soft white filled my eyes, His voice filled my mind. "God made people the way He did because the world is harsh. Other people are harsh. People can serve others if they choose. Family, leaders, whoever. But they shouldn't be forced to serve. And when those outside influences become too strong, people can resist. You all have it in you. You don't see it right now, but you are the map. Your mind, your heart, everything you are marks the map, provides direction. And it will always lead you out of the wilderness."

I felt myself calming. He was right. I knew Camael. I knew the courts. I knew the Churches. I knew them better now than I did the first time I stood trial. I knew how to examine, build arguments, look beneath the surface, manipulate the opposition....

"Maybe...I can do this," I eventually said.

Suddenly, the light of the Holy Spirit vanished from around me. I was back in my quarters, curled up on my couch next to my reading lamp.

I slowly unfolded and sat up. I didn't really look at anything. I just sat.

Suddenly, a putto, Mary, zipped into my quarters. She gave me a salute and said, "Miss Singer, your trial is ready to begin. You are requested in the Grand Courtroom immediately."

I wasn't exactly looking at her. "Do you need to bring me, or can I walk there?"

She thought about this. "You can walk. Otherwise, they would have sent a guardian."

I slowly stood up. My voice sounded flat and far away as I said, "I am walking there now."

Mary nodded, then wrapped her arms around my neck in a desperate hug. I hugged the tiny angel back as well as I could. She pulled back, gave me a salute, and flew off.

I took another look around my quarters, willing every detail I could into my memory. My small bookcase and the beautiful works they contained. The constantly lingering scent of jasmine. The feel of the rough carpet beneath my bare feet. Part of me was afraid I'd never know it again. The other part wanted to commit everything it could, to build a tally sheet. To know exactly what was at stake. What I could lose. I kept looking around until my gaze settled on the small table by my kitchen area. There were a few scrolls here, trials that had been heard but I hadn't returned them yet. There would be more trials. There would always be more trials. Everybody needs help.

I said a quick prayer to the Holy Spirit. "Please," I silently implored. "This is what I want. More than anything else. This is what I'm good at. What I'm made for. I don't want this to end. Please...please be with me."

I heard the Holy Spirit speak to me. "I am right here with you. I am with the mother whose child is sick. I am with the father hunting food for his family. I was with Jesus when the Disciples fell asleep and He was alone in the night, right until He died. I am with you always."

I felt my resolve steel. It was time to defend the next Hannah Singer. It was time to defend me.

I walked carefully from my quarters to the Celestial Courts, still cataloging everything. I heard the voices around me, saw the angels flying through the air, the colors, the sounds, the scents. I walked past the fountain at the center, remembering the bubbles that couldn't be made to go away. I hadn't thought about that in almost six hundred years. Funny what you think about when things are bleak.

As I walked, a thought struck me. I would have loved to have had

Michael by my side, just a little reassurance from my big brother that things would be okay. It was then that I thought, where was he? He wouldn't just abandon me at a time like this. Something was going on, but I couldn't imagine what.

I made it to the court building and continued my steady pace to the Grand Courtroom. I fought to keep my fear under control. How could I do this? There would be no one to defend me. I had to stand on my own, to make sure there was no doubt about the verdict. That was the bright side to this. Camael hated me. The Churches would have everything. The deck was completely stacked against me. If I could win, they would never be able to retry me ever again. This was their best chance to get me.

I got to the Grand Courtroom, the biggest court here. The Guardians outside the doors saw me and picked up on my vibe. The politely opened the doors for me, both whispering, "Good luck," as I passed. I smiled at them in thanks and continued up the aisle.

I have no idea what the Gallery was really like. I know it was jam packed, but I couldn't tell you about the discussions or anything. I was still in my personal haze, just working my way to the Celestial table. The only thing that made it through was Gallows, in the Gallery, and Michael, standing in front of the judge's bench between the two usual Guardians. He watched me. There was no mistaking the fear on his face. I had never seen him look so scared.

I got to the lead Celestial seat and just sat. I could feel my shoulders sagging, my head tilting just enough to the side that I could notice the angle. I didn't bother to look at the Church table. Devereaux would be the lead Church, no doubt Fairchild was a junior. I continued to prepare my mind for whatever they could throw at me. I needed something good, or I was a goner.

It was then that I felt a presence. A sinister presence. I turned to look at the Church table. Sitting comfortably between Devereaux and Fairchild was the devil himself, Lucifer. He smiled and waved at me. I locked myself further down. Lucifer wanted me. And it scared me.

The only other option I had was my petition. It was still mine. Even if the Tribunal ruled otherwise, it was mine until Camael slammed the gavel, ending the court session and making the ruling official. If the Tribunal said I was Cast, I had a small opening to pray to Jesus and get out of there. I just hoped it wouldn't come to that.

The chimes sounded, and everyone stood. We deployed our wings. Was it my imagination, or were mine drooping a little? They felt like they were. I saw Michael looking at me, giving me a little more strength.

The door by the Tribunal box opened, and twelve angels, wings already out, entered. They looked at me with concern. They couldn't just rule to approve my petition. The ruling would automatically go to the Churches, it was up to the Celestials to establish an exception. They were hoping I could do it. Me, too.

The door at the back of the court opened, and Camael came in. He watched me the entire time he came in, smiling like a hungry wolf. I could feel myself getting smaller. I fought the feeling. If I gave up on myself, it was over. I had to forge ahead. I had to have faith that things would work out.

Camael set a record scroll off to the side after making sure it was ready. He smiled out over the court, "Who is the Petitioner?"

"The Petitioner is Hannah Singer," I replied flatly.

"Speak up," Camael commanded.

I forced volume into my voice. "The Petitioner is Hannah Singer."

"And who are her Advocates?" he asked.

"Hannah Singer, acting alone."

"And who advocates for the Church?"

"Jeff Fairchild, Lucifer, and Pierre Devereaux, acting as lead," came the happy response on my left.

Camael was clearly about to ask me to take the stand, then remembered I wouldn't be able to speak at will there. Sure way to get a mistrial. "Miss Singer, your opening arguments, please."

I didn't flinch. I didn't deviate. I didn't change. Expecting sympathy from Camael was a waste of time. "I lived a good life in accordance with God's wishes. I should be allowed into Heaven. Thank you."

Camael looked at Devereaux. "Your opening arguments?"

"She was not just any Atheist. She flat out never believed. She didn't just have a different conclusion, her very thought process was an affront to God. Because of her thought process, we are seeing undesirables enter Heaven, ones that never should get in there. Make her pay for her crimes, and restore order to the court. She should be Cast Down. Thank you."

Camael looked at me. Opening arguments were over. What could I do? I couldn't think of anything.

I started slowly. "No one is undesirable in the eyes of God."

"Blasphemer!" Devereaux screamed.

Lucifer stood up. "I am proof she is wrong."

"You deny the charge of blasphemy?" Camael asked me.

I looked at Camael levelly. "I deny saying God loves all His children is blasphemy."

"Silence is golden!" Camael yelled, and smashed the gavel. A golden ribbon rocketed out of the impact point and sped down my throat. I would not be able to speak as long as court was in session.

Which gave me just a few seconds.

Devereaux looked ecstatic. Lucifer and Fairchild actually shook hands. Devereaux said, "Move for closing arguments."

Camael looked at me. "Are you going to voice an objection?"

I couldn't voice anything, and he knew it.

Devereaux smiled triumphantly at the Tribunal. "Under the rules of the court, in a case like this, the ruling automatically goes to the Church unless an exception has been created. None has been created. You must rule for Casting Down. Thank you."

Everyone then looked at me. I just held still.

Camael looked at the Tribunal box. "You have heard the Advocates for Hannah Singer state their recommended fates. You may now make your decision. You wish to confer?"

Ten...nine....

The lead Tribunal stood up, looking at the others in the box before speaking. He knew how it had to go. "We are ready to rule."

Eight...seven...

"And what is your decision?"

Six...five...four....

"Petitioner is to be Cast Down."

Three...two...one...

"So be it!" And Camael slammed the gavel.

Zero. "Call for a mistrial!" I yelled, ignoring the fear in my voice.

Camael rolled his eyes as streaks of light shot through the ceiling of the courtroom, illuminating the Churches, Lucifer, Camael, the Tribunal, and myself. It was the light of God, looking into our minds and our hearts.

Eventually, the voice of God was heard throughout the court. "Hannah was unable to properly represent herself. The trial must start over."

The lights vanished, and Camael looked at me. "Who is the Petitioner?"

I answered, "The Petitioner is Hannah Singer."

"And who are her Advocates?" he asked.

"Hannah Singer, acting alone."

"And who advocates for the Church?"

"Jeff Fairchild, Lucifer, and Pierre Devereaux, acting as lead," came the slightly less happy response on my left.

"Miss Singer, your opening arguments, please."

"I lived a good life in accordance with God's wishes. I should be allowed into Heaven. Thank you."

Camael looked at the Churches. "Mister Devereaux? Your opening arguments, please."

"Singer is an Atheist. She never believed. She defied God. She should be Cast Down. Uh...thank you."

Camael looked back at me. I thought hard, and found a straw I could cling to. "This entire trial is moot."

"How so?" Camael asked.

"The arguments presented at my original trial have been upheld numerous times and have been established as precedents. They have not been overturned. As such, all this trial is is a rehash of my original trial. With no original arguments, the ending is guaranteed. I am to be allowed into Heaven, Atheism or no."

"We have new arguments ready," Devereaux sneered.

"Then let's hear them," I said.

"The Bible says we are to be faithful to the Lord. You were not."

"How I lived my life was faithful to the Lord, whether or not I acknowledged His existence."

Devereaux looked at Camael. "Move to strike Singer's last argument."

"On what grounds?" Camael sounded ready to grant any Church motion.

"This is a redo of her original trial. She is not allowed to come up with new arguments."

That snapped me out of my fog. Did I just hear that right? "Why are you allowed to come up with new arguments and I'm not?"

"That's my question to ask, Singer," Camael stated forcefully.

I simply looked at Camael, fighting to keep the anger from rising inside me. Under the rules of procedure, both opposing council and the presiding angel are allowed to question motions.

Camael looked at me for a moment, then said, "Argument is struck," while cracking the gavel.

I should have requested the motion be denied. Then my question would be part of my argument and not shut out like that. Hang it all, Hannah, you're losing! You have to focus! It's your soul on the line!

Every attempt at redress was shot down as the Churches used their narrow definition to present new arguments. I just waited. There was no way this wouldn't be a mistrial.

Eventually, closing arguments came. I reiterated my statements. Camael looked at the Tribunal box. "You have heard the Advocates for Hannah Singer state their recommended fates. You may now make your decision. You wish to confer?"

The lead Tribunal stood up, looking at the others in the box before speaking. He knew how it had to go again. "We are ready to rule."

"And what is your decision?"

"Petitioner is to be Cast Down."

"So be it!" And Camael slammed the gavel.

"Call for a mistrial!" I yelled, the anger actually registering in my voice this time.

Camael's glare was even harsher this time, but my own warring emotions shielded me from it. Once again, the lights of God streaked down through the ceiling and examined us. Eventually, the voice of God was heard. "The trial unfairly favored the Churches. It must start over. And do try to get it right this time."

The lights faded, and I breathed a sigh of relief, not caring how obvious it was. I thought about praying to Jesus really fast, just getting this over with. Camael was giving the Churches every edge they could get. I had to fight a war on two fronts. I could take the Churches easily, even with Lucifer in their corner. But Camael? He refused to see anything other than what he wanted to see. And he saw me as the enemy. If only he could see in me the things God saw in me....

I suddenly fought to lock down my emotions tighter than ever. I felt like I'd just woken from a deep sleep. I felt energized. Empowered. Ready to take on the world. And not only did I not want Camael picking up on that, Lucifer, fallen or no, was still an angel. I needed him to stay on the starting blocks until I was ready for him to run.

It's star time.

Camael gave me an impatient look. "Who is the Petitioner?"

I answered flatly, "The Petitioner is Hannah Singer."

"And who are her Advocates?" he asked.

"Hannah Singer, acting alone."

"And who advocates for the Church?"

"Jeff Fairchild, Lucifer, and Pierre Devereaux, acting as lead," came the increasingly annoyed response on my left.

"Miss Singer, your opening arguments, please."

"I lived a good life in accordance with God's wishes. I should be allowed into Heaven. Thank you."

Camael looked at the Churches. "Mister Devereaux? Your opening arguments, please."

"Singer deserves to burn!" Devereaux practically screamed.

Camael turned his gaze on me, full bore. "Singer, you have yet to advance any sort of affirmative defense."

I kept myself timid. "But I shouldn't need one."

"Why not?"

Time to start clog dancing through the minefield. "I already have an approved petition. I have been determined to be worthy of Heaven. This trial shouldn't be happening."

"Angels approved that petition!" Fairchild yelled, shooting up from his seat. "Not God!"

"Angels are fallible?"

"You bet!" he screamed.

A sharp rap of the gavel drew everyone's attention to Camael. The only thing he hates more than me is being insulted, and Fairchild just hit him square. I took a quick read of the Tribunal. They were angry, too.

Lucifer stood up slowly and calmly. The leader of the Fallen attempted some damage control. "Are you denying that angels can do things contrary to God's will and intent?"

Time to rattle the cage. "Move to strike Lucifer's testimony."

Camael gave me a look that said, "Oh, please, have something I can use." "On what grounds?"

"Lucifer's own admission is that angels are fallible. As such, his presence here is potentially not in the interest of justice but some other misguided notion. Anything he offers should be rendered moot."

Devereaux, Fairchild, and Lucifer burst to life. "Motion should be denied!" they screamed in perfect unison.

Camael was about to hit the gavel, presumably to allow my motion, when Lucifer screamed, "Mistrial!"

Camael brought himself up short just before the gavel would have hit.

He looked at Lucifer as if he was ready to vault off the bench and ram his fist down his throat. And believe me, Camael has the strength and the skill to do it. "On what grounds should Singer's motion be denied?" he growled.

Lucifer smiled. "Singer is incorrect. Angels are not fallible. Just because we can and do do things counter to God's will does not mean we are fallible."

Michael asked, loud and clear, "What?"

"Otherwise," Lucifer continued, "God would not allow angels to sit in judgment. The entire Celestial court system would be moot."

Camael looked back at me. He was very disappointed in me. "Singer? Do you object?"

Full speed ahead. "Absolutely. Lucifer is wrong."

I had everyone's undivided attention. "How so?"

"Lucifer is not an actual agent of the court, only a temporary one. Unlike you and the Tribunal, he hasn't been educated in the Celestial courts and how they operate. You have learned how to prevent the fallibility Lucifer revels in from becoming an impediment to seeing justice done." It was subtle and no one else noticed it, but I caught Michael make a slight kissy face when I said that.

"I do not revel in fallibility," Lucifer smirked at me.

"You take joy in spreading as much intolerance and injustice as you can, and you are unrepentant about it."

"It's what he does," Fairchild said. "His whole purpose is to tempt and lie and cheat and destroy."

Lucifer glared at Fairchild. "I'm standing right here, you know."

"If the purpose of this trial is to see justice done, how can someone you admit exists for the exact opposite be an instrument to that end?" I asked. "Unless your end is to violate the purpose of the court."

"We are seeing if you can resist the devil," Fairchild growled.

"I'm not the one with him arguing in my behalf," I shrugged.

Devereaux's eyes popped. How he couldn't know he was setting himself up, I have no idea. Fairchild was much more...subdued? I knew Fairchild from watching him junior under Gallows. This wasn't like him. What was going on?

I moved to yank the rug out from under them. "Your arguments defy God's will. Do they not, Lucifer?"

Lucifer looked around in a panic. If he lied to the court, everyone would know. He went with what he did best – smooth talk. "You are on trial here, Singer, not our motivations."

"Incorrect. Your motivations cut to the very heart of the trial."

"We are seeing justice done. It doesn't matter what our motivations are, we are still using the courts for their intended purpose."

"Are you?"

"You think otherwise?"

"'The devil can quote Scripture if it suits his purpose.' The court has already done it's job. It ruled in my favor. All points raised in my trial have been upheld. This is actually a mistrial, not a trial."

Devereaux appreciated the conversation drifting away from his ally. "We do not retry other Petitioners because their fates are claimed. It's not our fault you never claimed yours."

"Are you saying you would contest other Petitioners again if you could?"

"Yes."

"So you are saying the angels are not just fallible, they are wrong."

I caught Devereaux's face scrunch up for a moment. Didn't matter what Camael thought, he wasn't making the final decision. And all the lobbying Camael could do wouldn't sway a Tribunal that not only would be feeling insulted, but would remember this insult at any subsequent trials he was involved in.

Lucifer rose to his feet. "It's not that the angels are wrong. The angels represent mercy and understanding. They are a vessel for God's will. The definition of what that will entails has changed over the centuries. The purpose of this trial is to re-establish what that will is."

I felt no fear as I looked Lucifer in the eyes. "The angels have always honored what God's will is supposed to be."

"You are incorrect, Singer. More people are getting into Heaven despite behavior contrary to God's will. Atheists. Prostitutes. Mercenaries. The understanding of what is God's will is being changed."

"God's will isn't changing. It never has. What has changed is what people *believe* God's will to be."

"People are corrupting it," Lucifer said.

I promptly gestured to Devereaux and Fairchild. "There's your proof that they are corrupting it."

Fairchild shot up. "Watch your mouth, heathen!"

I continued unphased. "Christianity is based on Judaism. Judaism teaches that all worthy souls get into Heaven, regardless of belief, be they Jews, Gentiles, or Atheists. That is God's will. You are attempting to change it."

Back to Devereaux. "Jesus said you must believe in Him to enter the Kingdom Of Heaven."

"Jews don't have to," I said with a shrug.

"You aren't Jewish."

"Don't have to be," I said calmly. "I accepted God and Jesus."

"After you died," Fairchild stated.

"You argue for deathbed declarations and deathbed confessions all the time. This is no different."

"It's very different," Fairchild said.

"How so?" I prompted. Oh, please, let him keep arguing. Nobody puts their foot in their mouth like Fairchild.

"Those people are still alive. You didn't accept the Holy Trinity until after your death. You wouldn't have been able to do any acts to testify to your new faith."

"Neither can those people on deathbeds, shut ins, anyone like that. And you still argue that it is acceptable. It doesn't matter when people come around, just that they do."

"It is a loophole," Fairchild growled. "It is an application of the rules not in the spirit of the law."

Thank you! "Then why does the Holy Trinity allow it to happen?"

Everyone was stunned into silence. I continued. "They don't have to do it. But They do. Because, ultimately, They want Their children to spend eternity with them. It's why there are so many ways to earn forgiveness. Because They don't want simple mistakes to prohibit anyone from getting to Heaven. THAT is their will."

The silence stretched out. Lucifer tried to break it. "They do it because They have no choice. Otherwise, God's creations would never make it to Heaven."

"Sure, They have a choice," I said. "It's not like God couldn't make us different. We could have been made more obedient. Never have left the Garden Of Eden. But we are what we are. And God loves us anyway. And He wants us to go to Heaven, regardless of our faults."

"Then what is the point of penance?" Lucifer responded. "If you are supposed to have faults, then you have nothing to apologize for. It's part of your nature."

Nice try, but not good enough. "In that case, no one should hate you, since you are only doing what God meant for you to do." Lucifer's brows knitted. I smiled as I said, "You are still God's little puppet."

The air around Lucifer flashed red and flames ran across his clothes. There's a reason Lucifer tempts so many with vanity – it's a subject near to his heart.

Suddenly, every angel in the courtroom, from Camael on the bench to Pahaliah in the Gallery, drew their swords and got ready. Lucifer is tough to rattle, but being at the center of dozens of angels ready to finish what they couldn't during the rebellion, and especially with the archangel fated to destroy him standing right there, got to him. Lucifer was genuinely afraid. Panicked. He got no sympathy from Michael, who was balancing his flaming sword by the hilt. He didn't even look at his target as he said, "Go ahead. I dare you."

Lucifer backed down quickly, sitting with a plop. Curiously, Fairchild and Devereaux hadn't budged an inch, and I saw the disappointment that Lucifer had been cowed so completely. I continued. "It is not our sins that damn us. It is the sins we do not rectify. It is the people we do not do right by. When confronted, both in life and in death, I did the right thing."

"You offended God!" Devereaux screamed.

"God forgave me," I said with a shrug.

"He shouldn't have!" he retorted.

"You are telling God what He should do?"

Devereaux froze in place. Fairchild jumped back in. "He is not putting himself ahead of God!"

"Yes, he is. He is offended by me. My existence is a violation of what he thinks is right. Doesn't matter what actually is right, since, according to those standards, I deserve my Heavenly reward. He knows better, and he is going to protect Heaven from the very people God wants there."

"Formality is necessary. It's why there are first communions, confessions, and so on!"

"Then why did Jesus live among ordinary people? He didn't live in an affluent society. He studied Judaism, but He didn't become a pharisee. He didn't minister to people who could give Him a comfortable place to live in the world. He lived among the sinners. The poor. The sick. Gamblers. Prostitutes. People who think they are damned by the circumstances of their lives. They had no formal instruction, just a desire to do better and help others." I leaned in and snarled. "And that's what I have done for nearly six hundred years."

Fairchild lightly drummed his fingertips on the table. I knew what that meant. It was his sign that he wanted to consult. Devereaux asked Camael, "May I have a few moments to consult?"

"You may," Camael responded. The trio at the Church table huddled and started talking. Usually, this was a good sign. It meant that they had nothing and were searching for some sort of argument. They were on the run. But I wasn't sure about this time. Something else was going on.

A quick look at Camael showed I had good reason to not coast. He was looking at them intently and occasionally shifting his eyes to me. The steel glint of his grey eyes had me gearing up. Whatever they wanted to try and do, he would help them. I had to be ready for whatever came my way.

On the edge of my consciousness, I caught some words. The voice was Fairchild's. I overheard him say, "Move for closing! You can't argue with her directly!"

"Shh!" Devereaux hissed.

Lucifer looked over at me and gave me a friendly smile while waving. Any other presiding angel, I probably could get away with giving the Leader Of The Fallen the longbowman's salute. But this is Camael's courtroom. I didn't trust any of this, so I ignored everything.

Eventually, the group straightened. Lucifer looked crestfallen. I knew what was happening. They were going for closing arguments. They all knew this was lost, none of them were going to get what they wanted....

...what was with Fairchild's smile?

"Move for closing arguments," Devereaux said with despondency.

If I tried for a denial, it could rile up Camael. My best chance was to run with them and keep sharp. "I concur," I said.

Camael nodded to Devereaux. He took a slow, deep breath, and began. "The whole purpose of this trial is to correct an oversight. One that has lasted for six hundred years. Singer has been an affront to God's order, God's wishes, God's rules. We are to love and honor our Creator. She did not.

"Some will say this is a tragedy, given the devotion and love Singer has shown since then. The tragedy is of her making. Had she accepted her proper fate all those centuries ago, she would not be holding your hearts hostage. The guilt that you would feel for doing the right thing is the result of her defiance. You should not feel bad for addressing this error. She should feel bad. She should feel guilty. Another set of regrets that will be hers and hers alone in the depths of Hell. Grant her what even a fallen angel like Lucifer knows – she should be Cast Down. Thank you."

I had to keep things even. None of my usual outrage. I had to address the Tribunal. And keep Camael from preventing that.

"God wants good people to have a Heavenly reward. Heaven is not just for Christians, and it takes more than Christianity to gain admission.

"None of these facts are in dispute in this trial.

"The entire argument advanced against me has nothing to do with established precedent. It has nothing to do with God's own rules, who allows all good people, Jewish, Gentile, or Atheist, into Heaven as long as they were good people. It is one of the central tenets of Judaism, the Word of God before Christianity. The only reason this trial is happening is because the Churches feel I don't deserve Heaven, regardless of God's wishes.

"At no point in my nearly six hundred years of service has God objected to me. I stand in His presence during trials by God. I talk with Him, visit Him, I am allowed within His grace. Few Churches get the opportunities I do, despite their assertion that their religious background makes them more worthy. In fact, neither of the Churches at the table today have even participated in a trial by God, let alone been with Him when not on duty.

"This trial borders on Misconduct. Why does it exist?" I fought to keep my attention, this wasn't the time for me to wonder that myself. I had the last word, and they couldn't challenge my statements now. "It exists because they do not want me. It has nothing to do with correcting an oversight. The Churches have argued points in defense of their own that I have argued for myself. Arguments that have been upheld. There is no legitimate argument. It is just a do over, because they feel they should have won...."

Uh-oh.

I caught Camael look at me. Some of my shock must have gotten out. "You have an additional point to make?"

I didn't dare look. I knew what was coming. I knew why Fairchild was so happy. I knew what this trial was all about. "We are to love each other, despite our differences. God allows these differences to happen. He allows us to be what we want. God wants me in Heaven, just as He wants everyone good in Heaven. If God had wanted otherwise, things would not be the way they are. Uphold His will, allow me into Heaven. Thank you."

I readied myself. Sure, I was ready to pray and claim my Heavenly reward, but I was more concerned about the Church table. Camael looked at the Tribunal and said, "You have heard the Advocates for Hannah Singer state their recommended fates. You may now make your decision. You wish to confer?"

The lead Tribunal stood up. "We are ready to rule."

Camael picked up his gavel and smiled at me. He was going to make my window of opportunity as small as possible. He lifted the gavel and asked, "And what is your decision?"

"Petitioner is to be granted entry into Heaven immediately."

I felt relief pour into me like cool water. Camael looked shocked. His jaw actually fell open and he nearly lost his grip on the gavel. He just glared at the Churches and said, with distinct lack of enthusiasm, "So be it," and tapped the gavel.

I turned to Devereaux and started to say, "Don't do it!", but I wasn't fast enough. He threw his head back and screamed, "Call for a mistrial!"

Camael's face darkened with rage. "No!"

Once again, shafts of light streaked through the ceiling and illuminated us, examining us and our thoughts. I winced as I waited for the inevitable. The voice of God was heard, declaring, "The trial has been just. The failure is Devereaux's for feeling anything other than what he thought should happen is unjust. The verdict is upheld. Devereaux is never to Advocate again."

Devereaux's face dropped. "No!" he screamed, but his plea fell on deaf ears. His wings vanished into blowing dust. He was done.

Camael glared at me. "You could've warned me, Singer." He then stomped down from the bench and out his door as the Tribunal filed out.

Lucifer turned to look at Fairchild. "You're good."

Devereaux didn't move. Didn't even flinch.

Michael came sauntering up to the Church table, a smile of anticipation on his face. Lucifer saw him approaching. He gave me one last look, said, "See you around, Singer," and vanished back to Hell.

Fairchild simply left his position and headed up the aisle to leave the court. Michael and I just looked at Devereaux. He still wasn't moving. Eventually, he mumbled something quiet.

"What?" I asked.

Michael didn't take his eyes off the deposed senior Church. "He said, 'It can't be.'"

"You know what he's talking about, don't you?"

"Yeah," Michael said glumly. "And I think we'll find out very soon that it can and will be."

Suddenly, Michael snapped to attention, listening to something no one else could hear. It could only be God Himself. Suddenly, Michael vanished in a flash of light.

I left the court with Gallows falling in with me, walking in perfect step, leaving Devereaux locked in his private thoughts. We got outside, and we saw several Churches rushing past, heading for the Campus where the Churches resided.

I flagged one down. "What's going on?"

"Vote was just taken. Fairchild is making a speech." And he rushed off.

That confirmed it. I was never really on trial.

The two of us knew what we would see when we got on Campus

grounds. All the Churches had gathered with Fairchild in the middle. Fairchild was standing on a miniature pedestal. The symbolism was just sickening.

Fairchild saw us and the friendly smile on his face was replaced with a serpentine grin. He turned to those around him and declared, "Today is a great day in the history of the Celestial Courts. Devereaux let his anxiousness get the better of him. He was so determined to win, he made questionable decisions. Like his decision to allow Lucifer to sit with him at trial."

Gallows looked crushed. Me? I was too busy studying what was before me.

"And this is Devereaux's legacy. The only senior Church to last exactly one case. His mistake was simple. It was a question of what he thought was wrong, not what actually was wrong. As a result, he did not have the information he needed.

"That changes now.

"I have the knowledge and the skill to restore our proper role in the Celestial Courts, making sure those who need to pay do pay, that those who deserve mercy get it. We know from our earthly studies that God wants people to live as He says. Those who do not obey will now have to answer for their insubordination. Our purpose has been steadily reduced, some by outside influences," and he looked at me, "and some from our own misguided efforts," and he looked at Gallows. "We know what God wants. And we will do as He wishes. I promise you this as the new senior Church."

Fairchild then looked me right in the eyes. He gave me a salute with his fingertips. I got the message -- "See you real soon, Singer."

Gallows simply said, "I want to go to Heaven. Now."

Suddenly, the two of us were outside the Pearly Gates. I thought it odd I was brought with, but I guess Gallows wanted one last goodbye. He greeted Jesus and St. Peter as well as he could -- you could tell he was just emotionally spent. He gave me a hug then went through the gates to the other side. He didn't look back once.

As the gates closed, I just stood there, trying to sort through what happened. I eventually wound up back in the Archives. I wandered around, then decided I wanted to talk to my big brother. I went to his chambers and knocked politely on the door.

"Come in," came Michael's voice. I felt my eyes fly open in surprise. Michael's voice was flat. Uninterested. Practically dead.

I went inside and saw Michael sitting at his desk. He was going over paperwork very methodically and mechanically, like a robot. He looked up, saw me, and said in that same flat tone, "Hello, Hannah."

I walked up carefully. I knew this wasn't a prank. This wasn't Michael's style. There was something else. "Michael? Are you okay?"

"Just fine. Why do you ask?"

I covered my mouth with my hands. "God took away your sense of humor."

"I had to pay for my insubordination," he said simply. "It will return to me eventually."

My own concerns vanished. This wasn't the Michael I knew. I couldn't imagine the torture he was going through, being unable to laugh, to appreciate, to feel joy.

I quickly fell to my knees and started praying to God. Prayers for others have a little more impact than prayers for ourselves. I didn't care what I sounded like or looked like as I felt tears start to fill my eyes. "Please, God," I said. "Michael was just trying to help. He had a hard choice to make. It's already making him suffer. Please, have mercy."

I suddenly felt the strength of God's light inside me jump. I looked at Michael. Michael had closed his eyes and tilted his head to the ceiling. I thought I saw a few white specks drifting around him. After a few seconds, he lowered his head to me and opened his eyes. They were smiling. And the rest of his face followed suit.

Michael shot from his chair. I barely had time to get to my feet before he enveloped me in a huge hug. I hugged him back as well as I could.

"I had to pay for my defiance, Hannah," Michael said, not hiding the relief he felt.

"You suffered enough," was all I said.

"You shouldn't have done it," he said.

I pulled back and smiled. "Are you suggesting that I actually made God do something He wasn't ready to do?"

Michael looked at me odd. "Are you suggesting that I could have ended that but I was punishing myself?"

"I would. And you have said how much alike we are."

Michael just looked at me with a smirk for a few moments. Then he folded me into him again. "Thank you, Hannah," was all he said.

Eventually, we pulled apart. He asked, "So, what brings you around?"

"I'm going to Earth for a little bit. Would you like to come with?"

We wound up outside Niagra Falls, on the Canadian side. We were able to get right next to it. The power of the water, the noise, it's awe-inspiring, be you human or angel. As we sat, Michael said the first thing. "Why is it the ones who talk so much about morality are the most likely to abuse it for their own ends?"

I thought about Camael. "Why is it the ones who never listen always complain they aren't told anything?"

We just kept sitting there. I finally broke the silence. "He scares me."

"Camael?"

"No. Not like this. Fairchild scares me more."

Michael looked at me. "Wow."

"I can't help it," I said. "Fairchild doesn't feel remorse for his behavior. He feels justified. That people deserve to be treated cruelly and heartlessly. That people can and should be shamed into living the way he thinks is right. That people ultimately bring their misfortune on themselves."

"They sort of do," Michael said. "Some people just don't want to resist."

"I don't mean things like that. I mean people who are trapped in a life with no hope of getting out. So they have to do things they know they shouldn't or are wrong. Churches are great at saying people should lead pure lives, but they can't bother to give people those opportunities. Those people aren't their problem."

"It's always easier to assign blame," Michael said. "To say that people deserve their fate or that there was nothing they could do. They don't realize how even just a tiny little gesture can make a world of difference."

"Man is meant to survive, not succeed."

"Survival is success," Michael said. "And success can translate, but it takes a lot of work and drive to make happen. And when things just don't go your way, it's easy for others to say you don't deserve it or you screwed up instead of something more complicated. How many inventions have humans made that, had they built and released them even five years later, would have been smash hits?"

"Timing is everything."

"That it is. And you're right – it's the people that don't understand that, that they do not control their own destinies as well as they think they do, that they are very much at the mercy of things outside their control, that are dangerous."

I sighed. "And it's why God needs us."

"Exactly," Michael smiled. "There's a big difference between serving the church and serving God."

And I felt the tension pour out of me, mixing with the water and falling away.

RUNNING FROM THE FAMILY

You can pick your friends, but you can't pick your family.

Ain't that the truth.

The whole point of family is a continuous, supportive unit. The young help the old, the old help the young. No one person can know everything. There are things that only life experience can prepare you for, leaving new adults out in the cold. There are things that age eventually prevents you from doing, leaving old adults out in the cold. It is a bond of love, honor, and respect that keep everything together.

Needless to say, when family starts turning on each other for various reasons, it gets really hairy. It's not supposed to be that way. But lines can be crossed. They do get crossed. And the problems are not limited to the living.

I had caught up with my case load and there was really nothing that needed my undivided attention. Looking at some downtime, I considered a jaunt down to Earth.

"Where are you thinking of going?" St. Michael asked me.

"I'm not sure," I told him.

"You could always go someplace like an amusement park."

"No, thanks," I told him.

"Still haven't shaken off Hampton Beach?"

"It was the most interminable experience ever. And remember, I died from the Plague."

I decided to go indoors for a change. I went back to my native England and went to Brookstone, the legendary London bookstore. I materialized and marched through the doors. I inhaled the scent of paper and ink, the faint whiff of leather mixed in there, the finish on the wood. It wasn't Heaven, but for the moment, it was an acceptable substitute.

I can pour through books quickly and easily, so I was adsorbing as much as I could. I had gotten to the mystery section when I heard a familiar voice ask, "Do you know where I might find the J.K. Rowling books?"

I smiled at Michael and leaned towards him. "Are you sure that *she's* the one you came here to find?"

Michael quirked a smile and said, "Follow me."

We wandered through the bookstore until we got to the Arts section. Michael looked for a moment, then pulled a book off the shelf. He held it up so I could see the cover. A picture in classic black and white. The man pictured was Caucasian, six foot two, brown wavy hair, green eyes, a smile of sophistication and good natured mischief. Not that I could tell that from the black and white picture, I had met him a few years ago. His name was Christopher Moore, and he had been an actor. Nice guy, very charming. He led a good life and was in Heaven. So it wasn't him that was the focus here.

I looked at who wrote the book. It was by one Harold Moore. "His brother?" I asked.

"Yes," Michael said, handing me the book. "Skim through this."

I started going through the book and my eyes got wide. Lots of stories that couldn't possibly be true. His petition had been approved by both sides, there wasn't even a trial. The Churches alone would have thrown the brakes on his Heavenly admission if this was right.

I thought it over and said, "Harold Moore has died?"

"Yes," Michael said. "What's more, the Churches filed No Contest."

I nearly dropped the book. "Are you serious?"

"Swear to God, Hannah. They won't explain their reasoning, so we probably won't find out about it until trial."

Churches could throw cases. If they knew they were on a loser, they would present a token case just so they could say they tried, but they didn't put much effort into it. "They filed a request for trial yet?"

"Sure have."

"Who's lead?"

"Jeff Fairchild." That didn't necessarily mean it wasn't a token case, just that the odds were against it. If they had made someone green the lead, that would have meant it was a tosser.

"Is this book in the library at the Archives?" I asked.

"Aren't they all?" he smiled.

I put the book back on the shelves and started walking past Michael. "We can just leave, you know, Hannah. No one will notice us."

"Before we go, I want to get some chocolate bars," I smiled. The only better chocolate was Swiss, and it's not just nationalism that makes me say that. Really.

With my precious cargo in hand, we returned to the Archives. I pulled out the life scrolls for the Moore brothers, and got to work.

Christopher and Harold Moore were born into a large family in a poor rural area of the American Midwest. The father barely kept them above the poverty line, working in a steel mill, hunting, and doing everything he could. Mom worked as a waitress. The four young ones were latchkey kids from an early age.

Although this might seem a harsh set up, the family had love. They also had fun. They actually enjoyed their lot in life, whether practicing shooting with dad or going to pumpkin chucking contests or whatever. The world might have looked down on them, but they didn't care.

The Moore patriarch never stopped drilling into his sons' heads that they should be striving for more out of life. Sure, they were happy as they were, but if there's a chance to be better, you should take it. Most of the kids didn't really have much opportunity, where they were combined with what education they could get. The state gave most of the resources to the cities, not the countryside.

The older brother showed a knack for working on cars from an early age and was doing informal business as a mechanic. The next oldest, the sister, was perfectly content to learn to cook, clean, and other qualities people in the area looked for in a wife. She wanted a family and kids. Harold was the youngest, and just couldn't get a handle on life. He found himself in continual trouble with the law and never finished middle school. The parents still gave him love, and what money they could, but you could tell they always hoped for better for him.

Christopher was a bit different. He was a natural performer. School plays, cracking jokes, everything. He also had classic good looks and an easy charm. He had star quality. Everyone said he should be in movies. Christopher thought, why not? With his parents' blessing, he took off for Hollywood after graduating high school to make it to the Big Time.

Breaking into movies is very hard. Christopher had an edge over most people there. Being from a rural area, he knew how to live on the cheap (including a stint in a public storage unit).

Christopher was trying to rely on his parents as little as possible. Harold had gotten married after two near pregnancies, and he and his wife were really having trouble making ends meet. Harold's love for his parents should have come into serious question when he and his wife visited every weekend and always asked for money. When the parents started saying no, they stopped visiting, and the parents had to go to them. The requests for money didn't stop, though, and the couple frequently found themselves with surprise bills and collections they weren't expecting (or so they claimed), and the parents had to bail them out, like when he needed a lawyer for selling stolen goods. Each time, they gritted their teeth and said, "Well, that's what family does – they look out for each other."

Christopher was getting nowhere. He was learning that Hollywood was full of people there trying to make it and it was very cutthroat, a marked contrast to back home where everyone was encouraging him. He also saw a lot of scams, such as several acting schools. People paid money to learn how to act, but people who went to acting school are everywhere there. People would leave Hollywood with their dreams dashed and the teachers at the acting schools stayed.

It was during an open audition (or "cattle call" as it is derisively known) that inspiration struck. Christopher was one of fifty in the small room (with another two hundred waiting outside). Everyone was dressed as the character they were auditioning for, everyone was staying in character, all in hopes of impressing the casting director. Everyone was portraying a casual guy. Hmm, he thought. There's a lot of competition to play casual guys, and not as much for sophisticated guys. Maybe that's where I need to look.

Christopher had never taken acting classes. Instead, he went to charm school. He went from a charming guy to a smart, sly, sophisticated dog in the Cary Grant mode. He got better clothes, and every time he left wherever he was staying, he got "in character".

One day, while having lunch, a casting director saw him and approached. A famous director was getting ready to shoot a law drama, and he thought Christopher would be perfect. It was only a minor role as a young lawyer in the firm working his way up, providing a counterpoint to the star's story, but it was a credit in a high profile movie. Plus, the paycheck was more than he had ever made in a year in his life.

The producer, director, everyone was impressed with how natural Christopher was on camera and how professional he was off camera. He was already getting other minor roles when the movie that started this all was released. There was the usual worship over the director's vision and people were talking Oscar just after seeing the trailer. However, Christopher caught a lot of eyes, and people wanted to know more about this person. Buzz started, and soon after that, offers.

Christopher's star was on the rise. He carefully chose a movie role that would play to his strengths and inked his first seven-figure deal. The movie came out. Audiences cheered. Critics raved. Women swooned.

One of the first things Christoper did with his newfound fortune was give some to his oldest brother. He had always wanted to open a dirt bike track. His brother was really sharp, however, and was soon leveraging the business into a stop on the professional circuit. With a generous gift from Christopher and his own smart bookkeeping, the eldest was able to pursue his ultimate dream, his own monster truck team. He was a good business man, but not so good at physics – he misjudged the incline and the truck went up, over, and on the roof. Fortunately, he had enough sense to reinforce the cab and belt himself in. A couple of broken bones, and he was back to redefining the phrase "compact car" before long.

Christopher's older sister got a lot of help, too. Dating prospects in town became limited because, well, she was the sister of a Hollywood movie star. Not many people were interested in what she offered for a family, just in what they could sponge off of Christopher. Christopher offered her a place to stay at his home in California. She didn't want to just crash there, so he helped her find a job, working as a seamstress in a TV studio costume department. While there, she met a gaffer. Swell guy, they were smitten with each other and got married. He wound up moving into the same house with her and Christopher. The guy thought the arrangement was just a bit odd, but it was cheaper than his little loft, and the family vibe was great.

The parents? Oh, they got a brand new house that they didn't have to fix up every year. Christopher flew out to visit them when he could, and if he was busy, flew them out to visit him. Everyone in town thought he was still the same great guy who grew up there. Everyone loved him.

Well, almost everyone.

Harold was the lone holdout. When Christopher's star started to rise, Harold started dropping hints that he was having trouble making ends meet. He thought he was being too subtle. In truth, Christopher was ignoring them. Things came to a head during a family gathering when Harold took Christopher aside and ripped him for being so selfish. Harold needed money, and mom and dad had given so much over the years, wasn't it time for his bigger brother to step up? Christopher immediately fired back that Harold was a selfish jerk. Christopher got lucky, but if he hadn't made it as an actor? The parents had no money from bailing out Harold, sometimes literally. Their brother and sister would be doing odd jobs instead of being self-sufficient. The three of them worked and tried to improve their lots in life, Harold just let his parents improve his lot in life. He took and took and took, often things they could have used themselves, like the older brother wanting to go to college to be a mechanic. The arguing continued until the two of them actually started coming to blows. Everyone separated them, and the party broke up. That was kind of a buzzkill.

Harold noticed people were asking him about the shiner he got from his brother. Everyone in town figured he deserved it. Those outside, however, gasped in horror. After all, Christopher was such a gentleman, and he was liked. Tabloids came calling, offering cash for dirt on Harold's brother. The tabloids offered to handle any legal heat, and Harold jumped at it. Even legitimate press started wondering. Never mind that if they dug into Harold's background, they'd find far more (and better documented) bad behavior. Harold wasn't news. Christopher was.

Christopher responded to this by refusing any contact with his brother. His siblings followed suit. The parents were still trying to smooth things over and keep the family together, unaware of how badly things had corroded underneath. Harold was able to leverage this into more sympathy for him and more money with more interviews. Professionally, he was Christopher's brother.

Then, one day, Christopher saw that Harold had moved to Los Angeles so it would be more convenient to do the professional guest circuit. The negative publicity was starting to cool Christopher's career. Interviews were less about his latest movie and more about the public falling out with his brother. Roles started to dry up as producers felt Christopher's off screen life was becoming a distraction. Christopher pleaded with Harold to give it a rest, but Harold refused, asking, "How else am I supposed to make money? It's not like you ever helped me."

When a plumb role that had "Oscar" written all over it was given to a young unknown instead of Christopher, he took action. First, he rewrote his will and gave most of his stuff away, including his house to his sister. He then used some industry connections to get a bunch of downers to help him with his stress. When he had enough to handle a large-sized nursery school, Christopher started downing them with shots of whiskey and was dead before you could say, "Shooting Star."

This only shook up the family worse as everyone started complaining about Harold and what could have been done to make things different. Yes, there was quite a bit of, "Well, if Christopher had just given him money, this wouldn't have happened." Harold didn't care. He was more in demand than ever to talk about the great talent that was lost. He fell in with a different crowd that was looking to use him for all kinds of boosts. That included the perks some of the less reputable ones provided, like drugs and prostitutes. Harold wrote a "tell-all" book about life with his brother that was no more accurate than anything else he sold. While celebrating his success with some hard partying, he overdosed. People at the party took him out to the countryside and made it look like a suicide to keep themselves in the clear. It happened almost a year to the day that his brother died.

Even though neither side contested his petition, Christopher wasn't in Heaven. God needed him to help his family work through their grief. Harold's death basically meant he had to start over again. But Christopher was just keeping busy. Once his family was fine, he'd be heading for Heaven.

Harold? Well, that was what we were going to sort out.

I walked to the courtroom, a casual smile on my face. This was so in the bag, it was pathetic.

I selected one junior, my favorite goto guy, Harold "Smack" Kowalski. He was a former sportswriter with one of the fastest minds I'd even seen. I would pay serious money to see him and St. Thomas Aquinas square off, but it would never happen. Aquinas was more concerned with philosophy and human nature, not Smack's area of expertise. If Aquinas ever tried talking baseball, though....

Entering the court, it was the usual turnout. The Church table had Fairchild in the lead position, Harold Moore in the Petitioner's seat, and, to the left of them, Jacob Palini. Palini thought he was slick. Fairchild didn't like him, but put up with him because his twist of mind could go in unpredictable directions and gave an edge over Celestials. Palini and Fairchild watched me enter and silently communicated their feelings for me. Harold, meanwhile, just smiled at me, like mommy and daddy were going to get him out of trouble with the principal.

Smack was at the Celestial table, second seat in from the aisle. He was reading a scroll with several columns of names and numbers. His pen, which he used as a substitute for a cigar, was working around the corner of his mouth, the only thing keeping his teeth from grinding.

I got to my seat and looked over his shoulder. "Hey, Smack. Whatcha reading?"

"Picking players for my baseball fantasy league."

I had never gotten a good look at a stat sheet like Smack used. It had more numbers than anyone else doing fantasy sports, here or on Earth. "What exactly is all this?"

Smack moved it over so I could see and started explaining the rows. There were normal stats from the games. There were stats we knew because we knew more about their bodies and spirits than they did. And then there was the last set of columns.

"They're what?"

"Drug usage," Smack said, eying a bunch of numbers carefully. "This group is for regular drugs due to injuries and such. This is for recreational drugs, from marijuana to blow. For a bunch of health nuts, they don't take very good care of their bodies. Some of them are on enough drugs to drop Keith

Richards. And then this is steroids."

"You track steroid usage?"

"Sure. Being juiced increases the risk of muscle damage plus other factors. They can cut someone's life and career short."

I took a good look at the list. "That many players are on steroids?"

"Oh, come on, Hannah. You know the human body isn't supposed to look like that."

Smack was right. Not only that, but alterations to the human body don't transfer to the spirit, so they turn up here looking like they did before the steroids, and the dichotomy could be hilarious at times. One guy? It was like comparing Mike Tyson to Urkel. "Are there any sports that don't have people on steroids?"

"Nope," Smack said. "I should know. I got to see it as a sportswriter. There are golfers on steroids. There are rap stars on steroids. I wouldn't be surprised if there were Little Leaguers on steroids."

"Little Leaguers?"

"Hey, they have age scandals all the time. 'The love of the game' is a bunch of bull."

I noticed one name on Smack's list in particular. He was taking so many performance enhancers, he could probably evolve into a new species. And yet, his stats were in the tank. I pointed and said, "He's having problems."

"Steroids boost strength, not talent. He's like the guy that won a dollar in the five dollar lottery."

"Shouldn't you be upset that there's so much rampant cheating?"

"I can't control it, all I can do is roll with it."

I shrugged and went into my own private world. I just stopped long enough to look at the seat directly behind me in the Gallery. Yup, Michael was sitting there. Nothing else entered my head until the chimes sounded, signaling that court was in session. We deployed our wings.

The door on the right opened, and twelve angels entered, wings already out. I breathed a soft sigh as I watched them take their places in the Tribunal box.

The door at the back opened to admit the presiding angel. Oh, Christ Almighty! Not Camael! Camael hated me. I don't know why, I don't know what I did. He's Silence Is Goldened me. He's barred me from advocating. Arguing in front of him is like walking through a minefield in variable gravity – just because nothing went off when you stepped there didn't mean nothing ever would. And as a lowly human, I had no recourse whatsoever.

Camael looked at me as he came in the door and smiled like a hungry wolf. I didn't flinch, didn't change expression, nothing to show any weakness or disrespect. When Camael looked to the front to watch where he was going (he tripped one time climbing the steps. I was the only one in court who didn't laugh. Guess who got reprimanded), I snuck a look at Fairchild and Palini. They were smiling. This was literally theirs to lose. And if I did anything that even smelled funny to Camael, he would clamp down on me like a rabid bear

107

trap. I started reworking my arguments and statements in my head. I quickly charted a new strategy. Thank God I didn't have Privilege, I needed the time.

Camael got to the bench and looked out over the court. With his compact build, he doesn't sit during trial, he stands. He looked at Fairchild. "Who is the Petitioner?"

"The Petitioner is Harold Moore," came the response.

"And who are his Advocates?"

"Jacob Palini and Jeff Fairchild, acting as lead."

Camael looked at me in silent challenge. "Who advocates for the Celestials?"

"Harold Kowalski and Hannah Singer, acting as lead," I responded evenly.

Camael eyed me for another beat before saying, "Will the Petitioner please take the stand?"

Harold Moore sauntered out and took his place in the dock. He didn't look the least bit worried.

"Mister Fairchild? Your opening statements, please," Camael said.

"Harold Moore has done nothing to warrant being denied Heaven," Fairchild said. I got my first real ray of hope in this whole thing. It was only for a split second, but I saw Camael's eyebrows arch ever so slightly and for oh so short a time. Camael doesn't like this, either. If I structured my arguments in a way that reflected his thought process, it should keep me out of trouble and still pot Harold. The way for me to do that was to exploit Fairchild's overconfidence. A statement like what he just made was loaded. He didn't do that unless he felt the case was a snap. Usually, that meant he wasn't thinking anything through. Good. This was already a headache, I didn't need it to turn into a migraine.

"He made a few Earthly mistakes, sure," Fairchild said. He was either oblivious to the damage to his own case he was causing or he was trying to throw it. And with Palini there, that wasn't likely. There had to be some weird angle that they were considering. "But compared to the love for his family, that is trivial. Especially his love for his brother. Grant his petition. Thank you."

Camael turned to me. I kept it simple and straightforward and with sins Camael found egregious. "Bearing false witness. Character assassination. Dishonoring mother and father. Disruption of family. Living a false life. Lying. Loving money. Lack of compassion. Blatant self-interest. Sloth, Wanton Disregard. Inappropriate drug use. Theft.

"That's not a few mistakes. That is not trivial. And the love he felt for his family was far from great. It was convenient. There has to be some great, noble act on his part to counter all the ill he has done. There is no noble act in his history. He should be reincarnated to make up for it. Thank you."

Camael didn't stop studying me, even after I said thank you. My nerves turned to steel, I didn't waver a bit. The silence continued to stretch. Camael was waiting for me to say something.

Fairchild was feeling the wind against his back. "Move for closing arguments."

"Motion should be denied," I said calmly. "We have not debated the merits of Fairchild's statements that Harold deserves Heaven."

"Motion is denied," Camael said with a quick pop of the gavel. "Well, Singer? Say what is wrong with Fairchild's assertion."

I thought carefully and said, "Harold's actions to his family are hatred, not love."

Fairchild looked innocent. "How is saving his brother from temptation and bad choices hatred?"

I saw an opening. If I did this right, I could get Fairchild to overplay his hand. "Harold didn't save Christopher from temptation or bad choices. Christopher did. His life is the result of his choices, not his brother's."

Fairchild blanched. I had advanced an idea the Tribunal could seize on. Harold's motivations were no longer Fairchild's to define. "Harold guided Christopher. He did it with his tell-all books and interviews."

"He exploited his brother, full stop."

Palini shot to his feet. "Christopher held back from doing certain things because he was afraid of what kinds of stories his brother would tell. He could not do any wild partying or anything because his brother would blab."

"Are you suggesting the only reason Christopher was a good person was because his brother was a tattletale?"

"Yes. Hollywood corrupts many, many people. People who are good begin worshiping all sorts of false gods. Sex. Money. Power. Themselves. Harold acted as a safety check."

"Christopher was incapable of the actions you are saying Harold kept him from."

"Says you," Palini retorted.

"He was never a partier to begin with. He was always responsible. His parents, his siblings, his friends, they all counted on him. He was boring. He was the reliable one. Look at his past, he had no interest in anything like that."

Fairchild smiled. "Move to strike Singer's argument."

Camael smiled happily. "On what grounds?"

"Privacy of mind."

Camael closed his eyes in delight as he declared "Struck!" and hit the gavel.

It took a lot of effort to keep me from screaming in rage. I could no longer argue Christopher's intent. Fairchild hemmed me in. I started thinking what other track I could take.

Smack shot to his feet. "Move to strike Palini and Fairchild's accusations of immorality."

Camael gave Smack a challenging look. The two of them mixed it up, but Smack was never in the danger I was. "On what grounds?" Camael asked.

Smack took his pen out of his mouth and used it like a pointer. "Moore's environment makes all the sins his brother was protecting him from interpreted sins, not absolute sins."

Camael laughed. Fairchild looked at him. "Drinking? Drugs? Sex?

Idol worship? How are those not sins?"

"How are Solomon's mistresses not sins?" Smack smiled.

Camael calmed down. All his rage was absorbed by Fairchild and Palini. "He was God's chosen!"

"How many people who aren't God's chosen in the Bible had concubines? You two are constantly griping about people with extramarital sweeties. Why do they get a pass?"

Palini piped up, "We've left that behind. Those were different times."

Fairchild looked like he was ready to spin around and punch Palini in the face. Smack kept going. "The environment they were in, slaves and concubines and shows of force were all considered part of everyday life, not sins. In that environment, the sins were interpreted, not absolute. Look at athletes who think cheating and juicing on steroids is just keeping up with the competition, not cheating. Same principal applies to Hollywood. All the temptations and earthly pleasures are par for the course, not something to be ashamed of. Look at Paris Hilton. The Kardashians. Bad behavior isn't frowned on anymore, it's celebrated."

"It shouldn't be celebrated, it shouldn't be rewarded," Fairchild countered. Come on, Smack, don't let me down.

"But it is. Christopher could have seized his chance and had no repercussions."

"Bad behavior is bad behavior, your motion should be denied."

Camael declared, "Motion is denied," and struck the gavel. Smack sat down, and I made a note to find him some scotch later.

I went right for the throat. "By your own statements, Harold's petition should be denied. He did wrong by exploiting his brother, telling lies for personal gain. Bad behavior is bad behavior." Fairchild turned red, whether from me getting the better of him or him walking right into it, I don't know.

Palini tried a rescue. "What he did wasn't bad behavior."

I couldn't directly engage him without risking Camael's wrath. I kept to things that, were Camael to rule any other way, would result in a mistrial. "His actions clearly demonstrate bad behavior."

Palini didn't realize he was going out on a limb, and a very flimsy one at that. "Only if you aren't looking closely."

Fairchild's face suddenly stretched. He knew what was coming. He turned to Palini and ordered, "Sit down now!"

"He did it out of love for his brother, plain and simple."

I didn't even blink. "Move to strike Palini's argument."

"On what grounds?" Camael grumbled.

"Privacy Of Mind."

Camael knew he had no choice. I would call for a mistrial in an instant, and he wouldn't have a leg to stand on. Glaring at me the entire time, he tapped the gavel as he said, "Struck."

Mad as Camael was at me, that was nothing compared to the fury Fairchild was sending Palini's way. Palini had sat down and hunched his shoulders a little. All that was left was for me to bring it home. I looked back at Camael and said, "He spent no time with his brother except when he wanted something. He lived separately from him and ignored him. In fact, most of the events he wrote about, he wasn't even at the locations in question. Harold lied to the world. That is inexcusable."

"I've heard enough," Camael declared. "Time for closing arguments."

No point in honking Camael off more than I already had. "The official position of the Celestials is that Harold led an opportunistic life and he should be reincarnated into servitude to make up for it."

Fairchild sounded deflated. "The official position of the Churches is that, heinous as Harold's actions were, they helped keep Christopher and his family out of trouble and his petition should be granted."

Camael looked at the Tribunal. "You have heard the Advocates for Harold Moore state their recommended fates. You may now make your decision. You wish to confer?"

The lead Tribunal stood. "We are ready to rule."

"And what is your decision?"

"Petitioner is to be reincarnated according to Singer's suggestion."

Camael rolled his eyes and droned, "So be it." He tapped the gavel, ending the session, and eyed daggers at me as he left the courtroom.

I walked through the hallways, steadying my nerves. Facing Camael was always rough. I pulled through this with minimal altercation, so I was happy.

I reached an intersection, and I turned instead of going straight. I decided to head to Michael's chambers. A little bit of time with him to lift my spirits.

I got to the door and knocked politely. "Come in," came Michael's response.

When I opened the door, Michael looked up and his face was a mess of emotions. "Hannah? What brings you around?"

"Is this a bad time?"

Michael quickly waved me in. I entered and shut the door. "Not exactly," he said.

"I can come back...."

"No," he said with finality. "But, I'm glad you're here. You want to know what Harold's trial was about?"

"Sure."

Michael went over to a set of bookcases. With a wave of his hand, one slid out, then its depth started shrinking. From the front, it looked exactly the same. He gestured to the open space and said, "If you'll go behind here, you'll get your answer very soon."

Part of me recoiled, thinking it was a prank. But another part of me knew Michael too well. This wasn't how he did pranks. I went into the gap. Michael pulled a book off the shelf next to me and gave it to me, then slid the bookcase back into place.

I stood there for a moment, wondering what was going on. I looked at the book Michael gave me. The Last Unicorn by Peter S. Beagle. Always a good read. So I turned to the side, sat down, and got comfortable.

It didn't take long before I heard another knock at Michael's door. A distinctive knock, one that filled me with dread. I heard Michael get up and open the door. After a beat, he said with a distinct lack of enthusiasm, "Camael. Good to see you again."

"You know why I'm here, Michael," he responded.

"Come in," he said. I forced myself to calm down. God only knows what would happen if Camael noticed Michael had altered the bookcase and started wondering why. Humans wouldn't notice, but angels would know.

I heard them cross to Michael's desk. There was a pause when Camael's footsteps stopped. I imagine he was looking for a whoopee cushion in the chair. I heard them sit, and Michael started without preamble. "That trial had to happen like that."

"Did it now?"

"Yes, and you know why. You've sat at the trials."

"Clue me in."

"We're starting to get too many people who think avoiding a bad life constitutes living a good life."

"They don't sin," Camael said, I bet with a shrug of his shoulders.

I could almost hear Michael shaking his head as he spoke. "The only reason they don't sin because they're afraid they'll get caught. If it weren't for that, they'd be doing all kinds of evil. Just as there can be good reasons for doing bad, there are bad reasons for doing good. It's not the what, it's the why. They are actually fine with this stuff. They haven't learned."

"Isn't the brother of a movie star kind of the wrong way to illustrate that point?"

"The Churches had to do it. They've been building their 'end justifies the means' defenses in this regard steadily lately. If they didn't try, they could be shot down as inconsistently applied. And with the way arguments went, it's set them back as far as using social intimidation as validation."

"And lucky me, I got to hear your pet argue."

"Wasn't luck."

I don't know how I kept still instead of dropping the book or hitting my head against the bookcase when I heard that.

Camael practically oozed distaste. "Such an expert manipulator."

"Watch your tongue," Michael said, suddenly forceful.

You could have cut the silence with a knife, the way it stretched on. Finally, Michael spoke, a bit calmer than before. "You heard Hannah argue because of how much you hate her. No one can say she got any advantages from you." I had suspected that was the reason. Just nice to know Michael and I were on the same page.

"Oh, wonderful," Camael said dryly.

"You don't want to see her so much? Be nicer to her. Make it so that presiding at her trials is a potential deficit, not an asset."

"No," Camael clipped.

There was a long, considered pause from Michael. "You do realize she's not going to quit because of you, right?"

I could hear Camael get up from the chair and walk to the door. He didn't open it, and I got scared he'd noticed the bookcase. "She will get no special treatment from me. She says she's the best ever. She better act it." I heard him open the door, step through, and slam it shut.

A chill fell over me once he was gone. It's not a good sign when you're afraid of an angel. Michael called, "He's gone," but I didn't move.

Nothing doing. Michael pulled out the bookcase and looked at me, sitting on the floor and forcing my nerves under control. "Don't let him scare you," Michael smiled. "He doesn't really mean it."

"Yeah, he does," I said, straightening up. Michael offered me his hand, but I refused it. I was strong. I had this. "What did I do to him?"

"I can't say," Michael said with a shrug as I passed him.

I stopped and looked at Michael. "Does Camael hate humans?"

Michael looked confused. "Why would he hate humans?"

"He's always been strict at trials. He...."

"Let me stop you right there," Michael said with a smile. "He doesn't hate humans. He hates opportunists. That's the reason for his beef with Adam in the Garden Of Eden. Angels, humans, anyone who uses others' weaknesses for their own gain, he hates."

"Is that what my problem is? He sees me as an opportunist?" Michael looked to the side, considering it. I didn't wait for a response. "Well, tough. Let him hate me for what I am."

"You're no opportunist, Hannah," Michael said.

"Yes, I am. I have to be. Everything I do in court is about seeing opportunity and taking advantage of it. It has to be that way, or souls will lose their Heavenly reward! If he doesn't like it, he can go burn!"

Michael started walking towards me, the smile never leaving his face. "Okay, maybe you are an opportunist. However, there's a key difference between you and others."

Michael was up to me. I tilted my head back so I could see into those amazing eyes. "And what difference is that?"

"You use opportunities to help others, and if you help yourself, it's not at others' expense. The opportunists Camael hates? Everything they do, they do for themselves. All they care about is themselves."

I sagged a little. I thought I had the answer. I couldn't have done anything about it, but at least the mystery, the not knowing, would have been over.

Michael simply gathered me to him and held me in a protective hug. I hugged him back as well I could. I resolved to find the answer one day. Would Camael and I be friends again? I resolved to find that answer, too.

MANY HAPPY RETURNS

With the declaration, "So be it!" and the smack of the gavel, another trial was over, another soul was on his way to Heaven, and another feather in the cap of Hannah Singer. I gleefully marched out of court and starting running through ideas in my head.

My case load was now clear, so I had time to do some reading. Not only did I have to consider what I would read, but where I would read. I felt like some music, and I know one of the angels has a string quartet that was meeting soon. I reflected on Claire Johnson, one of my juniors on grey area cases. She used to enjoy doing aerobics even though it isn't necessary up here. Typically, angels do choir music, other music types and groups exist but they aren't as common. Claire trying to do her routine to an angelic choir took some getting used to. Then she tried her routine to an angelic choir being led by St. Michael. Partway through her activity, the choir sang the theme from the TV show "Diff'rent Strokes." The cognitive dissonance was too much, and Claire never did aerobics again. To this day, Michael refuses to tell me if he did that just to mess with her, although it's not like I don't know the answer.

Asking around, today was going to be a great day. A jazz trio would be playing on the edge of the Blooming Meadow. I went to the library and grabbed the collected works of Noel Coward. Next destination? The Blooming Meadow.

I was almost there when I ran into St. Michael. Michael wasn't walking, he was actually flying carefully over the grounds at about a third story height. That's not usual for him. He saw me and landed deftly in front of me. "Hello, Hannah. Have you seen Harold Ginderson anywhere?"

My eyes popped. "He's back already?"

"Yup. Car accident. His kid's fault."

"He ain't getting his license anytime soon."

"You're more right than you think. The kid's twelve."

Well, that ceased all mental activity in my brain. "What happened?"

Michael clearly didn't have Gilderson's life scroll with him. He reached out to me with his right hand, putting his palm to my forehead. In a flash, all knowledge about Gilderson's most recent life entered my head. Gilderson was under a car doing an oil change and the kid released the jack. I saw that, as is typical of reincarnations, Gilderson did not look like his recent body, but still looked the way he did from his first lifetime, so he should be easy to spot up here.

I had never represented Gilderson in court, but I knew him fairly well. Gilderson had lived eight times so far. It wasn't that he lived bad lives. In fact, most of his petitions were just stamped "No Contest" by both the Celestials and the Churches. It was his family line. They desperately needed a stabilizing influence on their lives, and that was Harold Gilderson. He'd be reborn, and eventually gravitate to the center of the family. Sometimes, he'd cool his heels for a while before going back, which was how I ran into him in the first place.

When Michael removed his hand, that was when my brain resumed working and the question occurred to me: "Why are we looking for him? Hasn't he petitioned?"

"Nope," Michael said with a shake of his head. "All we know is he died and he hasn't turned up yet."

"I'll keep my eyes open for him," I said.

"Thanks, Hannah." Michael lifted off the ground and resumed his search.

I watched where I could, but short of going on an extended tour through the Valley Of Death (not possible, given the cases that were soon coming up), I couldn't do much. It was obvious Gilderson was hiding, but why was a mystery. After all, he wasn't going to Hell, he'd lived another good life....

...hmm. Maybe that was it. I decided to take advantage of the fact that I was the best Celestial ever. I grabbed some life scrolls for cases I had coming up and marched to my favorite spot, the Water Gardens. Everyone knew it was my favorite spot, so it wouldn't take much for Gilderson to learn it.

I acted casual as I went to my favorite spot. That meant sitting on the ground with my back against one of the water troughs. I kept an eye out for passers-by, knowing each time they would chase Gilderson back into the shadows. Eventually, while I was reading my fifth scroll, I heard him.

"Uh...excuse me...."

I craned my head and turned it so I could see over the trough. Just on the edge, ready to duck out of sight, was Gilderson.

"Hello, Gilderson," I smiled. "Want to talk about it?"

He shifted his eyes down, clearly having an internal debate with himself. He finallly sighed and crept out, watching around him and above him for anyone else. He stayed on the other side of the trough and lowered himself onto his knees, ready to duck behind it at a moment's notice.

"Gone straggler on us, huh?"

He was silent for a beat. "Yeah."

"Can I ask why?"

Another beat. "I don't want to go back."

I turned my head back to my scroll, but my attention was on him. "What makes you think you'll go back?"

"God keeps asking me to."

Aaaaaaaah, I thought. Now it makes sense why he kept filing new petitions. Each one was a separate lifetime, not penance.

God sometimes needs people to be born again. There's no real way to tell what it is, other than He knows it's important. Typically, God is more likely to send angels down to be born to help guide people and families. Angels are harder to corrupt, can get away with more, don't need the forgiveness of the earthly church, and what's more, are already in Heaven. God doesn't like delaying humans from gaining their Heavenly rewards unless it is really really necessary. And I guess, for Gilderson, it was. I mean, eight times around the block? With the same family line?

Not that Gilderson knew such things when he was born. The knowledge of the Afterlife isn't generally accessible to living beings because there's no frame of reference. A lot of people think they are just dreaming or imagining things when actually their brains have put something together and given them a glimpse of what lays beyond. Of course, the real trick is what is an actual unlocked memory and what is just imagination.

I got up and turned to look at him. He was actually shaking with fear. I leaned on the trough. "Come on. Was life really that bad for you?"

"...no."

I gave him a sympathetic smile. I said, "Say it. Go ahead."

There was a long, long beat. Then he said, "I want to go home."

I let out a sigh. Poor guy. God doesn't force anyone to do anything they don't want to. He always presents a choice, no one is compelled. But good luck getting someone like Gilderson to say no to God. "So you're going to struggle. For how long?"

His eyes darted around, like he was looking for attackers. He looked back at me and said, "I don't know."

"Until your family line is dead?"

"...I...I don't know."

I climbed up on the stone edge of the trough. The walls are wide enough, I could sit crosslegged across from Gilderson. "You know your family line needs you, right?"

He looked at me in exasperation. "They've needed me for eight lifetimes! They might need me for a ninth! Shouldn't they have learned by now?!?"

"Your family line keeps changing. It's never the same people. Is there anyone from your first lifetime still there?"

"No," he said, angling his head so his eyes said, "What are you, stupid?" "But they aren't learning anything. Certainly not passing anything down. Especially if I'm doing the same thing every time I'm coming back."

"So, you're just going to let them sink or swim?"

"Why not?"

"Because they need help."

"Haven't I done enough?"

"You know you haven't."

Gilderson just looked at me. "I've done plenty."

"Then why do you keep going back? God isn't going to compel you to do something you don't want to do."

"You expect me to say no to God?"

"You can," I told him. "People on Earth say no to Him all the time." I leaned towards him over the water. "We need to do this."

"...I...I want to go home."

I leaned back and could tell I was getting wistful. "So do I. I can go to

Heaven literally any time I want. And I don't. You think I've enjoyed the last seven hundred years?"

"Wait a minute. You have a judgment?"

"Sure do. Stood trial when I got here. You're surprised?"

"Yeah," he said. "I thought you were atoning or something."

"You've seen me all these centuries and you never knew?"

"No," he admitted.

I looked skyward. "I could never enjoy Heaven. Not right now. There are people in trouble. People who are scared. They think I'm their only hope. Some of them, Michael thinks I'm their only hope. And I know, lots of times, I am their only hope. I would be spending eternity thinking about all the people that I could have been helping and didn't. And how many aren't with me because of that."

Gilderson seemed to have forgotten his situation. "How much longer will you do this?"

"Until I burn out," I told him honestly. "When I'm no longer any good, when I can't help anyone anymore, I'll go. And not a moment before."

He just looked at me. Finally, he said, "I hate being alive."

"I know. You don't see the happiness of life, because you have to look out for the dangers. Life is hard. Frustrating. Dangerous. Disappointing. But you know what?"

"What?"

"It's because of people like you that it isn't so bad. That it's actually worthwhile."

He hung his head and I heard him sigh.

"You know, if God asks you to go back, it's because He needs you to. He doesn't like people missing out on Heaven."

"But I hate it there!" he yelled. He looked at me, and tears were forming in his eyes. "I hate every last minute that I'm alive! Every breath I take! Every tick of the clock! Everything! They don't because they don't know what they're missing!"

His head dropped again. I didn't know what to say to him. In court, no one can outthink me. But something like this?

All I could think to do was ask him, "So you're just going to straggle and hope for the best?"

He didn't move. He didn't say anything.

I started climbing down from my side of the trough. Once on the ground, I gathered up the scrolls and said, "If anyone else could do it, someone else would be asked. Whether you like it or not, you are the best one to live the life you get." And I walked away.

It was a while later. I was in the middle of another trial, a relatively simple one as my cases go. In the middle of arguments, I felt it. A tugging around my heart, energy enveloping it. God was reaching out to me. I tried to play casual, but a look at the presiding angel and the Tribunal box showed they felt God as well, they just weren't sure who He was reaching for.

We wrapped up, I won, and everyone filed out of the courtroom. I got around a corner, and saw no one in the hallway. I heard footsteps approaching, but they hadn't gotten anywhere where they could see me. I quickly closed my eyes and surrendered to the feeling. I felt the power envelop me as everything turned to white light.

I didn't need the light to pull away to know where I was. I was standing in the presence of God Himself. I dropped to my knees and bowed to Him. "Yes. What is your will?"

"Always business first with you, Hannah," I heard God's good natured voice say. I felt myself lifting up, my arms and legs straightening and head tilting up to look upon God. I was then set down, standing casually in front of him.

"I brought you," God said, "because someone wants to talk with you."

I didn't notice Gilderson there before. Then again, when you're standing in front of God, you aren't exactly looking around. "Hello, Singer," he smiled. He was completely at peace.

I walked up to him. "So, finally get to go to Heaven, huh?"

He turned his head slightly and looked sheepish. "Uh...not exactly."

God still sounded pleased. "I didn't have a mission for him this time."

I know the confusion showed on my face. "So why isn't he in Heaven?"

Gilderson didn't look at me as God said, "He volunteered to go back again."

Gilderson explained, "They have a couple of people in my family that know what's important."

"Going to make sure they get it right?" I smiled.

"It's one more lifetime," he smiled back. "Better to make sure."

We hugged and said our goodbyes as Gilderson vanished in a flash of light. I looked at God and asked, "He's going to be okay, right?"

God knew what I was asking. "Yes. He's at peace with his decision."

"Isn't it kind of a bad thing when people think the world can't get along without them? I mean, that's where ghosts come from."

"That's not the same thing," God said. "They do it because they think they are the best. He's doing it because, as much as they bother him, he still loves his family. He loves people. He loves the world. Making sure things are put right is the important thing."

I was silent for a moment.

"Please, Hannah. Ask," God said.

I took a deep breath and asked, "Are you disappointed in me?"

"Why would I ever be disappointed in you?"

"I'm still here," I said.

"If you are asking if you should volunteer to live again, no. Harry can help people by living. You can help people here. Believe me, I don't ask anyone not to go to Heaven if there are any better options."

"You haven't asked me."

"Do I need to?"
I smiled at Him, and just enjoyed His company for a while.

SINS OF THE FATHER

Whew! That was a relief! I had just finished a gauntlet, what we call advocating several cases in a row, like an assembly line. One gets done, either head for another courtroom or just wait and the next one begins almost immediately. Gauntlets are generally easy cases. No one rushes through the harder ones, when someone's salvation is actually on the line. Because of my skill, I could run tougher gauntlets than the other Celestials. I do gauntlets to lighten my case load and buy myself some downtime. Before this most recent one, I had done three grey cases in a row, with any time between them spent researching and working on defenses. I did a gauntlet of twelve cases (high for other Celestials, average for me), and was looking forward to settling down in my quarters with a cup of jasmine tea and my Oxford Book Of English Verse.

I had just returned my scrolls and stepped outside the Office Of Records when I saw him. St. Michael was walking past the Office Of Records in full blown Prankster mode. He was wearing clown pants and fuzzy slippers. His polo shirt was made from an iridescent material and covered at least three other polo shirts – I counted four popped collars. He wore 3D glasses, the old ones with the red and blue lenses. His head was adorned with a multicolored propeller beanie that spun so fast, it occasionally seemed to slightly lift off. He was pulling a red wagon chock full of wheezes. Rubber chickens. Air horns. Peanut brittle cans. Giant cans of shaving cream. A small clear bag with paper tapes you hide up your nose and then pull out when you can gross out the most people. Whoopee cushions. Noise makers. A soft plastic hammer that squeaked when you hit things. An air pressure water gun sitting in an ice bucket. For a brief moment, I wondered if this was what John felt like when he witnessed the Apocalypse in Revelations.

Michael turned and saw me. "Hannah! There you are!"

I screamed at the top of my lungs and ran around the edge of the building, ignoring the stares I was getting from others in the Archives. My mind was trying to process someplace I could hide where Michael wouldn't find me...

...I ran face first into a banana cream pie. I didn't bother moving. I just stood there with my shoulders sagging and I swore.

"Understandable and forgiven." Michael's voice was a mixture of amusement and apology. "Sorry, Hannah, but God help me, I couldn't resist."

I didn't do anything. I felt Michael pull the plate away, but I couldn't see anything through the complex sugars. Suddenly, it all vanished. Michael had waved his hand and I was cleaned up.

I let out a sigh. "All right, bring the rest of your toys. Let's get this over with."

Michael looked back in the direction we came from. "Oh, no. That stuff isn't for you. In fact, I was looking for you because I wanted to ask you to participate."

"Who's the victim?"

"A sleepwalker."

I came to attention. A sleepwalker is a person who simply waited to die. They settle into a routine and go day by day. They feel there's nothing to do, nothing to accomplish, so they stick to their familiar comforts and keep going until they stop. Basically, they run out the clock on their lives.

I thought briefly about the sheer amount of stuff Michael was hauling, and him asking me to join in. "That's five alarm stuff you're pulling around. Is it really that bad?"

"Worst I've seen in about a century," Michael said glumly. I walked up beside him, and my big brother put his arm over my shoulder. As we walked, he told me about Thomas Freeman.

Thomas Freeman was part of America's Baby Boom generation. The Boomers were basically a giant unexpected social experiment. America was coming off a major victory in World War II. With the private sector doing all it could to help the war effort, the country entered a time of unprecedented prosperity. Everyone was doing all right. It's telling that "Death Of A Salesman", America's only successful tragedy, came about at a time when everyone was insulated from fears of it happening to them.

When the kids started being born, it was literally in a different world. A book on child rearing by Doctor Spock came out, and shifted the attitudes of new parents determined not to be like their own parents. Some goods that were exclusive for years became easier to acquire, such as cars. The Boomers had a level of freedom and access to money their parents never had, resulting in another new culture, and the world changed again.

Just as their parents had figured they didn't need everything that made their own parents what they were, the Boomers figured the same about their own parents. Communication broke down as everyone felt no one else got it and they searched for answers among their peer groups. Reactions varied wildly, with parents suddenly needing to exert some sort of influence over their kids and the kids never having learned to heed that influence. Each rejected the values of the other. The reason for familial generations is to teach, to pass on knowledge, to protect each other from threats based on where they are in life, both children and adults. For many families, that connection stopped.

Thomas Freeman was an average member of the Boomers. Born at just the right time, he was too young for Korea and too old for Vietnam. He did as all kids do, embracing things that weren't new to society but certainly new to him. He saw the cultures change, but wasn't part of it. By the time Civil Rights and women's equality became forces to be reckoned with, he had finished college, was married, had three kids, all boys, and was working steadily in sales. There was simply no option to back out of the life he was drifting through.

Things were fine enough. Thomas and his wife were actually quite happy with their domesticity. There was just one little problem – Thomas didn't really know how to be a parent. As the head of the household, he was the disciplinarian. He was more than happy to help the kids get things they wanted, especially when his money was good. Acting up? He acted up himself when he was a kid. Wanting to do things like weekend road trips? He would have loved to have done that when he was younger. So his discipline could be a bit...lax.

The three boys didn't really do much with their lives. They saw no reason to. They had run-ins with the law. They overspent. They tried to start businesses that were practically doomed to fail. Daddy backed them up, giving them money from his savings or cosigning loans. And when the kids forgot to give the money for the monthly payments, he got angry. But he couldn't stay angry. The thought of putting his foot down and alienating his sons was horrifying to him.

Finally, Thomas retired. Well, sort of. He had a pension, and he had Social Security. But it wasn't much. They wound up having to sell their house and move into a smaller condo. Options were limited for them, now. Had to cut corners. Had to do without. Thomas' wife was resentful. The money they were saving was so they could get a travel trailer and tour the US. Not enough money for that now. She kept to her knitting and her coffee talks, and he stuck to watching TV and playing cards with his friends.

One day, one of the sons came up to him. He forgot to pay a credit card and if he didn't start coughing up, it was going to go to collections and really mess up his credit rating. Thomas checked his accounts. There was nothing he could give. Anything at this point would risk him and his wife losing their home. Basic survival instinct made Thomas call a family meeting. There, he delivered the bad news – there was no more money. Period. Finito. The end. The sons were basically cut off.

The sons cut off contact with Thomas.

They would make the obligatory calls on birthdays, anniversaries, and holidays. But beyond that? No contact. Thomas and his wife would sometimes try to visit, but the visits were strained and always had at least one request for money. The sons refused to visit. Why bother? They wouldn't get what they wanted, anyway. Thomas became depressed. It became even worse when Thomas and his wife found themselves a little behind and needed some money. The kids refused to help, saying this was how it was now. Thomas' wife managed to get a job as a greeter at a superstore. Thomas eventually stopped reaching out to the world. He just woke up, watched TV, and went to sleep. He didn't really talk with his wife anymore.

He became a sleepwalker.

Thomas didn't die so much as he just sort of stopped. It was peaceful. No pain. Heart tried to give one more pump, but just didn't have it in it. He had only been retired for about five years. Thankfully, his life insurance paid for the funeral, so his wife wasn't financially hurt. She also got a very nice payout. The kids came around for a visit as soon as she deposited the check. Just to make sure she was holding up okay, of course. She slammed the door in their faces and called the police on them for trespassing. She blamed them for her husband's death, and only spoke to them each once after that, and only long enough to say she was disowning them. She still had friends who were helping her along. Things would be shaky for her, but she'd be okay. The sons? Living off the government, taking odd jobs, and occasionally helping themselves to things, if you know what I mean.

Sleepwalkers are difficult. They turn up in the Valley Of Death and just find someplace and sit there. They literally don't do anything. Advocates touring to find souls can tell them everything about the Valley Of Death and they won't petition or anything. They just sit. So when one is found, everyone does what they can to snap them out of it.

Michael and I walked through the Ancient Forest, heading for Thomas. Michael was pulling the wagon, and we were going over routines we would use. I knew Thomas was in really bad shape because Michael told me, "Now, seeing a big guy get abused is funnier, so when we get to him, I'll be the straight man."

I looked at him in shock. It's not that I would never prank my big brother. It was the fact that I had almost seven hundred years of being on the receiving end of his pranks streaking through my mind when he said that. "An eye for an eye" is not about making the punishment fit the crime, but about not being excessive in punishment. But it was getting harder to hear that as another part of my brain screamed, "VENGEANCE IS MINE!!!"

Michael and I eventually found Thomas. He was sitting beneath a tree, legs bent up and looking at nothing. He was wearing a white undershirt, crew neck, with a few food stains on it. He wore plaid boxers, no socks or anything else. His thin grey hair was messy. The hair on his arms was all there, nothing worn away where he would wear a wristwatch. I felt tired just from looking at him.

Michael waved to him and shouted, "It's showtime!"

Thomas just looked at him.

Michael and I turned to the wagon and started going over our options. Each item had been engineered by Michael to also make special sound effects when they were used. It would be like a living Three Stooges routine. We decided to start small, with a seltzer bottle to the face and a mallet to the head. Michael stood out there as I came up with the items I needed. I stopped and just looked at him, unsure if I wanted to take the step.

Michael smiled at me. "Go on, Hannah. You've paid your dues."

I chucked my reservations aside and bounced right up to Michael. Seltzer to the face, mallet on the head. It made a bell ringing sound. "You win!" I screamed, sticking a cigar in his mouth that exploded once I left the blast radius. Michael was standing in the middle of a crater with more blackened char marks than a Cajun pot luck. We stood together, sang, "Ta-dah!" and took a bow.

Thomas didn't do anything.

I leaned over to Michael and whispered, "Tough crowd."

"See? This is why they invented the two drink minimum," Michael whispered back.

We went back to the wagon. Michael started reaching for really special miraculously blessed objects that did a lot more than just make noise, such as a full size trebuchet that simply flung Michael up, over, around, and straight into the ground when I pulled the lever. Michael remained the target as I inflicted all sorts of mayhem on him. The only thoughts in my head were, "It must be Christmas!" or "Maybe it's my birthday!" Eventually, Michael went for the coup de grace – a wrecking ball that hit him square (with me riding it like Major T.J. "King" Kong) and squishing him between sixteen tons of iron and one of the hardiest trees around. From somewhere in there, Michael managed to stick his hand out and give Thomas a thumbs up.

We heard Thomas snicker. Good. He was snapping out of it. Michael might have had it coming, but I still felt a little guilty about doing all this to him.

The wrecking ball vanished and Michael and I dropped to the ground, landing expertly on our feet. "Great," Michael said, rubbing his hands together. "So you're finally coming around, eh, Thomas?"

Thomas looked surprised. "You know who I am?"

"I'm St. Michael. Omniscience has it's perks, you know." Michael reached into his robes and pulled out a deck of cards. "Wanna play some poker?"

"No, no, that's fine," Thomas said quickly. He let out a sigh, then climbed to his feet. It was kind of surprising how much movement he had, given how old he looked. He easily could have been more active on Earth if he hadn't become a sleepwalker.

"This is Hannah Singer," Michael said while pointing to me. "She's a Celestial Advocate."

"What's that?" Thomas asked.

Michael gave him a quick rundown on how things worked. Thomas looked a little distant. "What are my chances of getting into Heaven?"

"I would say excellent. And if they aren't, that's what people like her are here for."

Thomas looked around for a moment. Michael and I knew what he was thinking. Michael asked brightly, "Would you like us to lead you to where you start the petition process?"

Thomas looked like a weight had been taken off his shoulders. "Yeah. I would like that."

Michael ran over to the wagon and grabbed the handle. He marched proudly past Thomas and I and said, "Follow me!" We fell into step, and Thomas seemed to be lightening up as we went. Everybody was happy.

I had finished up another batch of cases, winning most of them, and had just returned my scrolls to the Office Of Records. My schedule was clear now, and I was wondering what I was going to do for some down time. But walking through the Archives brought a shock. Sitting in one of the garden, sort of against a tree, was Thomas Freeman. He looked like he'd fallen back into sleepwalking.

I walked up to him and smiled. "Hi, Thomas! Remember me?"

No movement.

I couldn't understand it. He was doing so well. He was so happy and assured. What could make him....

My eyes popped. Something went wrong with his petition.

First stop on the train? Michael's chambers. He would know what happened. I did a speed walk through the court building and got to Michael's door. I politely rapped on it.

"Just a second," came Michael's response. I heard a couple of strange noises, and then he said, "Come in!"

I opened the door to see Michael standing there, holding a bucket of water at his side. I looked above me at the door jamb, and there was a collapsible shelf up there. I fought the urge to shake my head. There was work to do.

Michael smiled at me. "Hannah. I figured I'd be seeing you sooner or later. I have a case for you."

"Shot in the dark," I said, closing the door behind me. "Thomas Freeman."

"Give her a cigar," Michael said as he walked back to his desk, the bucket and water vanishing into nothing. "Churches are contesting."

"Any hints why?" I asked. I went to one of the two highback chairs in front of Michael's desk, checking for a whoopee cushion before I sat. Found one.

"None. But it's easy to figure out." Michael reached into his desk and produced a scroll with a tie around it.

I took the scroll, untied it, and started reading. I studied it in depth, then said, "It has to be the sleepwalker thing. There's nothing else here they could contest."

"Sleepwalking isn't a sin, though. Otherwise, every person who died in a nursing home would be contested."

"So the sleepwalking isn't what they are really contesting," I said, leaning back and folding my hands against my chin. "It's the result of what they are contesting."

It took me a few more seconds, then the answer hit me. "They're using Thomas to get to his sons."

"They're counting on a trial that they can use the court record against those three kids when they get up here."

I hated these kinds of trials. Admittedly, his kids were rotten and deserved some punishment. But the thing about punishment is it implies penance – you learn your lesson and become a better person. I wasn't convinced that was what the Churches had in mind.

"I'll lead," I said with certainty.

"My thoughts exactly," Michael said back.

I walked down the halls of the Celestial Court very easily. I wasn't worried. My guess about what was happening was proven right when I saw who my opposition was. Remy Gustov was a very nice, low key Church, typically handled easy cases.

I had been carrying a full armload of scrolls in front of me. I could barely see over the top of it. The Guardians opened the doors for me and I padded down the aisle that cut the Gallery in half, heading for the Celestial table on the right just past the divider.

I got to the table and simply dropped all the scrolls on top of it. I heard a gasp. I looked at the Church table and saw Remy there, seated in the lead Church seat, staring at the scrolls rolling around, some dropping off the table. He looked at me with despair in his eyes. "What'd I do to you?!?"

I smiled easily at him. "Relax. I'm just making sure I've got everything covered. You know how thorough I like to be."

"You don't have to be so rough," he said, slumping in his seat and propping his head up with his fist. "Trust me, this case is a loser for me."

I leaned towards him, keeping my head turned away but my eyes shifted to him and putting my hand by my left ear. "Care to tell me why?"

"A! Hem!"

We both looked at the interruption. Jeff Fairchild, the most senior Church, was standing in the aisle just on the other side of the divider from us. He looked like he couldn't decide who he should glare at, Remy or I.

Fairchild's voice resumed a more casual but no less threatening tone. "Now, now, Gustov. Singer is perfectly capable of winning this case on her own. You don't want to be accused of Collusion, do you?"

Remy turned and faced the front, looking unbelievably angry. Fairchild was very good at reminding his subordinates he was in charge. He didn't like having his authority questioned.

Fairchild looked at me. I shifted my mind into high gear. I had to make sure I didn't tell Fairchild I knew what was happening. He usually figures I'm smart, but I think the scrolls reassured him. "Overkill, Singer?"

"I don't fiddle about with half measures," I responded. "There's no such thing as overkill."

"I would think this would be a breeze for you, seeing as how we aren't going for Casting." Fairchild's recommended fate was guardian angel duty over the three kids. That was another good indicator what his plan was.

"Trying to lull me into a false sense of security?" I countered, adding a bit of anger to my voice. "Remy may be leading the case, but it's got your fingerprints all over it."

"Paranoia is never a good thing," Fairchild countered as he turned to sit down in the Gallery.

I went to my table and started organizing the scrolls. I made a pretty convincing layout, if I do say so myself. I knew Remy wouldn't be talking to me, so I sat down and waited.

I heard the court Guardians walking down the aisle behind me. After a moment, it registered that their pace was rather slow. I turned to look. Thomas was just sort of shuffling down the way, a distant look in his eyes. He was firmly stuck in sleepwalker mode again. I fought to keep my anger under control. There was no need for any of this.

The Guardians brought Thomas up to me and waited. And waited. And waited. Thomas didn't budge. I got up, went behind Thomas, and with my hands on his shoulders, steered him to the Petitioner's seat to the right of mine. I pushed him down to make him sit. Other than my outside influence, there was no movement from him.

The Guardians looked over the scrolls on the table and looked at me as if to ask, "Is all this really necessary?" I gently shooed them back by the judge's bench and sat down next to Thomas. I was thinking of something to snap him out of it. On the bright side, him speaking out of turn was probably not going to happen. He still needed to at least walk out to the dock for the hearing, though.

I reached behind him and grabbed his right arm. I then lifted it and placed his hand on top of his head. A thought struck me. I took his left arm and put his hand on his stomach. I then stood behind him and started trying to make him pat his head and rub his stomach at the same time. You think it's tough, try doing it the way I was doing it.

"That's not professional behavior, Singer," came Fairchild's annoyed voice.

"It's a lot more professional than this," I smiled as I took Thomas' right hand, made the index finger stick out, and put it up his nose. I had just about put it by his lips when Thomas wigged out.

"Welcome back to reality," I smiled at Thomas as I sat next to him. "Please stay with me, don't make me escalate."

"How would you escalate?" Thomas asked, sounding a bit worried.

I did what Michael did centuries ago when I asked the same thing. I stuck my own finger in my nose, then aimed my finger at Thomas' mouth. Doesn't matter that there's nothing up there or no germs up here, it's still effective.

"Truce! Truce!" Thomas yelled, at the loudest volume I'd heard since he got here.

"So, you clear on procedure?" I asked.

"Uh...can I ask you a question?"

"42."

He clearly wasn't a Douglas Adams fan. "...wat?"

"What's your question?"

"Why am I even going through this? What exactly did I do?"

I leaned close to him. "I'll tell you later. You just have to have faith in me. Trust me, you getting anything other than a Heavenly reward ain't happening. There's something else going on here. You aren't even a pawn in this, because your fate isn't even in doubt."

"You sure I'll be okay?"

"Trust me."

He went back to facing ahead, looking a little nervous. That's natural.

No matter how convinced people are of their chances, there's always that fear that something will go wrong. I had to keep up my act, though. I didn't want Fairchild to know I'd figured out his scheme until it was too late.

The chimes sounded. Everyone stood, and Remy and I deployed our wings. The door by the Tribunal box opened, and twelve angels, wings already out, entered. I hoped I kept my wistful sigh quiet enough that nobody heard. Especially the angels. Hannah Singer becoming an angel was as likely as those on Earth finding Jimmy Hoffa (I'm not being hyperbolic. Michael told me where he is).

The door at the back of the court opened to admit the presiding angel. In walked Uzziel. He's the angel of love, gratitude, and faith. He actually made the case a bit harder. Remy didn't usually play to the presiding angel, and that was good right now. I would have to make sure I dressed Thomas' behavior to his sons as simply asserting himself instead of abandoning them. If I did that, I should only have to worry about the court record.

I had to keep my mind focused. Uzziel is almost hypnotic. He just radiates peace and calm, and it's infectious, like if someone crossed Zen with kudzu. When he's not in court, Uzziel can often be found at the Equilibrium with Shalmana and her ministering angels. His gentle movements seemed to leave vapor trails as he moved. Long blond hair flowed from his head, a subtle expression that would make the Mona Lisa jealous, and his robes seemed to billow of their own accord.

Uzziel got to the bench and sat. He's extremely quiet, he doesn't speak unless he really needs to. He pointed to the dock on his left.

I said, "The Petitioner is Thomas Albert Freeman."

Uzziel pointed to me.

"Hannah Singer, acting alone."

Uzziel pointed to Remy.

"Remy Gustov, acting alone," he responded.

Uzziel gestured to the dock. Thomas looked at me in confusion. I whispered, "Take the stand."

Thomas was soon installed in the dock and just standing there, looking a little unsure. I gave him a smile and a nod. Just hang in there, this is between the Churches and me.

Uzziel pointed to me, indicating I should start my opening arguments. I did so. "Thomas has lived a good life. He held the Lord in respect even if he didn't go to church, he provided for his family, he never cheated on his wife, never got staggeringly drunk...there is nothing in his history to warrant a trial, let alone denial of petition. He should be allowed into Heaven. Thank you."

Uzziel gestured to Remy. He started speaking, and confirmed I was on the right track. "Freeman was not all he could be as a father. He turned his back on his sons. Towards the end of his life, he did not give them the help or love they needed. The three of them are facing a life of mistakes and messes. As their father, Freeman should help them, and guardian angel duty, watching over the three of them, is the best recourse. If the kids don't heed the lessons, the fault is theirs. But if they do, Freeman will have succeeded in the duties he took on when he became a father. Thank you."

That ending opening arguments. Usually, at this point, I would just move straight on to the boot. But I wanted Thomas to not be entangled in his sons' trials when they came up. I read their life scrolls, nailing them at trial would be easy, there was no reason for Fairchild to pull this number. So, how do I go about this....

Uzziel was just looking at Remy and I, waiting for someone to move. He turned his head from me to Remy and back, then held his hands out while shrugging his shoulders.

I quickly formulated a statement and fought to keep from smiling. "Thomas' sons have nothing to do with this."

I just know Fairchild blanched. Remy, good soldier that he is, kept on. "His sons actually have everything to do with this. Parents are supposed to provide for their children and raise them. He didn't."

"He tried. They didn't listen to him. The fault is all theirs."

"Thomas was too lenient with his sons," Remy responded. He didn't sound convinced. "He should have been a tougher disciplinarian."

"Did that work with your kids, Remy?"

Remy stopped dead as he remembered his own children. I continued, "You can only do so much. There are parents who do everything they can for their children, and they still do terrible things, from robbers to politicians. But I repeat myself."

Remy smiled a little, then refocused. "You aren't suggesting parents have no responsibility to their children, do you?"

"Not at all," I responded. "But responsibility is a two-way street. Love is a two-way street. Thomas showed his children love, they didn't reciprocate. They closed the two-way street themselves. Thomas had no connection to them through their own choice. There should be no connection to them now."

Fairchild shot to his feet. "There is a connection!" he bellowed at me.

The gentlest gavel crack I ever heard drifted through the courtroom. Everyone looked at Uzziel. He smiled admonishingly at Fairchild and waggled his finger at him. Fairchild bowed to him and apologized before sitting back down.

Remy looked at me. He didn't want to be here. Holding my hand so that Fairchild couldn't see it, I extended out my index and middle fingers on my right hand and crossed and uncrossed them, first one on top of the other, then under the other.

Remy got the hint. "Move for a recess for consultation with my superior."

Uzziel nodded his head and tapped the gavel. Once he and the Tribunal left the court, Remy and Fairchild did a speed walk up the aisle and out of court.

Thomas looked at me in confusion. I motioned for him to come to me from the dock, then rolled my eyes. I told you Uzziel was contagious. "You can come out, Thomas. We're in recess."

Once Thomas was up to me, I set his mind at ease by explaining what was happening. He looked confused still, but for a different reason. "Maybe...they should be allowed to win this."

"No," I told him with certainty. "This has nothing to do with family or obligations. Fairchild just sees a chance to nail someone extra hard, regardless of whether or not they deserve it."

"I...think...they do."

"I think your sons have to answer for what they've done, too. But the fact is, Fairchild is angling to get a harsher punishment than he would normally get."

"What does he get out of it?"

"Satisfaction. Fairchild doesn't take kindly to defiance of authority."

"Which explains why he keeps glaring at you."

"Ten points for Thomas Freeman."

"So you aren't defending my sons, you're just making sure they don't get railroaded."

"Right."

"What's going to happen next?"

"I expect Fairchild to take over the case. He realizes he has to get through me to get a ruling the way he wants it, and he knows Remy will never pull it off."

"What happens when he faces you?"

I gave him a million candlepower smile. "It's showtime."

We chatted a little more about my case histories and such. He really seemed fascinated by the Celestial Courts. He was particularly interested in what I thought would happen to his sons. He may have been hurt by them, but he still cared about them.

While we talked, I heard the doors at the back of the court open and the irritated footsteps of Jeff Fairchild slapping on the floor. It's tough to do an effective stomp when you're barefoot. I looked behind me and saw Remy. His expression was that of someone who got chewed out, but the punishment was more of a reward. The duo got past the divider and Fairchild took the lead Church spot, Remy took the next seat over.

Thomas whispered to me, "Showtime, huh? When does it start?"

The chimes sounded to reconvene court. I just smiled at him. Thomas went back to the dock.

I had to get this in quick before the Tribunal returned and I could no longer speak at will. "Senior Church leading a case like this. Overkill, Fairchild?"

"Burn," he growled.

"Paranoia is never a good thing," I smiled as I faced the Tribunal box to get another helping of divine vibes from the entering angels.

Uzziel came in through his door, took one look at Fairchild, and said, "Oh my God...." With a pained expression, he climbed up to the bench and sat. He actually pinched the bridge of his nose.

"A substitution has been made...." Fairchild started.

Uzziel held up a single finger, indicating Fairchild should please just give him a moment. I stole a quick look at the Tribunal. They had settled in, they weren't expecting this to be sedate anymore. Finally, Uzziel straightened, pointed to Fairchild, and used his two hands to mime switching something around.

"Yes, sir," Fairchild said with certainty. "Jeff Fairchild, acting as lead."

Our reputations precede us. Uzziel looked at Fairchild and I and made a motion with his hands like he was gently pressing down on something. He was asking us to keep it down. Sorry, Uzziel, you know I can't promise you that.

Uzziel tapped the gavel, and it sounded like a starter pistol. I made the first move. "Thomas has done nothing to warrant denial of petition."

"He failed his fatherly duties," Fairchild responded.

"Sez who?"

"The Bible says parents are responsible for their children. They are to raise them to be good, solid citizens and servants of God. By allowing his sons to do what they have, he has failed in his role as a father and has to atone for it."

Fairchild had a very simple endgame in mind. If he could get me to heap the blame for the kids' behavior on the kids themselves, he could use that at their trials to really let them have it. Not only did I feel that was cheating, but I don't like being used. The obvious response, the one he was counting on me to provide, was that the kids chose to disobey their dad, so everything they did wrong is their fault. However, I was facing Jeff Fairchild. I never make things easy on him if I have the option. And, boy, did I have the option.

"You're right," I said.

Fairchild just stared at me like someone hearing the whistle of a bomb dropping right above them. "You're joking."

"Why would I joke about you being right?"

"You never admit I'm right."

Well, there's a reason for that, I thought. But I said, "No joke, you are right. Thomas failed to do what he was supposed to as a parent. The proof is that he's on trial right now."

Thomas looked confused, but he did seem to trust me. Fairchild was now torn between allowing an obvious set-up to complete and stopping me from dragging the trial in a direction he didn't want. He ultimately did what I knew he would, get me to admit my logic so he could try to deal with it. "How is the fact that we contested his petition proof that he failed as a parent?"

I smirked inwardly. I had this in the bag. "It's proof because he is being tried before his three sons. As a father of disobedient sons, he should have killed them."

Uzziel started rubbing his face with his hand. It was the moment he was dreading, when things got ready to explode.

Fairchild tried to block me. "The Bible says, 'Thou shalt not commit murder.'"

"The Bible also says, 'Whoever curses father or mother shall be put to

132

death.' Exodus 21, verse 17. Also Leviticus 20, verse 9. And Deuteronomy 21, verses 18 to 21. 'If someone has a stubborn and rebellious son who will not obey his father and mother, who does not heed them when they discipline him, then his father and his mother shall take hold of him and bring him out to the elders of his town. They shall say to the elders of his town, "This son of ours is stubborn and rebellious. He will not obey us. He is a glutton and a drunkard." Then all the men of the town shall stone him to death.' Thomas has violated this with each of his three sons. Therefore, you are right, the sin is his. Kind of a light punishment for defying God, don't you think?"

Fairchild just blinked. In that moment, he knew exactly where this was going. He apparently decided not to fight it. "Move to change my recommended fate."

Uzziel turned his hand up to ask, "To what?"

"Immediate entry into Heaven."

Uzziel looked at me.

"No objection," I smiled.

Uzziel slammed the gavel. I just had to wrap this up. "The official stance of the Celestials is Thomas should be allowed immediate entry into Heaven."

"As is the official stance of the Churches," Fairchild said.

Uzziel looked to the Tribunal. Admittedly, they could come up with some other ruling, but no way they were going to.

The lead Tribunal stood and said, "We are ready to rule."

Uzziel tilted his head up.

"Petition is to be approved immediately."

Uzziel let out a visible sigh of relief and slammed the gavel. The angels started shuffling out.

Once Uzziel and the Tribunal were gone, Thomas dashed up to me from the dock. It was the happiest I'd ever seen him. "Thank you!" he said. "Thank you so much! I don't know how to repay you!"

"I didn't do this so you would owe me something, I did it because you needed help and it was the right thing to do. Now, go."

Thomas dashed for the Petitioner's exit on the left, waving to me the entire time. Once he was through, I turned to look at Fairchild. He was enraged.

"How dare you shield those brats," he said.

"I didn't shield them from their trials, I shielded them from you," I responded tersely.

"They put him through Hell," he responded, equally tersely. "They disrespected their father. They should pay."

"So, with everything they've done, the greatest sin, the one that makes you want a piece of them, is how they treated their father?"

Fairchild thought for a moment, then said, "Yes."

I looked at him levelly. "It's not the what of your actions, it's the why. Children can be excused for defying their parents."

"There's no excuse for it."

"A father who encourages his children to commit immoral acts? A father who doesn't actually care for his kids? Absentee parents? Children have the responsibility to defy that when they get to a place where they can. Otherwise, every illegal and unethical act can be excused by asking daddy."

Fairchild just looked down at me. "You probably defied your parents."

"Yes."

"Refused the gender roles?"

"Duh."

"Are you even a virgin?"

"Why? You offering?"

"BURN!" And Fairchild stormed out of court.

I had just returned my scrolls and stepped outside the Office Of Records when I saw him. Thomas Freeman was heading my way, and when he saw me, his face lit up and he made a beeline for me. I was a little taken aback. Thomas was now wearing white robes with a brown overrobe.

Thomas started shaking my hand excitedly when he got up to me. I was still sorting through everything. He noticed how quiet I was. "Miss Singer? Are you okay?"

I snapped out of it. "What happened?"

Thomas stood with his legs apart and his fists on his hips. He triumphantly declared, "God made me an offer I couldn't refuse! I'm going to be a guardian angel for a while!"

"Well, at least it's God's decision, not Fairchild getting his way."

Thomas looked at me blankly for a moment, then seemed to figure it out. "Oh, no. I'm not a guardian angel to my kids. It's for my wife. The kids are starting to work her over, and she needs some extra help. And that's me."

I smiled. "Well, I'm sure you'll be fine."

"Sure, I will," he responded. "Lots of angels are offering to back me up if I need it. They don't like what my kids are trying to pull, either. With their guidance, and maybe a little bit of their muscle, she's going to be just fine."

We said our goodbyes. My insistence, he wanted to talk more, but I reminded him his mission had to come first. He raced off to get started, a man who felt his life was worth nothing, but his Afterlife was worth everything.

THE DARKEST SECRET

There are many mysteries in the universe that humans try to figure out. Faith. God. The spirit.

The two greatest are love and sex.

Love is a mystery because of its amorphous nature. Love is love, but it is expressed and experienced in a variety of ways. There are different kinds of love. There's family love. There's romantic love. There's sexual love.

That last one usually gets the most interest.

Part of what made the foundation of Judaism so unique was its approach to sex. Many cultures saw sex as a public act, what with fertility rituals and so on. Judaism held that it was a private act, something you didn't just do for the sake of doing it. This carried over into the teachings of Jesus when Christianity was founded. As a result, a sort of disconnect happened, making sex not just another part of the human make-up, but something that had to be conquered and controlled and, depending on circumstances, ashamed of.

And so a physical act that God meant to be pleasurable (think about it, it's not like He had to allow it to feel good) became something confused and rife with opportunism. Sex became a bargaining chip, a means of control, something even those in the Bible were subjected to. And because people don't understand love or sex, they will confuse one with the other.

Or even incorporate them in ways they shouldn't.

It was the early part of the 21st century. I was walking down the halls of the Celestial Courts, heading for St. Michael's chambers. I hadn't seen him casually in the last few days, and that usually meant something was bothering him. I was determined to cheer him up. I had with me a picnic basket full of sandwiches, jasmine tea, and lawn darts. Lawn darts is one of the few games someone can actually beat Michael at, as long as you actually play the game. He will eventually get bored and start tossing the darts straight up in the air to see what kind of height he can get (I don't care if I'm invulnerable now, I still run away).

Michael's door was closed, so I knocked on it lightly.

No answer.

I gave the handle a quick turn. It wasn't locked, so there wasn't any sort of consultation going on. Michael didn't usually lock his door when he wasn't in there. Angels know who is going in their private areas, what they are doing, and when, and only a fool would attempt anything with the most powerful archangel. Michael trusted me, but wherever he was, he would instantly know as soon as I opened the door and set foot in there.

I took a quiet breath, then took action. I pushed open the door and walked inside. I looked around, just in case Michael was in here and just so wrapped up in something, he didn't hear me. Nope. I was the only one there.

Well, not for long. Two Guardians appeared outside Michael's doorway, looking in at me as best as they could – their huge muscular frames seemed to be shoving each other out of view. The one on the right spoke. "St. Michael requests us to bring you to him right away."

That caught me by surprise. Like I said, Michael trusts me, so the fact that he sent Guardians shocked me. But it's his chambers. I stood straight and resolved, like I was facing a firing squad. "Yes, sir," I said.

Both Guardians arched their eyebrows, then relaxed. The one on the left said, "No, you aren't in trouble. There's been a putto looking for you. You just helped Michael find you faster."

I didn't even bother to sort anything out. A putto searching, Guardians immediately turning up, and no sign of where Michael was. Something very bad was happening. "Overlook Peak?" I asked as I walked forward.

"Yes," both Guardians said as I got up to them. Overlook Peak is the highest point in the Afterlife, and Michael only goes there when there is something really bothering him. Whether he needed his best Celestial or his best friend, he was going to get her.

One of the Guardians picked me up in his arms like a newborn baby, and everything around me shifted and swirled as, with the speed of angels, we turned up on Overlook Peak. It is towards the edge of the mountain range, and gives a spectacular view of the Afterlife. Getting up there takes a lot of time and a lot of effort unless you're an angel. There's a very narrow ledge around the face that leads to the outcropping. One wrong step, and you're in for a long ride and tumble that would make a postal package feel sympathy. The Guardians, however, were flying, their mighty wings holding us in the air for the remaining portion of the trip. We got up to the level with the small outcropping, barely larger than a picnic table.

I gasped when I saw my big brother. He was sitting with his legs dangling off the edge of the outcropping, and he was slumping forward. It almost looked like he was going to tumble forward off the ledge. His eyelids were being pulled down, and his usual smile was no match for gravity. This wasn't Michael.

The Guardian carefully placed me on the outcropping so I was sitting next to Michael, same position and everything. They both gave Michael a salute, which he returned with a weak wave, and they departed, leaving just the two of us.

We were both silent for a while. The only sound was our breathing, deep and steady. I needed some way to break the ice.

I reached out to the middle of the back of Michael's robe and tugged it down, like I was calling the butler. Michael slowly swiveled his head to me. He smiled weakly, but at least it was a genuine smile. "Hi, Hannah," he finally said.

I gave him a smile as I attempted to reach my arm across his back but only got halfway. "What's it all about, Michael?"

His smile vanished. Whatever it was, this was bad. "I think you should just see."

That caught me by surprise. "You can't just tell me?"

"You're going to wind up Advocating one of them, I can guarantee it," he said.

If it would help get him out of this, I was up to it. "Where do I go?"

Michael simply touched my shoulder, and everything settled into a view of nighttime Earth. We were standing in the middle of the street of a suburban area. High income, the cars and SUV's parked along the sides proved it. We were facing a very nice house, two stories, probably furnished basement – these kinds of places always have that.

Looking at the house, I felt a chill. Despite its idyllic appearance, there was something WRONG with it. It was like standing near a block of ice. You could feel the numbness reaching out for you, affecting you without touching.

"That's it?" I asked Michael.

He just nodded.

I steeled myself up. "Wait here. I'll be back."

"Be ready, Hannah," Michael said as I walked, making me stop and look at him. "It's just...."

I nodded to him, and resumed walking up to the house and passing through the door.

I found myself in a very nice living room. Everything arranged just so and clean. I thought about trying to sense the imprints around me, but I could feel the darkness emanating from somewhere in here. Not only did it feel strong enough to drown out any impressions, but the darkness would tell me everything. I wanted to make sure I was in the right frame of mind to face whatever it was.

Plan B – Power Of Observation. I started taking in the room around me, building a profile of who all resided there. That was when I noticed the first problem. There was no clear number. There were no different elements to indicate different people, different mentalities, different aspirations. It fused together. This was a bad sign.

I continued to look around, hoping for some sign of individuality. I noticed the second problem. Lots of stuff here had no real timeframe. There was nothing to indicate when it was acquired or how long it had been in their possession. Nothing reflecting current events or moors of the times. No newspapers. No magazines. Standard issue TV and cable box, VCR, and one of the then new DVD players, but no media or channel guide. The residents more or less walled themselves off from the world here.

I looked deeper, and noticed something else missing – sexual identity. You can usually get a rough idea of someone's sexuality from their home. Whether they are gay, straight, or bi, if they are conservative or adventurous, if they are active or not. Nothing. Not a hint of any sort of human interaction, despite the couch occupying the place of honor squarely in front of the TV. Not only that, but no other chairs or other sitting furniture. Not a lot of guests. Like I said, walling themselves off from the world.

I could see the kitchen right off to the side. I walked inside. On the counter was the mail. I took a quick look and got two names, Candice Birkett and Maya Birkett. Judging from the bills, Candice was the breadwinner of the house. Maya's name only appeared on correspondence relating to Candice. Mother daughter....

...oh, please, sweet Jesus, no.

I carefully crept up the stairs to where the bedrooms would be. The darkness got stronger, I was getting colder. I started to feel chilled. At the landing, the room at the end of the hall, where I figured the master bedroom would be, gave off the frightening sensations. I decided to look in some other rooms in the vague hope that I would be proven wrong.

I eventually found Maya's bedroom. Twin size bed, perfectly made. Judging from the microscopic dust no human eye could see, it hadn't been slept in for a while. Everything pointed to her being just out of high school. I soon found a box under the bed. Inside were college mementos, nothing to indicate she graduated but she wanted to return there, to those days.

I took a deep breath and walked into the hall. I walked slowly towards the master bedroom, as if I was trying to give the scene on the other side time to change into something else. I got to the door, then pushed my head through.

Inside, the scent of sex assaulted me. In the master bed were Candy and Maya. They were spooned together, naked under the covers. Cathy was perfectly happy, smiling in her sleep with her hand on her daughter's breast. Maya looked sort of happy, but her posture was borderline fight-or-flight. It wouldn't take much for her to curl into a fetal tuck. As I sensed the contentment in Candy, I sensed the barely contained turmoil in Maya.

I don't remember leaving the house. I got outside, and Michael was just standing where I left him, heartbreak and despair evident on his face. I got to him and just stood in front of him. I finally asked, "It just started, didn't it?"

"A few days ago," Michael said, anger creeping into his voice. He glared at the window. "All the animals of the world will gladly die to protect their children. And the one human Maya should have been able to trust has corrupted her for her own ends."

I wrapped Michael in the best hug I could. He returned it, his arms enclosing me. I couldn't see or hear anything about the world around me. It was like Michael was trying to take me out of it, hiding me away in the safest place he knew.

I knew I needed to get a jump on Maya's case. She may still be alive, but she wouldn't be forever. And Jeff Fairchild, the most senior Church, enjoyed trying to Cast sex abuse victims. Spirits don't have physical bodies, but I suspect Fairchild didn't even have a heart when he was alive. Not that there was any danger to Maya. It is nigh impossible to Cast sex abuse victims. As long as they don't perpetuate their evil, they are pretty much in the clear.

It was a good thing I started my review early. I wound up with her case a lot sooner than expected.

Candy Birkett was a case study in how much people can get wrong about intimate relations. There's having sex, there's making love, and there's masturbation, simply using the other person's body for your own pleasure. Candy felt emptiness in her life as a child thanks to distant parents. Her own lack of social skills, combined with her ambitious nature, kept her from people who she should have bonded with and gotten support from.

Candy saw landing a man as a way to get the attention she craved. She lost her virginity at fourteen, working her way through boys with ruthless efficiency. They did all kinds of things for her, and all she had to do was what she was enjoying – Candy's body was very sensitive, and it made the sexual experience a lot more for her than for other girls.

Candy eventually landed a guy. They got hitched before she was out of high school as soon as she turned eighteen (thanks to her grades, she was still a sophomore) before dropping out. She wasn't using him exactly. He was a good guy and was crazy about her. However, they were in love with who they were at the time, not what they would always be. Because it was based on transitory parts of their personalities, it didn't take long for them to change and not be the same people they thought they were in love with. Quickie divorce, and Candy was on the prowl again.

Candy found another guy, and made a similar mistake – she was focused on what he could be, not what he was at the time or always would be. Basically, this marriage was a rehab project. This one started falling apart even faster, with him feeling Candy was trying to manipulate him into becoming something he didn't want to be. Candy saw the writing on the wall, and decided that, before he left, she was going to get pregnant. Why? Because a baby would love her no matter what.

Maya was conceived during a drunken night. The father left the picture a couple of months later. Candy had been trying to keep it subtle, but he was no dummy and recognized the signs. She still managed to get some decent child support from him.

Candy was not what would be considered an ideal mother. While being arm candy to keep herself in a comfortable lifestyle, she was also raising Maya. Maya's basic personality was somewhat suggestible and pliant. Candy, in her quest to make sure her daughter loved her, unknowingly took advantage of that. Mother knew best, and made sure Maya did as she thought was right. Maya would notice things that were contradictory or that conflicted with her own observations, such was which people could be trusted and which would stab her in the back. Any action Maya took was invariably incorrect, she either wasn't trusting enough or she wasn't smart enough, depending on the outcome. The only thing Maya learned was to doubt herself. As a result, she became more and more dependent on her mother to navigate life and right from wrong. And Candy was happy with that arrangement.

Candy eventually felt something was missing in her life. She noticed it because sex wasn't very satisfying. Sex is always better with someone who really cares about you, they aren't just using your body. Candy just couldn't figure out what the problem was. Even when she was in a relationship, the sex was great at the start, but eventually the thrill would just sort of fade out. She longed for the feelings that came from being with someone close to you....

That was the trigger. Somehow, the neurons fired in such a way that Candy realized her daughter, who she had to love her no matter what, could be manipulated into being what she wanted – a lover.

Candy knew she had to be at least a little subtle. She had no guarantees Maya would actually agree to this. She resorted to what is known among child molesters as "grooming." Little touches that could be argued were innocent and the victim is misconstruing them. Encouraging secrets. Indebtedness. Reminding her that she was supposed to love and support her. Creating an atmosphere that what was going on was normal.

Maya started to panic. This clearly wasn't normal. After all, none of her friends had anything like this going on. Candy said it was just because they were so much closer, they had a relationship that no one else could have or would understand. The touches from Candy became more intimate and sexual. Candy had managed to get Maya to cuddle next to her on the couch as they watched TV one night. Candy's hand became bold and brought Maya to orgasm. Maya was shocked and confused, but Candy continued to reassure her that everything was fine.

Maya's resistance was failing. After all, she had crossed a lot of lines, and there was no going back from them. Her confusion and despair provided the opening Candy needed. On that fateful night, just a few days before I first saw them, on the altar of Candy's bed, Candy sacrificed her daughter's soul to her.

Candy was happier than ever. In her daughter, she had someone who loved her no matter what in any way possible. She did not see the psychological damage she had done, and didn't care to. After all, this was only wrong because society says it's wrong. There really wasn't a problem. Maya's development pretty much stopped that night. She was trapped in the world her mother made.

Maya's psychology was spiraling out of control. She knew, just knew, that this was wrong. But her mother had done a good job grooming her. Maya couldn't pinpoint where exactly things went wrong, somewhere she could have done something different and this wouldn't have happened. Any time she expressed her doubts, Candy would tell her that Maya wanted this, too. After all, she could have resisted, but she didn't.

Maya's beautiful mind broke one day a few years after that night. She was living at home, not really seeing anyone else, not even as friends, which suited her mother just fine – she didn't have to share her with anyone. Candy had gone out to get some groceries for them (Maya almost never left the house at this point, she was paranoid that someone like the neighbors knew the truth about her). But a car accident happened, head-on collision. They were going too fast to allow the cars' safety features to do anything. Candy was dead.

When Maya opened the door and saw the cop standing there, she was confused. When she got the news, she lost it. What would she do now? There was no one else she could count on. Anyone who learned of her past would think she was a freak. She had no job, no boyfriend, no recent job history, and property taxes were coming up. Not helping was the computer in the house – Candy had started a web site to help other women warp their daughters into becoming their incestuous lovers. The computer that served the site was in the house (no need for a real server. Small comfort, they didn't have more than five actual subscribers. Everyone else was doing the atrocity tourism thing). What if anyone found it?

Neighbors called the police when they saw Maya out in her backyard smashing the computer tower with a sledgehammer. One well-placed swing was all it would have taken. Maya just kept swinging and swinging, not even stopping when blisters formed and ruptured on her hands. Maya was catatonic and spent a couple of days in one of the hospital's Second Floor Suites. She was given medication to keep her balanced. Doctors thought it was just maternal loss that was the problem, they never guessed the real depth. Maya calmed down enough to get out and get home, making sure any further evidence was as gone as it would get. She didn't bother with the medication, she felt she didn't deserve it. Once the house was in order and everything she could find was gone, Maya collapsed on the floor and her heart mercifully gave out.

Candy was nothing if not shrewd. She didn't petition and took time to get an overview of the Celestial Courts, how things worked, what the processes were, and, most importantly, how everyone reacted. I saw her in the Gallery a few times during my trials. Michael and I kept our little visit just between us, so she didn't know I knew who she was. I kept everything together, I didn't want to tip my hand. Camael had to notice something awry going on, as I argued differently when I knew she was there. He did look at me odd a few times.

Candy also saw Fairchild and how he operated. His reputation preceded him, and it was obvious that Candy was toast as far as he was concerned. She also had a good idea that I wouldn't be very lenient and merciful to her. Fairchild would lead just so he could Cast her, that would guarantee me arguing for the Celestials, and I was going to move for Casting, too. Candy wanted into Heaven and to stay out of Hell. She needed an edge.

Candy knew her daughter would be along sooner or later (although it was actually a lot sooner than she expected) and sort of camped out outside the clerks' office. She wasn't doing anything wrong, so no one could really stop her from loitering. It was shortly after her research into how we worked and her waiting game began that Maya snuffed it. Maya was dazed out of her mind, fearing she was going to Hell. Her numbness outweighed her fear, and she sort of drifted to the Celestial Courts to petition.

Fairchild and I were in the middle of a case discussion. I was walking away from him as he yelled at me for not only daring to oppose someone getting Cast, but managing to dig them out at trial and get their petition suspended. "Are you even listening to me?!?" Fairchild screamed at me.

I stopped dead in my tracks and spun to look at him, surprise on my face. "Jeff Fairchild! How long have you been there?!?"

If Fairchild's eyebrows dropped any lower, they'd become a mustache. "I am sick of your indifference to established order!"

I leaned into his face. "I'm upholding God's established order, not yours!"

"My order IS God's established order! Just like the Israelites! I am upholding their legacy! I am just like the Israelites!"

"If the Israelites had been like you, God would have written the Ten Commandments in crayon!"

"*BURN!!!*"

A shout of, "Mom?!?" interrupted our civil (for us, anyway) discussion. We looked, and saw Maya standing just around the corner of one of the buildings. She had been heading for the clerks' office, and saw her mother waiting by the door.

Candy rose to her feet and smiled. "Hello, Maya."

Maya was rooted to the spot, uncertain whether to flee or scream in terror. Candy simply walked with spring in her step up to her daughter and wrapped her in a hug. Not a normal, loving, reassuring hug. A lovers' embrace.

Maya was stiff as a board and her mother moved her side to side, the closest she could get to rocking her. Candy whispered something in her daughter's ear. I couldn't hear it, but I could read her lips. "Together. We'll get through this together."

I suddenly remembered Fairchild. I turned to look at him. His face was a complete mess of confusion. After seeing how Candy's hands were roaming over Maya's body, he finally galvanized into some sort of action. He moved towards the two like a poorly controlled marionette. "Stop that," he said, his voice uncertain if it should be booming or horrified.

Both girls turned their heads to him. Maya moved closer into her mother's embrace, trying to disappear. Candy smiled broadly and asked, "Why?"

"D...did that girl call you, 'mother?'"

"Yes, she did," Candy said with pride as Maya looked away.

"Well...you shouldn't be touching her like that."

"We both like touching each other like that. In fact, we touch a lot more than that."

I shot my hands into the air with just their index fingers extended and crossed them above my head. Five Guardians appeared just as Fairchild screamed, "You whores!" and rushed the pair.

Three Guardians flying tackled Fairchild to the ground, then hauled him away, one on each arm and the third grabbing his legs. Fairchild kept screaming, "Jezebels! Harlots! I'll damn you both to Hell!" as they left. The other two just looked at Candy and Maya. Angels know all about humans, and they knew about these two long ago.

I strode forward between the Guardians, glaring at Candy. "Release your daughter. You have hurt her enough."

Candy dropped her arms. Maya tried to burrow further in. "I'm not hurting her. She needs me."

"You don't feel the slightest remorse for destroying your own child?"

"I didn't destroy her. She wants this. We both want this."

"Oh, yeah. I can feel her pride."

Candy didn't bother acknowledging Maya's paralysis. "We should not be penalized for rejecting something that is wrong only because society says it is."

"It IS wrong."

"The Romans had no problem with it."

My temper flared up. "Why is it that, every time you idiots want to justify sexual selfishness, you point to the Romans? The Romans allowed rape and baby raping and other stuff until they saw the effect it was having on their society. Then they outlawed it. It wasn't society that proved it was wrong, it was human nature."

"Human nature at the time," Candy smirked. "It was an unenlightened time."

"Amber Lynn."

"Who?"

"An American porn star active during the late 1980's. Made a lot of movies, including one where she was part of an incestuous family. Her brother was also a porn star, but they never told anyone they were related. They kept it secret until they were scheduled to do a scene together, and they came clean."

Candy just looked at me. "So?"

"Lynn was part of a society that saw sex as liberating and something you just did if you felt like it, and even she didn't cross the line."

"She didn't have the courage we do. We see nothing wrong with what we did. We made each other happy. We gave love and companionship. Just like any other loving couple. You aren't really going to punish both of us, are you?"

"Not both of you. By the time I'm done, Maya will be spending Eternity in Heaven, and you're going to burn like London."

Candy smiled at me. "We'll see about that."

"Count on it." And I turned and stormed away.

I didn't really do that much advance work. There was no need to. Candy Birkett was toast, and Maya Birkett was saved. Nothing to it. I could phone their cases in.

I forgot to take something into account, however, and that was the unpredictability of humans that Michael likes to point out. I had no clue what was coming. I was in the Water Gardens, having finished up some case reviews. Candy and Maya hadn't petitioned yet, so I was doing my usual stuff. Today, the beauty of the Afterlife just got to me. I stood on the ledge for one of the water troughs and started walking along it. Soon, I did a slow but deliberate about face on my toes. I was doing a very slow, very undynamic, but very definite dance on the ledge, moving to my own private music.

I was in the middle of another turn when Michael suddenly appeared in front of me on the ledge. His sudden appearance startled me this time, enough that I lost my balance. Michael reached out and grabbed the front of my robes to keep me from falling in. He pulled me up as I grasped his giant meaty hand with both of mine.

"Thanks, big brother," I said. There was no sarcasm in my voice. Michael's a prankster, but he wouldn't just do something like this. Something happened, and Michael needed his best Celestial right now.

"Sorry about that," he said. "It's about the Birketts."

"I take it they finally petitioned?"

"Fairchild is trying them together."

This wasn't good. It meant that they would share the same fate. And they shouldn't. "They are exploiter and victim. They can't be tried together."

"Already been approved."

Which meant there was a presiding angel assigned to the case, since he or she would have to go along with it. "Who's the presiding angel?"

Michael looked at me guiltily. "Camael."

If my eyes had gotten any wider, they would have overtaken my head. Camael is a very dedicated angel and he absolutely hated me. Any chance he had to smack me down, he did.

I dropped down from the wall and started pacing back and forth, brow furrowed and hands behind my back. "What's Camael's game?"

"You don't think he's doing this just to hack you off?"

"Not this time. There are too many ways for him to make me miserable in court, and he never uses Petitioners as pawns. Camael is harsh, but he's sympathetic. There is no way he'd put Maya through this without a good reason. No, it's a game."

"Does the game matter?"

I looked at Michael as I walked. "You bet, it does. If I'm going to dig Maya out of this, I have to figure out what my limits are with Camael, what I can get away with now that I can't get away with normally. I need to come up with a way for their fates to be separated at trial. This is actually for the best. If they are tried separately, Fairchild can use one case to prop up the other. If I separate them like this, he can't do that." I stopped and quirked my head. "I'm thinking I need to interview Candy and Maya in order to figure something out."

"Which one do you want to see first?"

"Both at the same time," I responded. "They'll be on trial together, that's the dynamic I need to work with. I need you to...."

"I already cleared your case load," Michael said, holding up his hand. "I know you."

"Thank you."

Michael just looked at me. "How? How can you do this?"

I stopped dead and tucked my finger under my chin. Michael had just asked the million pound question. I needed to separate the two. Break the bond Candy was maintaining.

Desperate times, desperate measures. I had to gamble that my mind was faster than everyone else's put together. "Got the trial request?" I asked.

Michael looked surprised, but nothing more than that. He immediately produced the request for trial. With a snap of his fingers, a quill appeared on one of his fingertips. I unceremoniously grabbed it and started filling out the request. Michael was leaning over my shoulder as, by Recommended Fate, I put, "Immediate approval of petitions."

I gave Michael the quill and started rolling up the document. Michael just looked at me. "You're playing right into Candy's hands."

"I know," I said. "Sit on this for a little longer. I need to plow the road first."

And we went our separate ways.

Candy and Maya were staying at the Interim, like all souls who had petitioned and were awaiting trial. They had been given separate rooms, but Candy more or less invited herself to share her daughter's room.

I marched down the hall with nothing in my hands, no life scrolls, no nothing. I had a guardian with me, however. I was going to enter with a show of force.

I got to the door and just looked at the guardian. Angels can enter and exit any room here in the Afterlife, even Advocates. I didn't know if the door was locked or if Candy would try to keep me out. I didn't want to bother with finding out. I turned so I would be looking in the door as soon as it opened. The angel thrust his hand to the door and it flew in.

Inside, Candy was sitting on the edge of a chair. Maya was seated on the floor in front of her, her back to her mom and nestled between her thighs. Candy was doing her daughter's hair. Their situation made the image repugnant.

The angel was infuriated, I could feel it radiating off of him. Maya scrunched down a little lower. Candy looked at me without the slightest concern in the world. "Hello, Miss...."

"Singer," I supplied, knowing she was still working her game. I strode in, closing the door behind me. Everyone in the room could still feel the glare of the angel on the other side.

"What brings you around?" Candy asked with a chirp.

"I'm here to ask you to have mercy on your daughter."

Candy looked taken aback. Maya just froze in place. "What are you talking about?" Candy asked with mock innocence.

"You've watched me at trials. You know I'm not as stupid as you're treating me," I said, coldness in my voice. "You're piggybacking."

I caught Maya's interest. "Piggybacking?"

"Candy knows she has no chance of getting into Heaven on her own for what she did to you," I told Maya, locking her gaze with mine. "So she's tying herself to you as a package deal. In order for her to be Cast, they'd have to Cast an innocent person like you, too. She's using you."

"I am not," Candy said, but there was no defiance in her voice. It was more like someone dismissing a rumor that may be true, but can't be proven. "My daughter and I don't use each other."

"Then stand trial separately," I stated.

145

"It wasn't my decision," Candy said. "That one guy...Fairfield?"

"Fairchild," I corrected crossly. I do NOT like being played for a fool.

"That's right," she said happily. "He made the decision to try us together."

"You can oppose that," I said. "The will of the Petitioner does factor in. It's a last chance to do the right thing."

"I am doing the right thing," she said.

"You destroyed your daughter's life while you were alive. You are now risking destroying her soul by sending her to Hell."

"You won't let that happen," Candy said.

"I might not have a choice. Fairchild is very good at traditional rulings. He's the most difficult challenge a Celestial can face. Biblical law says what you did was wrong. I could create an exception for Maya. I can't for you, you did this willingly. And with the two of you being tried together, Casting you may be more important than saving her."

"Are you saying you suddenly have no way of beating Fairchild in court?"

I felt my eyebrows knit. "You are putting me in a very repugnant situation."

"I'm sure you'll do what's best for Maya," she said simply.

I turned and walked as calmly as I could out of there. Once outside the Interim, I started stomping. I was sorting through everything in my head. And nothing looked good.

At this point, there was nothing else I could prepare for the trial. I had all the facts available. Camael hated me, and I didn't count on it being less than the hatred he would feel for Candy. Fairchild not only already had the presiding angel on his side, he had enough ammo that Maya was practically doomed, thanks to the connection Candy encouraged him to make. Candy knew I would want to save Maya. And by tying their fates together, she would be saved if I could save Maya. But that was a mighty big "if".

This was the worst kind of trial. I had no clear plan of attack, no firm defense. I would be flying blind, hoping something would happen that would separate their fates and enable me to save Maya without rewarding Candy's selfishness.

And come Hell or high water, I would find a way.

Trial came up before I knew it. I had buried myself in my thoughts, going over every angle, every possibility. In fact, I was so focused, I didn't even realize trial was about to start. A guardian came to get me. I started to panic. Once trial begins, no one in or out aside from, generally, putti running messages and the occasional angel. But the guardian sought me out with plenty of time to spare. Michael sent him after me. My big brother always has my back.

The guardian simply whisked me to the courtroom. I didn't bother to stop by my quarters. When cases have a high probability of Casting, I like to bring my sword with me. It was given to me, possibly earned, the first time I faced Lucifer in court and won. I liked to have it there as a reminder to myself and to him in case he showed up. But when Camael was sitting, I never do that. I worry it would look presumptuous. I already had an uphill battle this time, I didn't want to make it worse.

I got into court and walked down the aisle. Michael was already in front of the bench, standing where the two Guardians of the court were usually stationed. Michael is always on hand when Lucifer makes an appearance as he is his specific foe, the angel fated to ultimately destroy the devil when the time comes. No one beats Michael, not even the ultimate traitor.

I got to my table. There were no scrolls here, and I brought none with me. I sat down and just waited. I didn't have to look to my left to know Fairchild was there. I could feel the happiness in him. He was going to get to Cast two people, and he was going to beat me. His day couldn't get much better than that.

Eventually, the two Guardians for the court entered. They were escorting the Petitioners. I looked over my shoulder. Candy looked like she didn't have a care in the world, that the case was in the bag. Maya looked like she would rather have never existed. The Guardians had to nudge her once in a while to keep her up to speed. The Guardians brought the duo to my table. They looked at me with uncertainty – how in the world can I save the innocent soul wrapped up in this mess? I was glad I didn't have to talk. I had no answers to give.

Candy took the usual Petitioner's seat next to the Advocate, putting Maya third seat in. Still controlling her daughter, still controlling who she interacts with. Maya sat with her shoulders hunched, like if she could draw her head into her body, she would. Candy squeezed her daughter's knee and said, "Don't worry. We'll be together forever."

The Guardians, by this point, had taken their positions in front of the judge's bench, one on each side of Michael. I continued to stir things over in my head. I had a plan of attack. It was my only option. And I only had one chance to make it work.

The chimes sounded, and everyone in court stood. Those of us with them deployed our wings. I got myself in the right frame of mind. Angels can sense human emotions if they are strong enough, and I didn't want to give Camael anything to feed off of. I had just gotten my poker face up when Camael entered, coming through the door at the back of the court at the same time the twelve angels making up the Tribunal entered through the door on the right.

Camael got to the bench and waited for the Tribunal to get situated. He was the only angel who never sat at trial, he stood. I faced ahead and still like a palace guard. I could still see Camael. He didn't even look at me. He looked at Candy and his expression was furious. Didn't matter that I was her defender, the fact that Camael seemed to hate someone more than me was a tiny measure of relief.

Camael slammed the gavel, and the Tribunal and Gallery sat. He continued to bore through Candy as he spoke. "Who are the Petitioners?"

"The Petitioners are Candy Birkett and Maya Birkett," I answered without betraying any emotion.

"And who are their Advocates?"

"Hannah Singer, acting alone."

"And who advocates for the church?"

"Jeff Fairchild, acting alone," came the breezy reply from my left.

Camael looked at Fairchild, and for the first time I could remember, a look of distaste appeared on his face. Camael then looked at me. "You ready, Singer?"

That caught me by surprise, although I betrayed none of it. I simply said, "Yes, sir."

"Will the Petitioners please take the stand."

Candy walked Maya out to the dock. Once inside, Candy stood with her arm low against her daughter's back, lightly touching her hip. Maya was bewildered and petrified. She wanted to be somewhere else, but where could she go? My heart went out to her. Hang in there, kid. I'm working on it.

Camael was all business. "Miss Singer? Your opening statements, please."

Opening remarks weren't going to do me any good. Rather than waste my time and brain power, I threw my turn. "The position of the Celestials is that the Birketts are misguided and should not be punished for their mistake. Their petitions should be granted."

Camael looked taken aback. "That's it? That's all you have to say?"

"For the moment, yes." I got it then. For the duration of this one case, I was being given a reprieve. Camael wanted Maya saved somehow without letting Candy off the hook, and I was the only chance of making that happen. And he couldn't do much to help me, or Fairchild could seize on the difference in his behavior and have a shot at a mistrial. What was I going to do?

For now, nothing. It was time for Fairchild's opening arguments. He looked very relaxed. "I'm amazed we're actually having a trial about this," he smiled, confidence dripping from his words. "These two have committed the most heinous act that can exist without taking another life. The act of incest if forbidden. It is wrong. It is an abomination. The reason for so many people around the world is to seek out others, build new families, create new values. If incest were allowed, there's be no need for anything other than family lines to exist.

"Sex is a beautiful act bestowed upon us by God. But it is meant to be experienced under specific circumstances. And one of the chief qualifiers is that it is not between family members. Family is to reinforce each other, not intertwine their lives and end their futures. Candy and Maya are guilty. There is no doubt. Their life scrolls prove it. They should be Cast Down. Thank you."

I took a quick read of the Tribunal. They looked fearful. They didn't want to Cast Maya, but with them being tried together, they could not rule for separate fates. What one got, the other would have to get. Their hands were tied, so they would have to rule a specific way unless I came up with an exception. In other words, business as usual.

It's star time.

Camael was watching me carefully. I started with my opening gambit. "Move to separate the fates of Candy and Maya."

"On what grounds?" Camael asked.

"Inconsistently applied."

Fairchild looked unmoved. "Motion should be denied. I've always recommended incestuous lovers be Cast."

"But you've never asked for them to be tried together before," I countered.

A good start. Fairchild was on the defensive almost immediately. If he wanted to Cast both of them, he had to justify it somehow. "I'm allowed to change my mind and do things differently to correct an oversight."

"An oversight?"

"Otherwise, what would be the point of having a Church Advocate? You could just say, here are the rules, here's why they don't apply, and that would be it. Churches are needed to adapt, and adaptations have to start somewhere."

"Like here and now."

"Why not? Is it because it makes it that much harder for you to win?"

And just like that, the hot potato was dumped back in my lap. "No, because it makes it that much harder to see justice is done."

"Two people who willingly conducted an incestuous relationship? How is justice being denied?"

"Maya didn't enter into it willingly."

Fairchild immediately turned to Camael. "Move to strike Singer's statement."

"On what grounds?" Camael asked.

"Privacy Of Mind," Fairchild smiled.

Camael just looked at me as he hit the gavel and said, "Struck."

I fought the urge to swear. God respects the privacy of our thoughts, and poking around inside your head isn't allowed. However, that's for more extreme circumstances, when the actions spoke louder than words. Privacy Of Mind flat out didn't apply here.

The decision increased my chances of getting a mistrial, but Advocates try not to make that move. It irritates the presiding angels (and I had enough problems with this one as it was) and also made you into a troublemaker, impacting your effectiveness. Besides, during a mistrial, God makes the decision, and there was still too much in the way of saving Maya from being Cast. And Fairchild The Fink friggin' knew it. I couldn't count on a mistrial, I had to fight my way through, right here and right now.

Fairchild may have blocked my immediate path, but he couldn't block the side road. I looked at him, to keep my anger from focusing on Camael, and said, "My point still stands. Maya didn't want this."

"Prove it," Fairchild said.

"Look at her in the dock," I said. "She isn't returning her mother's gestures."

All eyes went to the dock. Candy positioned her daughter's arms for her, but Maya didn't move a muscle on her own. Her eyes were wide with fear. When Candy reached out to caress her cheek, Maya's head jerked to the side.

"Ah, yes, love is wonderous," I deadpanned. "It's too bad I never got to experience something so real."

"She returned plenty of her gestures back on Earth," Fairchild returned, an edge entering his voice. He knew I was getting points on the board.

"She was coerced. She didn't do it of her free will."

"Those actions were her free will," Fairchild countered. "Her free will changed from being a living ambassador of God to being her mother's plaything."

My head snapped to the bench. "Move to strike Fairchild's last argument."

"On what grounds?" Camael asked.

"Privacy Of Mind," I said.

"Motion should be denied!" Fairchild yelled. "This is completely different from Singer's circumstances."

I looked at Fairchild, and said to him but meant it for Camael, "Are they now?"

Camael had only one option or his hypocrisy would be exposed. He didn't need another mistrial or another lecture from God about what he was doing. "Struck," he said, as he lightly tapped the gavel.

Fairchild was caught. If he wanted to prove Maya was a willing participant, he had to use her actions to prove it. And there was more than enough in her lifescroll to show she wasn't.

Fairchild then did what he usually does when the pressure is on and there are no easy answers – he made the worst move possible. "Candy? Maya? You both wanted this, didn't you?"

I fought to keep my emotions down, but inside, I felt the sun bursting inside me. Petitioners don't talk unless addressed. And any information they volunteered was admissible. Fairchild just threw out the advantage Privacy Of Mind gave him.

Candy gave Maya a couple of squeezes. "Come on, honey. Tell the truth."

Maya squeaked out, "I...I guess so...."

Fairchild smirked at me. "An admission of guilt."

"It is not guilt," Candy corrected loftily from the dock. "We are in love. It's just a different kind of love. One that is beautiful and loving. We should not be punished. After all, isn't God all about love?"

I choked down my temper. "Just because you accept it doesn't mean Maya does."

"She does accept it," Candy said happily.

"Maya? Tell the truth – you know what your mother did to you is wrong, don't you?"

"I did nothing to her other than love her," Candy stated.

Camael flashed with anger. "The question was directed at Maya, not you."

"It might as well be directed at me," Candy said, not even flinching under the angel's gaze. "Our love unites us. We are in this together. We are sharing the same fate, so I might as well speak for her. If we are not together, we wouldn't be standing trial together. We deserve to be in Heaven together, loving each other forever."

My mind suddenly jumped back to something Candy said. We are sharing the same fate....

Suddenly, I heard a "Ding!" sound in my mind and thought, "Ideeeeeeaaaaaaaaah!" I looked at the bench and said, "I withdraw my motion to separate the fates of Candy and Maya."

Every eye in the court darted to me. Camael looked like he wasn't sure he should go along with it or not. However, he is bound by procedure and said, "Motion is withdrawn."

Candy was smiling. It was the smile of a puppet master, knowing her ruse finally paid off. She had me on her side and she was safe. She don't know me very well, do she?

While everyone was still caught up wondering what exactly I was up to, I made my next move. "Move to change my recommended fate."

Candy's expression shifted a little. She knew times like this was when I got dangerous. Camael looked genuinely curious for a change. "And what do you seek to change it to?"

I kept my expression neutral. "Divine Intervention."

Oh, that didn't go over well with Fairchild. "Motion should be denied!" he screamed.

Camael smashed the gavel and shot Fairchild a warning look. "Control your outbursts, Fairchild. Now, what grounds do you have to oppose?"

Fairchild knew his motion was lost. The best that could be hoped for was that arguing would get me to change my mind. If Camael denied me, I would move for a recess and simply change my recommended fate with Ernie Haley.

Most Advocates don't sweat when Divine Intervention comes into play because it is almost impossible to get. It is asking God to suspend the normal rules the world operates under to make an exception. And the more blatant the exception, the harder it was to get because the longterm effects were unknowable. But Fairchild knew this was a sure thing. The angels wanted to save Maya, and this would enable God to do whatever was right. Which meant separate fates. And Fairchild couldn't Cast either of them.

I took a quick read around me. The Tribunal was smiling – Maya was off the hook now. Camael was smiling at Candy with pure evil. Fairchild looked fighting mad. Maya was still scared, as if not believing God could possibly be merciful to her. And Candy's face was barely concealed panic.

Fairchild's only option was to work the Tribunal and get them to rule as he wanted. Candy would never get the mercy of the Tribunal, and he had to paint Maya with the same brush to score his precious double Casting. He plunged straight in. "They don't deserve Divine Intervention. They deserve to be Cast. Even Maya agrees."

Candy held her daughter tighter. Her eyes darted around. There was an edge in her voice as she said, "I do not deserve to be Cast."

"Yes, you do!" Fairchild declared. "Maya's behavior shows she knows it is what she deserves. And you, after all, initiated it."

And then Candy said the single most despicable thing I ever heard. "I didn't want to. Maya wanted it."

Candy knew she was done one way or the other, and was now hoping to pass the blame onto her daughter. A fury consumed me that tinted my vision red. "How dare you continue to use your daughter for your selfish ends!" I screamed.

Maya had started moving a little when Candy said her words. She had moved enough to pull away from her mother a little. "No..." she said, her voice barely a whisper. "No...I never wanted this...."

"Yes, you did," Candy said, tightening her grip on Maya.

"You...you did things to me," Maya said.

"They were innocent, you misinterpreted them."

Maya started to struggle to break her mother's grip. "No. I said they were wrong."

"No. You took them the wrong way. I became your lover because you wanted it."

Maya froze. "I didn't want it."

"Yes, you did," Candy said smoothly. "I did it to take care of you. Now, you need to take care of your mother. Like I always say, 'Take care of your mother.'"

In that moment, you could hear Maya's mind shatter. From underneath the fragments, the most horrible sound in all Creation erupted. The cry of a fallen angel, and it came from human lips.

Maya started screaming. She would stop long enough to take a breath, then begin screaming again. She violently threw off Candy's grip and walked backwards out of the dock. She never stopped screaming. There were no words, just noise. No words could ever express what the noise could.

Suddenly, ten ministering angels appeared in the courtroom right in front of Maya. I caught Michael and Camael look at each other. Apparently, they both called for them, resulting in the huge number in attendance. Usually, the presence of one ministering angel is enough to calm someone. But even with ten beings of peace and healing, Maya continued to scream that horrible sound. Ministering angels started grabbing her limbs and lifting her in the air. Maya continued to scream as the ministering angels flew her out of the courtroom and off to the Equilibrium.

Once the ministering angels were gone, the court was silent as a tomb. Camael broke the silence. "Maya Birkett is unfit to stand trial. She will be tried again on her own."

Yes! Maya was out of the woods! She was as good as in Heaven. All that was needed was for Shalmana, the leader of the ministering angels, to do her stuff. She had handled far worse, she would be able to rebuild Maya's shattered mind.

My happiness was short lived, however. Now, I had work to do. I knew what was coming next, and looked at Camael with anticipation. He looked at me and said, "As the nature of the trial has changed, I will give both sides the chance to change their recommended fates. Singer? You wish to change yours?"

I glared at Candy. She actually flinched. I steeled myself up, knowing the implications of what I was about to do, but I knew I had to do it. It had to be this way. "Yes, sir. The official Celestial position is Candy should be Cast Down."

Candy's jaw dropped. "You can't do that!"

"Silence Is Golden!" Camael barked, and smashed the gavel. A golden ribbon shot from the impact point and zipped right down Candy's throat. She would not be able to speak until session was over or Camael released her. All that was left was for Fairchild to say he supported Casting, and the trial would be over.

Camael looked at Fairchild. "Mister Fairchild? You wish to change your recommended fate?"

With perfect calmness, Fairchild said, "Yes, sir. The official position of the Church is Candy should be reincarnated to teach her a lesson."

If it were possible, I would have dashed across the court and started beating Fairchild's face in. Camael and I actually looked at each other at the exact same time, and he looked ready to do the same. In that moment, it was back to the old days when I first arrived and it seemed we could communicate just by looking at each other. If Fairchild got reincarnation, not only could Candy's case not be used for Maya's defense, but he could try to delay a hearing for Maya, meaning that, when Candy came around again, he could take another shot at trying and Casting them together.

Casting is a horrible thing. There's no doing over, there's no escape. Anyone with a heart does what they can to keep from asking for it. I had already made up my mind and made peace with the decision. Now, none of that mattered. Not only did Candy's evil deserve the fate I recommended, but if I succeeded, Maya would be safe forever. I had to win this one.

First order of business was to shut Fairchild down before he had a chance to think. "Move for closing arguments," I said quickly.

Fairchild looked happy. "I concur."

Camael looked at Fairchild like he was the biggest fool in the universe. "Very well," he said.

Fairchild looked at me. "Well, start your arguments."

I wasn't done yet. "I was originally defender. I originally had Privilege. You go first."

Fairchild looked to Camael. "As both sides are now contesting petition, move for the bench to determine who goes first."

And that was when Camael's sympathy for me ran out. "Singer, you first."

Well, it had to happen sooner or later. Not that it really mattered. Fairchild would have to address way too much in his closing arguments, arguments he was now writing on the fly. That's something I can do, not him. "The official position of the Celestials is Candy should be Cast Down."

I looked at Fairchild and held my hand out to him as if to say, "Take it away, buddy." Fairchild actually went pale. "Move for a recess so I can review the case."

"Motion should be denied," I jumped in. "Fairchild has reviewed the case to the point he was not only ready to go to trial, he was ready for closing arguments. He felt he was ready then, he should be ready now."

"I need time to bolster my case," Fairchild said.

"You think that's possible? Remember my first motion in the case?"

Fairchild blinked. Here was someone guilty as sin, and he was arguing for leniency with no justifiable reason. Anything he came up with would be shot down with "inconsistently applied."

Fairchild finally saw the writing on the wall. He took one last look at Candy, regret clear in his eyes. Not about what was going to happen to her, but that he wasn't going to be the one to do it, and what this meant for his chances of Casting Maya. "The official position of the Churches is Birkett should be reincarnated, given another chance to get it right."

Candy's eyes widened with fear. She couldn't speak, but I saw her mouth, "No...you can't do this to me...."

Camael turned to the Tribunal. "You have heard the Advocates for Candace Birkett state their recommended fates. You may now make your decision. You wish to confer?"

The lead Tribunal immediately stood. "We are ready to rule." No one corrected him. And from the fearsome expressions on the angels' faces, there was only one way this would go.

"And what is your decision?"

"Petitioner is to be Cast Down."

Camael fixed his glare on Candy as he declared, "So be it!" and slammed the gavel.

I started steeling myself for who was coming. All around the courtroom, the clean white stone became splotched with red marks. The red spread from them like bleeding wounds, and sounds in the court took on an ominous echo.

Candy stumbled back in the dock as the light of the room was swallowed up in shadow. She dropped down on the floor, curling into a fetal tuck. She squeezed her eyes shut and covered her ears with her hands. She was rocking herself.

I watched carefully, preparing for the sights that were coming. Finally, the last of the stone was blotted out by the red. With no warning, the structures of the courtroom broke into pieces from the bottom up and fell away. Everyone was still standing where they would be if the room was still there, but we were standing in the middle of a red swirling tornado. It was huge. The top reached on, with only stars visible in the opening at the distant top. But looking down, you saw it. Hell. Fire. Stone. Demons flying beneath us. And the anguished cries of the souls condemned to spend Eternity there.

Several of the souls noticed the column and knew what it meant. Once it touched down, they raced for it, ran into it, struggled to climb it. They wanted out. They wanted to escape. As their hands and feet struggled for purchase, they started moving closer where they could be viewed. They barely looked human anymore. Their hair, their features, vanished under skin that had turned bright red from the fire and heat. From the back, you couldn't even tell their genders. They climbed and scrambled up the fire, shrieking and crying the entire time. I forced myself to look, to not ignore them. Fairchild simply ignored them. He was dismissive of them.

A figure walked into the center of the tornado, right under where the center of the court would be. He started rising, flapping his arms as he rose. It would be funny if it wasn't for the situation or for who it was. The most beautiful angel. The ultimate betrayer. Lucifer, the devil himself.

I looked at the other angels. The Tribunal was ready if anything got out of hand. Between Camael and Michael, though, there might not be anything left of Lucifer for them to beat up. I kept a sigh of relief bottled up inside me. Camael might not stop Lucifer from coming after me again, but Michael sure would.

Eventually, Lucifer rose up until he was level with me, Fairchild, and the Gallery. He smiled at me. I remained still. He then turned to Michael. "It's that time again already?"

Michael didn't say anything. He just kept glowering at him. Realizing he wasn't getting anywhere with Michael, Lucifer turned his attention to Fairchild. "Long time, no see. How have you been?"

"You cannot tempt me, Satan!" Fairchild declared loudly.

"I already have once," Lucifer shrugged. If Fairchild felt any remorse for allowing him at the table when he was having me retried, he didn't show it.

Finally, Lucifer turned to me. "Plenty of room for you in the palace, Singer," he smiled.

"You've had enough chances," was all I said.

"You call those 'chances?'"

"What? They don't count because you didn't get what you wanted?"

Lucifer was about to say something when suddenly, part of the court erupted with a brilliant white light that bleached out the red tornado of fire and made those climbing it stop all movement. I knew what it was. Michael had produced his flaming sword. Lucifer was on thin ice, and Michael was ready to break it. No idea why, Lucifer hadn't done anything yet, but he must have been moving to do something. My big brother always has my back.

Lucifer turned and looked at Michael in surprise. Whatever he was doing to anger Michael, he had no clue what it was. He wasn't doing anything I hadn't handled before. But we both trusted Michael's judgment. As I relaxed, Lucifer got more nervous.

"Well," he said, clearly unsure what exactly had Michael ready to go, "I guess I'll just take what I'm allowed and go." Lucifer gave a little smirk and took a step towards me. Next thing anyone knew, Michael had moved next to him and his flaming sword lowered in front of Lucifer's eyes like a toll gate. Michael didn't look the slightest perturbed. It was like he was just hoping for something to happen now so he didn't have to wait for the Apocalypse to kill him.

Lucifer then started to slowly turn around the court. "Let's see, who am I to take?" Candy continued to huddle in midair, even though she was in plain sight. Lucifer saw her and smiled. "Yeah, you'll do for now."

Lucifer went up and rose up a bit like he was climbing into the dock next to her. Candy was shuddering and shaking. Michael had willed his flaming sword away but remained standing where he was. The lost souls were screaming and howling again, struggling up the column of flame. I refused to feel pity for Candy. Lucifer simply stood above her and said, "See? This is your first mistake. Regret. You'll never find peace in Hell if you try holding on to your humanity."

A smile of pure evil appeared on Lucifer's face. He stood on the other side of Candy, where the courtroom wall would have been. He lowered himself until she about waist high from him. He then flicked her with his finger, sending her drifting across the courtroom and towards the fire.

Candy realized what was happening. She uncurled and started scrambling in the air, her movements in vain. She looked at the angels in the Tribunal. She looked at me. She looked at Camael and Michael as she floated past, screaming, "No! Help me! Somebody! Save me!"

Candy looked behind her in terror, seeing the flames and damned souls getting closer. When she was about ten yards away, she stopped. She started to relax, then she was flung into the flames.

I steeled my nerves as Candy's cries of anguish joined the chorus of pain. Her skin started to redden from the heat. Her hair fell out. Her eyes widened as much as they could as her inhuman sounds reverberated around us. She started trying to scramble with the others, towards the top, where they did not know what awaited them, but it beat an eternity of pain.

Lucifer closed his eyes, tilted his head, and snapped his fingers. The tornado of flame came to a stop and started spinning the other way. As it drained down, the souls within the fire went with it. Every moment, it went faster, until it was back down in Hell, and demons flew around gathering up those who tried to escape.

Lucifer took one last look at Michael, as if reassuring himself his ultimate destroyer hadn't moved any closer. He then, with his eyes on me the entire time, rocketed back down into Hell. Once he touched down, the red colors retreated, exposing the courtroom again. I kept myself focused as Camael and the Tribunal somberly left.

The doors of the courtroom opened, allowing the rank and file to enter and exit. I was numb as I walked up the aisle and out the door. Usually, an encounter with Lucifer, with seeing Hell, with seeing someone condemned to it, for those to be actions you approved of, takes a little bit of time to recover from. But I didn't bother. I couldn't. I had work to do.

I had stopped by the Office Of Records to get what I needed from Russell. I could feel my shoulders being pulled down by more than gravity, how my feet were lifting flat instead of bending normal as I walked. I felt my neck scrunch, and my eyelids trying to follow suit. Didn't matter to me. Shalmana would have Maya fixed up before I knew it. That meant her trial was coming up. And I was going to win it for her.

I got to my quarters, making a beeline for my couch. I didn't bother to make any jasmine tea, I wasn't sure how much time I would lose. I had several scrolls spread out on the floor when I heard a knock on my door. "Who is it?" I called without taking my nose from my work.

"'Who is it?' Usually you know it's me from how I knock," I heard Michael's voice say as he came in.

"What's on your mind, Michael?" I asked.

"Any chance of some eye contact as we talk?"

"Maybe in a minute, I need to finish this review."

Suddenly, the scrolls rolled up and slid across the room and in the air. Then landing in a neat pile on my table, right next to where Michael was standing. He had his hand out, palm up.

I wasn't in the mood to be pleasant. "Give those back. Now."

"You're exhausted," Michael said.

"Spirits don't need rest," I countered. I couldn't tell if the droop of my eyebrows was the result of my irritation or not.

"Yes, you do," Michael said. He was standing with perfect posture, as if he were judging me from on high. "You are still a human spirit. You do not have access to the reserve of strength and energy that we angels have."

"I don't need it," I said tersely. "I am just fine."

"No rest for the weary?" he asked.

"Nice try, but I'm not weary."

"Hannah, you have no cases coming up, you just faced Lucifer again, and you dealt with a truly evil person. You need rest."

"Maya needs me more."

"Her case is a piece of cake."

"No, it isn't. Fairchild tried to Cast her. He will try again. We both know it. And until I see her walking through the Pearly Gates, I won't stop."

Michael rolled his eyes. "I was afraid of this," dragged out of him as he pressed his flat hands together like he was praying. He held them up by his head, tilted his cheek to it, and closed his eyes.

And my world went black.

When I came to, my eyes were still closed, but I felt I was lying on something soft, softer than anything I had ever known. The sounds around me, the scents, what I was touching – I had to be in the Equilibrium.

I opened my eyes, preparing myself to adjust to the normal colors around me instead of the typical dynamic colors of the Afterlife. Standing in front of me, at the foot of the bed in proper robes, was Michael. He looked a little contrite but ultimately not the least bit sorry for knocking me out. In his left hand was a bouquet of roses, beautiful full bloom roses. Nestled among the ones in the front was a card with the words, "Forgive me," on it.

I told him to commit a sexual act with himself and gave him a V.

"Understood and forgiven," Michael chuckled as he made the sign of the cross at me with his right hand.

I started struggling to get out of the bed. Between the comfort of it and its lack of form, I was having trouble gaining purchase. "Well, I'm rested up now, so you can't say I'm not up to advocating Maya's case now."

"Maya's case has already been heard."

I looked at Michael as if he was planning to hand me over to Lucifer. Michael touched the card on the front of the flowers. It now said, "Please forgive me."

Rage propelled me out of the bed and right up to him. I grabbed the front of his robes and pulled his face down to mine. "How dare you!" I screamed.

Michael didn't even flinch. "I led her defense," was all he said.

"And what was the ruling of the Tribunal?"

"Reincarnation."

I felt like I was standing under a huge waterfall. "I could have saved her!" I started slamming my fists against Michael's chest. "I could have saved her!" I kept screaming as my fists slowed and emotion caught up to me. Eventually, I stopped swinging and just leaned forward, my forehead to Michael's chest. "I could have saved her...."

Michael dropped the flowers and scooped me up into a protective hug. All I could do was wrap my arms around him as best I could as all my tears, my frustrations, my anger poured out of me. I was done with words for now. There was no other way to express my feelings.

Eventually, I calmed down. I whispered, "I could have saved her."

"No, you couldn't have," Michael said firmly but with understanding. "It's why you were working so hard on her case. You were looking for that one edge that would get her a fate other than what she had to get."

Michael was right. I knew Maya was going to have to go around one more time. Her mother had broken her understanding of love, and unless you know what love is, you can't get into Heaven. But I was angling that there was some way to affirm that she still knew love, that she should be allowed in. Unfortunately, I ran into one of the hard facts of the Afterlife – angels know all about the people they see. It is still their decision, and they wouldn't have gone along with what you say.

"...I'm sorry, Michael...for hitting you...."

"I'll forgive you anything," Michael said, and I heard the smile in his voice.

I pulled my head back to look him in the eyes. "Anything?"

His expression didn't change. "Yes, Hannah. Anything."

I felt my insides cool down. Michael took me back in the hug. "I'm not worried about you doing something that I can't forgive. You don't have it in you."

I was silent for a little longer. "What kind of life is she looking at?"

"She's getting an accelerated course," Michael said. "She's going to be born with retardation."

I pulled back. "Isn't that going to make it worse?"

"The parents are good parents and more than up to what is needed," Michael smiled. "Once Maya's life is over, she will have seen, experienced, and returned protective, unconditional love. And with Candy's case unable to be used against her, she's in."

I shuddered a little when Michael said that name. "Why? Why did she have to do that?"

"Corrupt her daughter?"

"And take so much pride in it."

"We wish we knew."

"You angels?"

"And God. What Candy based her actions on were things God allows people to feel and enjoy. He can't remove them without taking away from the fulfillment of those who would never abuse it."

"It all comes down to a person's choice."

"And God's faith that they will ultimately do right."

We stood, embracing each other, for what seemed like forever. Just being held by Michael feels better than anything the Equilibrium can provide. He asked, "So, you recovered from doing what you had to do?"

He meant me Casting Candy. It's like making the decision to kill – you're never quite the same when you realize you were fine with such a horrible action. "Yeah," I whispered, "I think I'm okay."

"You have a little time," he smiled as we separated. "Nothing heavy coming up on the docket for a while, should give you a chance to get your legs back under you."

We talked as we went, exiting the Equilibrium. The stark sensations felt good to experience again, and I went off to the Office Of Records to get the scrolls I was going to need.

Having gathered them, I went for my favorite spot in the Water Gardens. I had to make sure I was back on top of things before the next grey case came up. But when I got around the corner, I saw Camael standing imperiously by where I usually sat.

I didn't even break my stride as I stuck my emotions away and locked the box. I don't like showing fear, especially to someone who would likely abuse it. I nodded at him as I entered.

"Singer," he responded by way of greeting.

I went to one of the troughs and sat down on it, choosing which scroll to read and diving into my work.

"Are you just going to ignore me?" Camael asked.

I kept it in neutral. I lowered the scroll and looked at him, waiting.

"Anything you want to say to me?" Camael asked.

"Nothing comes to mind."

He quirked his head, clearly trying to get a read from me. He knew me and my reputation, and I think it threw him that I didn't behave around him the way I did around any other angel. "Nothing about how the case went?"

"Who am I to criticize how you run your court?"

"Not even for me agreeing to let them be tried together initially?"

I kept my movements subtle. I started shifting my eyes left and right around the area.

"There's no one else here," Camael said. He actually sounded insulted that I didn't trust him. "You can speak freely with no repercussions."

Yeah, I totally believed that. "Yes, sir."

The silence continued to stretch between us. It was starting to get to him. And me. This wasn't like him. He usually did his intimidation routine and took off. He was sticking around. Why? I didn't explore the question, I didn't trust it not to distract me and let him get a read on me.

Camael walked closer until he was right in front of me. He leaned in until his face was all I saw. I kept calm. I refused to blink. He said, "You aren't afraid of me."

I said nothing.

"Not even the tiniest trace of fear. Why is that?"

He was trying to open me up. I kept shut.

"I hold your future in my hands, you know," he smiled. "I can make amazing things happen for you. I can make things impossible for you. And I would be justified in whatever I did. You know, I can tell your precious big brother that I'm not sure you're being honest with me. That I don't believe you are truthful. That grants me a lot of leeway."

"Mm-hmm," was all I said, calm as a lake on a windless summer day. Besides, Michael knew both of us too well to fall for anything like that.

"So tell me what keeps you from being afraid. Just tell me the truth, and I'll walk away right now."

I wasn't sure what he was after. I felt myself getting nervous. Whatever answer I gave him, I was scared he'd twist and use against me. The emotions were starting to stir. So I reached for the one thing that always relieved me.

I thought of my judgment. I was cleared to enter Heaven at any time I wanted to go. I had earned it about seven hundred years earlier. Almost a century ago, Camael tried to take it away from me. But he didn't. The judgment was mine. If Camael's treatment of me ever became an impediment to Petitioners getting justice, I would leave with a clear conscience that I did everything I could, I didn't let them down.

I must have changed emotionally, I caught Camael's subdued reaction. The best cover is a simple extension of the truth. I told him, "I'm not afraid because we are both dedicated to our duties. We both defend God's mercy. And as long as that remains true, I have nothing to fear."

"That's the present," he told me. "What about your future? Aren't you interested in your future?"

"I'll deal with my future when it becomes my present," I told him.

"You're keeping that from happening," he said challengingly. "You can't go on like this forever. Sooner or later, you're going to have to face your future."

I let a little fire come to the surface. "My future doesn't matter to me. The futures of the souls who need mercy do. And I will do my duty and defend them as long as I am able to."

"You sure you're not just stalling?"

I went back into neutral. "I have a judgment in my favor. One I have fought for several times. Why would I stay here if I didn't want to?"

Camael just looked at me for a few moments longer, then started walking away. As he did, he called over his shoulder, "You can't run from your future forever, Singer. Sooner or later, you have to face it."

I watched him leave, then stayed for a little longer. I didn't want him to think he spooked me. I eventually left and headed for one of the choir theaters, hiding out under the stage to do my reviews.

I couldn't really focus on the reviews. I kept thinking about what Camael was implying. Advocates usually burn out after three hundred years. And here I was, bearing down on seven hundred. I didn't feel like I was losing it. I felt better than ever. Did Camael know something I didn't?

I shook it from my mind. I was certain I hadn't given Camael anything he could use against me in court or that honked him off. And if I was wrong, I would deal with it. I wasn't going to Heaven as long as I could avoid it. As long as I was needed.

I let out a sigh, and was able to focus on my reviews.

ACE OF CLUBS

I let out a sigh. This was taking longer than it had to.

Middle of a court session, Jegudiel was the presiding angel. He was sitting at the bench, his chin propped up on his fist and looking like he was ready to fall asleep. The Tribunal wasn't doing that much better. They sat ramrod straight, but it was an act – their drooping wings gave them away. My two juniors, Del Sierra and Claire Johnson, looked like two kids in detention with nothing to keep them occupied but afraid of doing anything that will keep them there longer. The junior Churches were also clearly having trouble keeping their eyes looking in the same direction. On the bright side, cases where one side rambled on way too long were a snap to win. Of course, the real challenge was getting there.

It helped that I didn't have Privilege. Churches approved petition, Celestials opposed. Jeff Fairchild, the most senior Church, was leading with his two regular flunkies, Burke Finley and Edward Fiedler. They tried hard to be extensions of their leader, but this was really putting them to the test. The subject of our debate was Carl Clifton. Clifton had been a bishop, but very much enjoyed being an authority figure. No wonder Fairchild liked him so much. And Fairchild always tried to go the extra distance for his fellow church authorities.

As much of a struggle as it was, I still listened to Fairchild's opening statements. I mined any information I could find out them, but this time, it was like trying to find a cup of tea someone poured into the ocean. Mmmm...tea. I love jasmine tea. St. Michael offered to have one of the taps in my quarters replaced with one that poured fresh jasmine tea instead of water when I opened it....

I slapped my face to bring myself out of it.

Jegudiel looked at me in confusion. "Something wrong, Singer?"

"Mosquito," I said without blinking.

Fairchild sneered, "There's no bugs up here." He was clearly hoping to nick me for interrupting his opening arguments.

"Human nature and force of habit." I said again, still facing resolutely ahead.

Jegudiel decided to nip this in the bud. "Fairchild? Please...." There was a definite hesitation there. "Please continue."

Eventually, Fairchild finished. All eyes turned to me, pleading for mercy. Fortunately, this was in the bag already. I just had to keep it succinct. "Clifton cared nothing of those under his charge, only for how he could use his position to further himself. He was more interested in climbing the ladder than doing right by his flock. He should be reincarnated into servitude to atone for it. Thank you."

I saw a couple of angels in the Tribunal box shift a little. Things usually got interesting when Fairchild and I argued. Then again, after those rambling opening arguments, watching slugs have sex would be more interesting. And faster.

Fairchild wasted no time going after my assertions. "He fulfilled the duties of his position."

If he thought he caught me napping, he was wrong. "He only did the basic requirements."

"That's good enough, isn't it?"

"If he lived a good life, sure."

"You're saying he didn't?"

"Once he became bishop, how much time did he spend interacting with his flock? Zero. He only associated with others at a similar station to him or a station he aspired to."

"Nothing says people have to associate with those they don't want to associate with."

"There's a difference between isolating yourself due to values and isolating yourself due to arrogance."

"It was values that separated him from other people."

"So other people without his level of training, his access to power, have no worth?"

"That's not what I mean by values. His values are clearly different from ordinary people. There was nothing wrong with him seeking others with similar values to associate with."

Fairchild gave me an opening, and I took it. "Plenty of people share his values."

"Like who? The people you successfully get into Heaven all the time?"

"Golfers."

Fairchild looked completely confused. "What do golfers have to do with this?"

"Clifton was a golfer."

"There are lots of different golfers."

"Yes, but plenty Clifton could have associated with."

"He was above them."

"Then why did he bless his clubs?"

Fairchild must have missed that detail in Clifton's life scroll. "Well, sure, he had his clubs blessed," he said, standing on thin ice and hearing the cracking. "He's a bishop, right?"

"He didn't have them blessed because he's a bishop. He had them blessed because he wanted to be a better golfer. Just like any golfer with a lucky routine."

Fiedler shot up. "It wasn't luck, it was to make his game better."

Fairchild slapped his hand to his face at the own goal Fiedler just scored. I siad, "Abuse of authority and seeking an unfair advantage. He cheated."

Fairchild glared at Fiedler and kept glaring into his eyes as Fiedler withered down into his seat and faced the front. Fairchild then looked at me, and I saw the despair in his eyes. He knew this was lost. He went on too long in his opening arguments, and I gave no quarter.

Then, his face lit up. Inspiration had struck like a hammer. He turned to the bench and said brightly, "His behavior should be excused as human nature."

Interesting. Of course, Jegudiel was having none of it. "Given the complaints Singer has mentioned, I would think a set of golf clubs is the least of your worries."

"The golf clubs are a symbol, if you will," Fairchild said, still bright as the sun. "The behavior that made him get his golf clubs blessed is the whole reason he behaved the way he did."

Oh, no. This can't really be happening. I said, "Interesting idea, that golf is the lynch pin of his bad behavior."

"It is human nature, something YOU are constantly reminding me of," Fairchild said.

I saw that gleam in his eye. It was the look he had when he knew he had the case in the bag. Oh. My God. Is he in for a surprise. "You're saying that he views everything in life the same way, so his behavior is just a logical conclusion."

Fairchild actually leaned back a little. "Yes. That's exactly what I'm saying."

"It doesn't make him any less wrong, just more consistent in his wrongness."

Fairchild glared at me. "I'm saying, what about walking a mile in his shoes?"

"I did. And my conclusion is, he's a plonker."

"You are taking his actions out of context."

"What a shame we can't live out his circumstances and can only judge him by his deeds."

"Ah, but you CAN live out his circumstances!"

"You're suggesting that I be born and live his life?"

"No," Fairchild said. "Besides, that wouldn't do any good. You don't make the final decision." He looked cheerfully at the Tribunal. "But they do. And there is a way to experience his circumstances without being born. Especially since being born won't be the same, no one will have his exact personality and life situation."

The Tribunal just blinked at Fairchild. He just kept smiling at them, like whatever he was suggesting was patently obvious. When the silence continued to stretch like a fresh cheese pizza, Fairchild filled in the blanks. "A round of golf!"

Several on the Tribunal looked like they'd rather the Apocalypse started, and they would make time on their calendars if need be.

"How exactly is a round of golf supposed to provide insight into his mentality?" I asked.

"It will enable me to put his behavior into context," Fairchild said. "Everything he did ties into his personality. A round of golf will condense all those elements and make it easier for me to...."

"Redress his behavior?" I smiled.

"...to explain his behavior," Fairchild said, his smile slipping a little. "We are to provide the best defense for our charges that we can. This will aid immeasurably in my defense."

Jegudiel looked at me. "Singer? How do you feel about this?"

I didn't want Jegudiel or any of the angels on the Tribunal to think I was manipulating them. I simply said, "I have no opinion one way or the other, I defer to the wisdom of the angels."

Jegudiel leaned towards me. "Singer, I am giving you the opportunity to object without repercussions."

I looked at the Tribunal. Some of them were pleading with their eyes. So. Not. Good. I stood at parade rest and said, "I do not feel that is prudent of me, sir."

Jegudiel looked at the Tribunal in apology, then at Fairchild. "So what do you suggest?"

"A foursome," he smiled. "Me, Clifton, you, and an angel from the Tribunal. One round of golf. And then, my defense will become clear."

"Well, I am the presiding angel. Not only is my opinion immaterial to proceedings, but I've already tried golf." He then looked at me, still apologetically. "Singer? I think you should be the fourth."

Figures. This was why I was already thinking what I would need to make the day tolerable. "I have said I defer to the wisdom of the angels. I will respect your will."

And so, the arrangements were made, the angel from the Tribunal was chosen, and things were put in motion for a court case to be decided over a round of golf.

I should explain something really quick. It's not that golf is a bad game. It's just not my game, and it's not the angels' game, either.

There are games here in the Afterlife. After all, Eternity can get boring. There are lots of games based on what humans play on Earth, and a few that are specific to the angels. Humans can play, but the angels either restrict themselves to keep it fair (the lowliest angel is greater than the greatest human) or they hold special tournaments just for them. Those are the ones you want to watch. They are just amazing.

One such angelic game is a one-on-one competition. You each get half the pitch, and a "glow", or a floating orb of light, is thrown back and forth, trying to get it past your opponent. Hit the wall behind them, and you score a point. You can try to english the glow or give it more oomph or whatever. St. Michael is the best at the game. Actually, he's the best at all games. No one beats him, not even other angels. All you can hope if you face him is that you go the distance and that he doesn't plow through you like a cop car through a fruit stand.

With the session in recess while everyone got ready for golf, I headed over to the pitch. Michael was already there, leaning against the wall with the entrance and waiting for me. He was wearing royal blue gym shorts and a white T-shirt with blue lettering that said, "Let's get physical!" He wore sweatbands on his head and wrists, which was odd – I never saw him sweat, but he must have been after the whole package. Nothing else explained the leg warmers. The sweatband on his head bunched the top of his hair up so it looked like a crop of medium brown crabgrass. He had one of those digital sports watches, but this is the Afterlife, where there is no real concept of time, so the display was blank. He had two bottled sports drinks at his side. "Hannah! You finally made it! Ready to go?"

I walked up to him and sighed. "Sorry, Michael, no. The case isn't over, we're just in recess."

Michael picked up the bottled sports drinks and handed one to me. He touched the side of mine, and the blue liquid turned brownish. I smiled gratefully, knowing full well he had turned it into jasmine tea for me. I took a healthy swig as he asked, "Is the case that tough?"

"No," I said, replacing the cap. "It's in the bag. Fairchild is arguing human nature."

Michael let out a short laugh. "You're kidding."

"Nope. He is trying to write a novel in a language he does not understand." And I explained the case to him.

When I mentioned I was going to have to play a round of golf, Michael looked at me like my dog just died. Then his face lit up. "You know what you need? A caddy."

I felt my mouth quirk into a smile. "You offering?"

"You bet!" he said. "A good caddy knows the course and can give advice. Whatever course is chosen, I know them."

I have to admit, it would be nice to have my big brother with me. Although not so much from an advisory standpoint as he would keep me from being bored out of my skull. "You're on, partner," I said as we shook hands.

"So, when does the match begin?"

Suddenly, a putto, David, zipped up to us. "St. Michael, Jegudiel requests a meeting in your chambers. You and a few others."

"Tell him I will be there and to contact anyone else he needs."

David dashed off, and we barely resumed our conversation when another putto, Solomon, appeared and approached me. "Miss Singer, Jegudiel requests you attend a meeting in St. Michael's chambers."

"Tell him I'm on my way," I said, and Solomon rushed off. I looked at Michael. "Gee. I wonder what that could be about."

We walked to Michael's chambers, talking about anything else except golf.

A crowd had gathered outside Michael's chambers. Jegudiel was there, rolling his eyes and shaking his head as Fairchild spoke to him, likely about the case, the game, or both. Standing around, looking uncertain, was Maasataa. She was the lead Tribunal, and I guess she drew the short straw. Also there was Metatron, imposing with his pale and thin appearance, dingy white robes, and white hair. It struck me as odd that he was here. After all, he wasn't on the Tribunal deciding the case.

Michael saw everyone, gave them a warm smile, and yelled, "Greetings! What are you waiting out here for? My door is always open."

That, in and of itself, was true. Michael never locked his door when he was gone. He never needed to. First, only a select few could enter his chambers when he wasn't there. Plus, no one can desecrate an angel's chambers, to say nothing of the mightiest archangel. Also, Michael knows exactly who is in there and exactly what they are doing, which I found out when I went there to look up some old maps one day. But Metatron spelled out the primary consideration. "We would rather make sure there are no...obstructions."

Michael smirked and charged through his door. Nothing happened.

Metatron and Jegudiel went through. Nothing happened.

Maasataa went through. Nothing happened.

I closed my eyes and prayed as I went through. Nothing happened.

Fairchild stomped through and a bucket of water hit him as soon as he got past the jamb. I focused my gaze on Metatron and his fierce disapproval. It was the only thing keeping me from laughing.

"Ha ha, you're a sport! That's what I like about you!" Michael crowed as he came around with a towel and offered it to Fairchild. Fairchild just stared at the towel like it was radioactive. Finally, Michael took the towel and walked back to his desk, looking for all the world like he couldn't believe anyone would misunderstand his completely innocent gesture.

Michael sat down at his desk and picked up a scroll he had off to the side. He held it to his temple and said, "Aaa, the answer is, 'Why would you want to do that?'" He then unrolled the scroll and said, "'St. Michael, can we have your permission to hold a golf outing to help settle this case?'"

"It's relevant. You can even join us for a round," Fairchild said. He was working really hard to sell golf as Big Time Fun.

"No, thanks," he said with a smile. "Caddy duties for Hannah. Not that I want to, she doesn't tip worth beans."

"Aw, Michael's afraid he'll lose," Fairchild teased.

"Nope. Golf just isn't for me."

"What could possibly be better than a round of golf with me?"

"Kickboxing," Michael said with a bounce of his eyebrows and an evil grin.

Fairchild gulped audibly. He probably remembered that one match between me and Michael where a good shot from him sent me flying over the ropes and into the audience. Not that that's the worst thing that's ever happened to me in our bouts, it's just the worst Fairchild witnessed. After all, it was the only time I didn't catch him smiling when I got nailed.

Michael returned his attention to Jegudiel. "So how is this supposed to work?"

"A foursome."

"How are teams divided up?"

"How about Clifton and Maasataa on one team, so she can see Clifton and his behavior develop."

Fairchild and I looked at each other. That meant we were going to be a duo. I was ready to tough it out. Not Fairchild, though. "That would be unfair," he said in a rush.

Michael gave Fairchild his undivided attention. "Explain."

"Maasataa is an angel. She will automatically excel at the game. Clifton will not face the kind of pressure he normally would. So it would be best to pair her with Singer or I."

Michael looked at me, and we silently communicated the barnyard epithet that described Fairchild's logic. "Fine," he declared. "Fairchild and Maasataa, Hannah and Clifton."

Metatron usually looks like he finds the world distasteful. This, however, was a whole new level. "I'm with Fairchild's team?"

"Why would you be on a team?" Michael asked.

"He's going to be my caddy," Maasataa said.

Michael looked at him in surprise. "You?"

"I happen to like golf," Metatron sniffed.

"You would," Michael said with a chuckle.

"Burn," Metatron declared.

Michael continued unabated. "Decision is made, I'll have one of the courses made up, and we'll meet to conduct this grand experiment. Now, shoo."

I walked to the appointed golf course, golf bag slung casually over my shoulder. I felt a little strange. Because of movements, I figured my robes would only get in the way, so I wore what seemed to be regular golf attire – white shorts, royal blue polo shirt, and a sun visor. My right hand rested on the golf bag, and my left carried a pair of cleats, each with a white ankle sock (with a pom) tucked into it. I was still barefoot, I wasn't going to traipse across the Archives in those.

The Afterlife has several golf courses. Because the game isn't so popular up here, there's no real need to show up early to beat the crowd. I headed for the designated...clubhouse, I guess. The stone building looked more appropriate for the Celestial Courts, but it's not like they're going to redo architecture just for this.

Inside, the rest of my foursome and others were milling around. Maasataa was wearing pure white, polo shirt and skirt just above the knees, her long brown hair pulled back in a top knot. Jegudiel was also here, just to observe and keep things official. Both he and Metatron were wearing their robes. Michael was here, wearing a white T-shirt with khakis and red high tops. A matching baseball cap adorned his head. Fairchild and Clifton, however, were dressed like a golf joke. Both wore plaid pants that contained seemingly every color, including some God Himself did not create. They wore polo shirts with...piping? Blue piping on pink shirts? Fairchild was wearing a tam o'shanter with any colors his pants somehow missed. White shoes and a white belt (sometimes referred to on Earth as a "full Cleveland") completed the look.

Michael saw me standing there, just blinking at them. "What?"

"I never thought I'd hear myself say this, but Michael? You're underdressed."

He looked at Fairchild and Clifton. "Yeah, I know." He then held his hand up, ready to snap his fingers. "I can fix that, though."

Everyone else except me instantly yelled, "No!"

Michael made a face like a kid who was just told no ice cream, no matter what mommy and daddy promised.

It was then that I spotted him. Harold "Smack" Kowalski was hanging just on the periphery. He was waiting patiently with his pen hanging out the side of his mouth. You're probably wondering what he was waiting for. Let me put it to you this way – his trademark fedora had a piece of card on the band that said, "Press." I walked up to him and smiled, "Official coverage?"

Smack took the pen out of his mouth and held up a small notebook. Usually, people trying to chronicle things just use a record scroll, which takes things down automatically. Smack, however, had been a sportswriter for over fifty years, and this was in his blood. He didn't participate in any of the games, but would sit up in a makeshift press box with an old manual typewriter and pound away at the keys. No complaints from me, I loved reading his coverage.

I leaned close to Smack's ear and whispered, "Make me look good."

"I'm a jounalist, not a plastic surgeon."

"Burn," I laughed. I then walked up to Clifton and asked, "Ready to hit the links?"

"We're partners?" he asked, blinking in confusion.

"Team of destiny," I said, reaching out to shake his hand.

He meekly shook mine, clearly unsure if he could trust me. I looked at Michael. "Is the course ready?"

"You bet!" he crowed. We all walked over to the door that led to the course, and Michael pushed it open.

The sight that greeted us was just amazing. Eighteen holes. In miniature. Bumpers closed off the individual courses from each other. A windmill about half my height stood on the first hole, its blades swinging around to block the hole you had to shoot through. Small loops dotted other places. A wooden bridge stretched over a tiny creek. One course required you to put the ball into a water stream that went into and out of a vase held aloft by a porcelain mermaid. And the last hole was a sort of skee-ball machine that would add or subtract more strokes to your score depending on where the ball landed.

Fairchild and Clifton just stood in silent shock, taking in a sight they clearly didn't bargain for. Fairchild eventually dropped to his knees. He tapped Clifton's leg, and Clifton dropped down next to him. They bowed their heads while praying. Fairchild said, "Heavenly Father, we thank you for this wonderful course, to prove your mercy is great, and your wisdom is unending. With this, your will will be done, and others will be shown...."

I stopped paying attention at that point. I couldn't help it. Michael had stepped back so he wouldn't be seen. He was leaning against the wall with his shoulders heaving. Michael was doing that really hard laughing, the kind where you laugh so hard, no sound comes out. Maasataa and Jegudiel looked like they wanted to laugh, but didn't want this to end. I have no clue where Metatron went. He doesn't like anyone thinking he isn't completely serious, so chances are he was...uh, practicing mirth control. I was fighting to keep my laughter from bursting out just to see how long Fairchild would go on, but the more you fight laughter, the stronger it gets. I was so afraid I was going to break this up.

Turns out, I didn't have to. Fairchild must have finally remembered he was in the presence of the Greatest Prankster In All Of Creation. Literally, it was like a switch got flipped. I couldn't see his face, but I saw him suddenly straighten up as he stopped talking. His head ever so slightly tilted to the side, and his shoulders went up, swallowing his neck. He shot to his feet and turned on Michael. What he thought he would accomplish against the greatest archangel, I have no idea.

Michael went up to Fairchild and patted him on the head as he said, "Aw, aren't you cute?"

Michael then snapped his fingers and the image of the miniature golf course vanished, revealing the actual golf course. The trees, the greens, curved in graceful lines that nature would never create. It was like viewing a stationary ocean that you moved through. It wasn't as good as nature, but I had to admit, it did have its own beauty. I did notice it was far more expansive than a regular Earth golf course. Spirits are capable of more than living beings, so the course was adjusted to allow for this.

By now, the group had reformed. More or less. I looked at Jegudiel and said, "Wait a minute. Where's the caddies for Fairchild and Clifton?"

"My decision," Jegudiel explained. "We are to see how they handle adverse situations, and I didn't want them ascribing blame on anyone but themselves."

Fairchild looked a bit miffed at this. Clifton looked scared. After all, he was facing a sportsman's worst nightmare – anything that happens is your own fault.

We stepped outside, making our way to the first tee. Michael was carrying my golf bag. I saw him touch it, and it sparkled for a moment before returning to normal. I knew he wouldn't do anything to give me an advantage, which only made me wonder what else was going to happen.

We stood around, and Jegudiel came up, holding his right fist out to us. "I have a number of tees in my hand. Fairchild, you have Privilege. Odd or even?"

"Even," he guessed.

Jegudiel opened his fist. Four tees. "You want to go first or second?"

"First," he said without hesitation. Everyone gave him room as he teed up a ball.

Fairchild was about to drive off when he stopped and looked at Maasataa. "I apologize," he said with a bow. "Where are my manners? Ladies first."

"Then why didn't you let me go first?" I asked.

"You're no lady," Fairchild hissed.

I held out my hand to Michael, who promptly put a five pound note in it as I said, "Told you it was a sucker bet."

"Burn," Fairchild said as he grabbed his ball and stepped out of the way for Maasataa.

Maasataa put down a golf ball, making sure it was soundly on the tee. She walked over to Metatron, who was holding her golf bag. She looked at the contents for a moment, then asked him, "Which one is the driver again?"

I took a quick peek at Fairchild. He looked like he was having second thoughts about this.

Metatron produced the driver from the bag and gave it to Maasataa with a bow. Maasataa took the club and went up to the tee. She had done her research. Her stance was right. Her swing was perfect. She scored a hole in one.

Wait....

Everyone was looking at her in confusion. She noticed. "What?"

"You got a hole in one," Metatron explained.

"Isn't that the goal?" she asked.

"Humans rarely, if ever, get holes in one."

Maasataa realized her error and reteed up. She put mental and physical blocks on herself so that she was subject to the same limitations and mistakes as humans. Well, humans in the Afterlife, at any rate. Still, she was sharp enough that she hit a nice shot off the tee and down the fairway.

Clifton looked at me and gestured for me to go before him. I walked up to Michael, who said, "What would you like, Hannah?"

"Driver and a ball, please?"

"Who are you, Cinderella?"

"Har har." At least, he didn't go for the dirty joke I was expecting.

"What I meant, Hannah, was what ball would you like?" Michael reached in a bag pocket and produced three different balls. They were standard white, electric blue, and...camouflage?

I pointed to the camouflage ball. "Question: why?"

Michael smiled. "You can't play if you can't find any of your balls."

Ooo, now THAT'S temptation. Just sitting back at the clubhouse drinking lemonade until everyone else came back. But, unfortunately, this was official business. I plucked the electric blue one out of his hand, and he handed me my driver.

I teed up and got ready, taking a couple of quick bounces on my feet to keep myself fluid. I lined up my shot and swung, knocking a good shot down the fairway but off to the side. Still, not too shabby.

Fairchild was next. He had just swung back when he stopped and looked at Michael.

"You're freezing at the top of your swing," Michael pointed out.

"What are you up to?"

Michael looked insulted. He's a prankster, but he's also a sport. "Nothing."

"My golfing record is excellent. You don't want me to win."

By now, I was standing behind Fairchild. The only ones who could see me were Jegudiel, Metatron, and Michael. I shifted my eyes to Fairchild and touched the side of my nose. They got the message. Michael simply said, "I am doing absolutely nothing, I promise."

Fairchild went back into his stance and hit the ball, sending a small bit of turf flying behind it. Fairchild glared at the divot and then at Michael. Michael simply arched his eyebrows. Fairchild replaced the divot then stood aside as Clifton teed off.

As Fairchild and Clifton started walking, I noticed Maasataa, Jegudiel, Metatron, and Michael were hanging back. Better bring them up to speed quickly. I went up to them and said, "Fairchild is trying to create an excuse for his case. How can he prove his point when the Greatest Prankster In All Of Creation is waiting to do something?"

Michael looked at Fairchild, and a sinister grin appeared on his face. Immediately, Maasataa, Jedugiel, and Metatron started walking to join the group, the first two whistling innocently as they went. I looked at Michael. "Do I want in on this?"

"You're already in on it," Michael said, hoisting my bag and walking off. "You'll know what to do." For the first time, I wasn't sorry I had to play golf with Fairchild.

Play was fairly sedate. Fairchild made par, Clifton bogeyed. Smack already had five pages of his notebook filled out. Maasataa got par. I was getting ready to putt, lining up my shot. I stood at the ball, readied to swing, and started going, "Nananananana...."

"Noonan!" Michael started yelling. "Noonan!"

Sank it for a birdie.

Michael turned the golf bag upside down. None of the clubs came out. Instead, a saucer dropped out, then a tea cup, then what had to be jasmine tea poured out. My big brother reverted the bag as I picked up the tea cup and said, "Thank you." We then walked off to the next hole.

The game was going as well as could be expected, I guess. I was actually doing pretty well. Michael commented that I was a natural at it, but I really wasn't enjoying the game. I'll stick with my stuff, thanks.

Fairchild made par on the next two holes, then scored a birdie. Clifton would either bogey or double bogey. I'm not sure if it was because he didn't have his precious clubs or if it was because the pressure was on him. Maasataa, meanwhile, was never more than a stroke over or under.

On the fourth hole, a par five, Fairchild eagled. His delight subsided pretty quick. He took his ball out of the cup and actually started walking with a swagger. Anyone that didn't hit the ball in the same neighborhood as he did was getting looked at down Fairchild's nose. I didn't care. Fairchild had to do a lot better than that to get to me. Besides, I was doing this to win a case. I didn't want to give him anything he could use against me and bolster his human nature claims.

After the ninth hole, I looked over the scorecard with Clifton. Fairchild was clearly in the lead, Maasataa in second, and Clifton and I bringing up the rear. Clifton was fit to be tied. "This is the worst round I've ever played in my life," he grumbled.

I didn't like losing, but I couldn't let this get to me. It was just nine more holes, and then I could wrap the case up and get on to something I actually liked, like reading. "Were you always this bad?"

Clifton cowered a little. I took a look around and said, "Everyone is scattered, it's just the two of us."

Clifton let out a sigh and said, "Yeah. I mean, that's why I blessed my clubs. I hate being...a nothing."

I looked at him and smiled sympathetically. "You know how the ruling has to go."

There was a long beat before he looked at me. "What kind of life am I looking at?"

"I didn't name any families, so that would be up to God to decide."

Clifton sniffed. I looked, and could see his eyes starting to tear up. "I'm never going to make it to Heaven, am I?"

"You aren't finished yet," I told him.

"I...I don't have it in me. I mean, I want to be...."

"Everyone does," I told him. "Everyone wants to be better than they are. There's always something missing, something they would improve. The trick is to know where to look."

"How would I know where to look? I mean, when I'm reborn, I won't remember any of this."

"You will know what's missing. It's a spiritual need. All the possessions or money or power in the world will never get rid of it." I looked ahead. "Besides, you're assuming you'll be stumbling around in the dark while you're alive."

He looked at me. "What kind of help will I have?"

"Your life is your help," I told him. "God will put you in an environment to learn to cope with whatever is keeping you from Heaven. You might get an angel to help if the people around you aren't up to it. God wants us all to go to Heaven. Do you think he'll put you someplace that will make you worse?"

He didn't look relieved, but he didn't look as terrified, either. "What do I have to learn? What am I looking at?"

"Have faith," I said. "God loves us all. Why do you think it's so hard to go to Hell?"

Play resumed. Fairchild was doing very well, but Maasataa was starting to find her rhythm. She clearly had figured out the proper way to swing, take the environment into account, everything. She got a birdie on the tenth hole, and never did any worse. On the thirteenth hole (a par two, the shortest hole just so no one has to be there longer than necessary), she scored a hole in one. Fairchild, however, was in the groove for distance hitting. He completely overshot the green and wound up in the rough. It took him three more strokes to sink it.

Fairchild glared at Michael. "What?" Michael asked.

"That was your fault," he said.

"I had nothing to do with that."

"You pushed my ball too far."

Metatron stepped up. "Michael did not affect your ball in the least."

"Then he did something to me!" Fairchild yelled as he stalked up to Michael. "You gave me too much oomph!"

Michael looked at Fairchild levelly and said, "I swear to God, there are no effects on you."

Fairchild was taken aback. Up here, if you swear to God and you don't mean it...well, the results aren't pleasant. That shook him up enough, though. He retrieved his ball and we resumed play.

It was all downhill from there. Literally. The fourteenth hole was at the bottom of a dramatic incline. It's a par five, and plenty do it in two strokes – one to get to the top of the hill, and then one very very long putt to the hole. Angle your shot right and play how the green slopes, and Bob's yer uncle.

I got it in four strokes. I didn't get to the edge of the hill where I could see the green and needed another gentle shot. Looking back, I should have just knocked it up and over to the green. I mean, I knew exactly where it was, and I would have gotten a three out of it. Instead, I misjudged the distance to the green and missed the hole, needing an extra stroke.

Maasataa got it in two. She got the ball almost perfect on the edge of the hill. She chipped the ball up, bypassing the incline entirely. The ball bounced on the green, losing momentum each time, and dribbled into the cup.

Clifton got it in seven strokes. He was too distracted. I'm actually surprised it didn't take him more than that.

Fairchild? Fairchild melted down like Chernobyl. He stood at the tee, casting suspicious glances at Michael. Finally, he swung, and sliced right into the woods. He looked at Jegudiel and said, "Move for a mulligan."

"Denied. Play it where it lies," Jegudiel said instantly.

"Move for mercy?" Fairchild said, smiling awkwardly.

"You want me to add twenty strokes to your score?" Jegudiel asked.

That got Fairchild's attention. After all, he was still way ahead, Maasataa was the only one close enough to take the lead from him, and this would move him close to dead last.

Fairchild stalked into the rough to play the ball where it landed, eying daggers at Michael the entire time. The ball wasn't in too bad a spot, and he was back on the fairway in short order. Fairchild then hit the ball down the way just a little too hard. It went over the edge of the incline and kept on going, the angle carrying it off the path and into rough grass far outside the green. Quick shot onto the green, and he glared at Michael as he made his putt. Too much, the ball rolled right past the cup.

Fairchild straightened and stalked up to Michael, the club he was gripping definitely curving a little in the middle. "Knock it off!"

Generally, angels don't like being treated like that. Michael, however, was infinitely calm as he said, "I'm doing nothing."

Fairchild grinned at Jegudiel. "Michael is interfering in the trial."

Jegudiel rolled his eyes. "Michael is doing absolutely nothing."

Fairchild looked confused. He looked at Metatron, who he knew wouldn't put up with that stuff. Metatron just shook his head. Then Fairchild declared, "He's giving the others an advantage!"

Jegudiel looked like he was about to reach his limit. "What part of, 'absolutely nothing,' are you failing to understand?"

Fairchild went back to his ball, finally making his putt. But he was clearly distracted. Michael just looked innocent.

The rest of the game went along those lines. It was starting to become a contest between Maasataa and myself as Fairchild lost the lead he had built up. Clifton wasn't doing well, his head wasn't in the game. When I took a one stroke lead over Maasataa, the change in Fairchild was dramatic. He steeled his jaw and was determined not to lose to me. Fairchild looked at everyone with angry eyes and wouldn't speak a word.

Eighteenth hole. The longest one, a par seven. By now, Fairchild had sent up enough divots to open his own sod farm. It actually took him three tries just to get off the tee, and that only made the ball dribble off onto the turf. Eventually, we made it to the green. Fairchild was pacing back and forth as I got ready to putt from the edge – a long distance, but certainly within my capabilities. I had just started to swing when Fairchild let out a short, wet hack. Everyone watched as the ball slowed during its roll, standing on the edge of the cup before dropping in.

When I looked at Michael, he was standing behind me holding a dynamite plunger. "Plan B," he smiled as it vanished.

With that putt, I was now ahead of Maasataa – the best she could do was finish a stroke behind me, which she did. Clifton got his putt, a bogey. That left the green completely clear for Fairchild to begin.

Fairchild was in a tight spot. He was only one stroke ahead of me. If he sank this putt, he would win. Miss, and he would tie me. His hands were starting to shake a little as he approached the ball. He gave the ball a firm tap, sending it towards the cup.

The ball caught the edge and rimmed out like a basketball.

Fairchild was working to calm himself down. He approached the ball again, taking his stance. He closed his eyes and mumbled something. Uh oh. Was he praying to God to win the game? Everyone else must have noticed it, because everyone except Clifton took a few steps back. Clifton noticed what we did, and took a few steps himself.

Fairchild opened his eyes, smiling peacefully as he tapped the ball. It rolled straight and true towards the cup, then at the very last moment, veered off hard to the right and zipped off the green.

Fairchild slammed his putter against the ground and uttered a four syllable word describing someone having intimate relations with his maternal parent.

Suddenly, Fairchild pulsated with light and shadows before vanishing into nothingness, his putter dropping impotently to the ground.

Michael went up to pick up the putter, looking at the scorecard as he went. "Well, I guess I'll just mark him down for the maximum strokes for the hole. Come on, the clubhouse is awaiting."

Trial resumed shortly after the game ended. Boy, it felt good to be back in my robes again. With no Fairchild, Fiedler attempted to take over the lead spot. But with no real idea what Fairchild was hoping to get from the golf game, he was lost.

I kept my closing arguments simple and focused. "The central point the Churches have attempted to establish is that Clifton's behavior is just human nature and should be excused. This is shortsighted. It's one thing to get caught up in things, to be so focused on the now that you don't see the effects. It is another to be focused on yourself. This is the key to the case.

"People pray on the spur of the moment for things they shouldn't all the time. Kids pray to ace pop quizzes in school. Boys and girls pray that a certain someone will ask them to dance. Drivers will pray that they don't hit too many red lights so they won't be late for work. And, of course, people playing games will sometimes pray for a little extra help so they can win.

"Fairchild was right – Clifton getting his golf clubs blessed is a symptom, a logical result, of his thought process. The very thought process that made him behave the way he did as a bishop was the same thought process that had him bless his clubs. Placing it with the other examples is wrong, however. Those are spur of the moment, to make the immediate time better. Clifton's actions were premeditated and for achievements he felt he should have regardless. The other examples are aspiration, Clifton's actions were entitlement.

"The entitlement is the crux of this whole thing. Clifton's crimes were not of direct harm. They were crimes of omission. He deserved better, and did what he could to get and retain it. Yes, the golf clubs and the golf game are metaphors. Clifton has accepted that he ultimately does not deserve what he seeks. He is on his way to humility, to earning his Heavenly reward, he just needs a little further work to get there. He should be reincarnated to make that happen. Thank you."

The Tribunal took a look at Clifton in the dock. He simply nodded his head sadly at them. He didn't want to go around again, but he knew it was for the best.

The Tribunal ruled as I recommended. Clifton would be going back with a good family and helping to maintain the family business. The only way he wouldn't get Heaven next time was if he willfully blew it. And there was no way that would happen.

The case over, I politely excused myself and dropped down to Earth. I was outside the gates of a monastery. It's an old one, going back centuries. They know about us. And they know me in particular, so I didn't bother to wear anything other than my robes. I politely jangled the bells outside the gate. Eventually, the door opened. David Smith, one of the monks, opened the door, saw me, and smiled. "Lady Singer!" he beamed. "What brings you around?"

"Just coming to visit your new helper."

David nodded and held the gate open for me. I didn't expect him to say much. The vow of silence doesn't mean you can't say anything, just no unnecessary talking. Idle chatter was out, but I didn't mind. Listening to the wind and the birds and the occasional escaped note from a chime or bell was enough for me.

I visited here often enough, I knew where to go to find the gardens. God had sent Fairchild here as an agent to help a little bit and cool him off. As an agent, he would feel everything a human would, including exhaustion. Oh, and repugnance. This was the time they spread the pig...uh, waste to help fertilize the crops.

Sure enough, Fairchild was there, looking absolutely miserable. Each shovelful was accompanied by a grunt. He saw me and his face soured. "Enjoying the view, Singer?"

I thought about it. I wanted to see Fairchild take it on the chin, but not like this. Victories in court are far more satisfying. "You know me better than that."

He just kept glaring at me for a moment before getting back to work. After all, God was watching him. He looked at me and asked, "Feel like lending a hand?"

I looked up to Heaven and said a quick prayer. "God said, 'No.'"

Fairchild stopped and looked at me. "Would you have really helped."

I didn't smile. "Why wouldn't I?"

Fairchild ran through some options in his head, then went back to work. I sat on the grass. "You heard what happened to Clifton?"

"Yeah," he growled.

"You wouldn't have won anyway."

"I should have," he griped.

"Human nature?"

"Yeah. You, of all people, should have understood that."

"I understand human nature. You have no concept of human nature."

"Says you."

"Everything you argue in court, every time you oppose me, every time you try to get your favorites out of the clinch, you deny human nature. To you, mankind has no business being anything but perfect followers of God."

"It's not that tough," he said. "The instructions are right there."

"You will excuse people despite the instructions, or deny people their weaknesses or fears or whatever makes them skip the instructions. You don't judge people based on their faith and their worth. You judge them based on whether or not you approve of them."

"I'm a good judge of character," he sniffed, then wished he hadn't sniffed, judging by the momentary burst of green that appeared in his face.

"That's the difference between you and me," I said. "I judge based on who they are in relation to God. Whether I like them or not doesn't matter, they get my best because God wants them to have my best. You decide who gets your best. And it's completely arbitrary."

"Do you mind, Singer? The sooner I finish this, the sooner I can get out of here." And Fairchild ducked his head.

I shook my head as I stood. Fairchild hadn't petitioned yet. Something told me, if he ever did, he wasn't getting into Heaven for a long long time.

ABOUT THE AUTHOR...

Peter G is a card-carrying Renaissance man. When he's not working his office job, he is either making his own computer games or creating stories. A comic book fan since the black and white boom, Peter G's first officially published credit came in the Morbid Myths 2007 Halloween Special. Since then, his comic output has included dark superheroes (The Supremacy), an online comic strip about the office environment (Stress Puppy), an existential fantasy series (Head Above Water), his first all-ages comic about a little girl who becomes friends with a mermaid (Sound Waves), a slapstick cartoony series (Red Riding Hood), and, of course, his first collection of Hannah Singer, Celestial Advocate stories in the imaginatively titled "Hannah Singer, Celestial Advocate", followed by "On A Wing And A Prayer" and the current volume you hold in your hands. He lives in Illinois where he spends most of his time complaining about politics and watching movies.

Made in the USA
Charleston, SC
02 July 2013